John Griffith London (born **John Griffith Chaney**; January 12, 1876 – November 22, 1916) was an American novelist, journalist, and social activist. A pioneer in the world of commercial magazine fiction, he was one of the first writers to become a worldwide celebrity and earn a large fortune from writing. He was also an innovator in the genre that would later become known as science fiction. His most famous works include The Call of the Wild and White Fang, both set in the Klondike Gold Rush, as well as the short stories "To Build a Fire", "An Odyssey of the North", and "Love of Life". He also wrote about the South Pacific in stories such as "The Pearls of Parlay" and "The Heathen". London was part of the radical literary group "The Crowd" in San Francisco and a passionate advocate of unionization, socialism, and the rights of workers. He wrote several powerful works dealing with these topics, such as his dystopian novel The Iron Heel, his non-fiction exposé The People of the Abyss, and The War of the Classes. (Source: Wikipedia)

Literary works:
The Cruise of the Dazzler (1902)
A Daughter of the Snows (1902)
The Call of the Wild (1903)
The Kempton-Wace Letters (1903)
The Sea-Wolf (1904)
The Game (1905)
White Fang (1906)
Before Adam (1907)
The Iron Heel (1908)
Martin Eden (1909)
Burning Daylight (1910)
Adventure (1911)
The Scarlet Plague (1912)
A Son of the Sun (1912)
The Abysmal Brute (1913)
The Valley of the Moon (1913)

THE ABYSMAL BRUTE
&
THE FAITH OF MEN

JACK LONDON

PRINCE CLASSICS

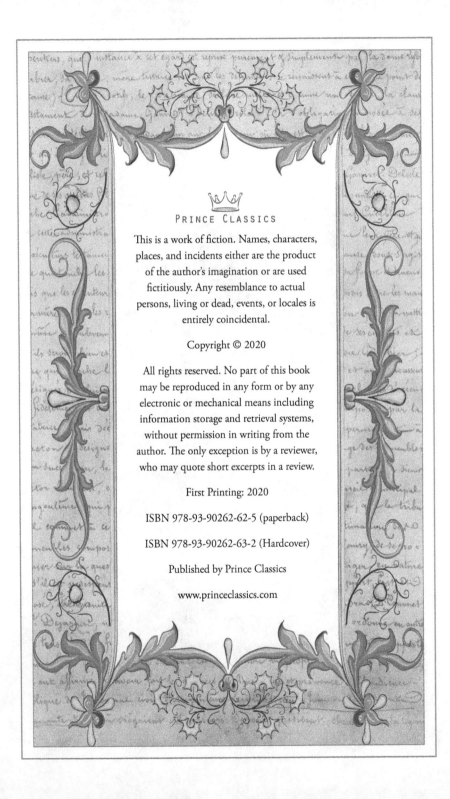

PRINCE CLASSICS

First Printing: 2020

ISBN 978-93-90262-62-5 (paperback)

ISBN 978-93-90262-63-2 (Hardcover)

Published by Prince Classics

www.princeclassics.com

Contents

THE ABYSMAL BRUTE
&
THE FAITH OF MEN

THE ABYSMAL BRUTE

I

Sam Stubener ran through his mail carelessly and rapidly. As became a manager of prize-fighters, he was accustomed to a various and bizarre correspondence. Every crank, sport, near sport, and reformer seemed to have ideas to impart to him. From dire threats against his life to milder threats, such as pushing in the front of his face, from rabbit-foot fetishes to lucky horse-shoes, from dinky jerkwater bids to the quarter-of-a-million-dollar offers of irresponsible nobodies, he knew the whole run of the surprise portion of his mail. In his time having received a razor-strop made from the skin of a lynched negro, and a finger, withered and sun-dried, cut from the body of a white man found in Death Valley, he was of the opinion that never again would the postman bring him anything that could startle him. But this morning he opened a letter that he read a second time, put away in his pocket, and took out for a third reading. It was postmarked from some unheard-of post-office in Siskiyou County, and it ran:

Dear Sam:

You don't know me, except my reputation. You come after my time, and I've been out of the game a long time. But take it from me I ain't been asleep. I've followed the whole game, and I've followed you, from the time Kal Aufman knocked you out to your last handling of Nat Belson, and I take it you're the niftiest thing in the line of managers that ever came down the pike.

I got a proposition for you. I got the greatest unknown that ever happened. This ain't con. It's the straight goods. What do you think of a husky that tips the scales at two hundred and twenty pounds fighting weight, is twenty-two years old, and can hit a kick twice as hard as my best ever? That's him, my boy, Young Pat Glendon, that's the name he'll fight under. I've planned it all out. Now the best thing you can do is hit the first train and come up here.

I bred him and I trained him. All that I ever had in my head I've hammered into his. And maybe you won't believe it, but he's added to it. He's a born fighter. He's a wonder at time and distance. He just knows to the second and the inch, and he don't have to think about it at all. His six-inch jolt is more the real sleep medicine than the full-arm swing of most geezers.

Talk about the hope of the white race. This is him. Come and take a peep. When you was managing Jeffries you was crazy about hunting. Come along and I'll give you some real hunting and fishing that will make your moving picture winnings look like thirty cents. I'll send Young Pat out with you. I ain't able to get around. That's why I'm sending for you. I was going to manage him myself. But it ain't no use. I'm all in and likely to pass out any time. So get a move on. I want you to manage him. There's a fortune in it for both of you, but I want to draw up the contract.

Yours truly,

PAT GLENDON.

Stubener was puzzled. It seemed, on the face of it, a joke—the men in the fighting game were notorious jokers—and he tried to discern the fine hand of Corbett or the big friendly paw of Fitzsimmons in the screed before him. But if it were genuine, he knew it was worth looking into. Pat Glendon was before his time, though, as a cub, he had once seen Old Pat spar at the benefit for Jack Dempsey. Even then he was called "Old" Pat, and had been out of the ring for years. He had antedated Sullivan, in the old London Prize Ring Rules, though his last fading battles had been put up under the incoming Marquis of Queensbury Rules.

What ring-follower did not know of Pat Glendon?—though few were alive who had seen him in his prime, and there were not many more who had seen him at all. Yet his name had come down in the history of the ring, and no sporting writer's lexicon was complete without it. His fame was paradoxical.

No man was honored higher, and yet he had never attained championship honors. He had been unfortunate, and had been known as the unlucky fighter.

Four times he all but won the heavyweight championship, and each time he had deserved to win it. There was the time on the barge, in San Francisco Bay, when, at the moment he had the champion going, he snapped his own forearm; and on the island in the Thames, sloshing about in six inches of rising tide, he broke a leg at a similar stage in a winning fight; in Texas, too, there was the never-to-be-forgotten day when the police broke in just as he had his man going in all certainty. And finally, there was the fight in the Mechanics' Pavilion in San Francisco, when he was secretly jobbed from the first by a gun-fighting bad man of a referee backed by a small syndicate of bettors. Pat Glendon had had no accidents in that fight, but when he had knocked his man cold with a right to the jaw and a left to the solar plexus, the referee calmly disqualified him for fouling. Every ringside witness, every sporting expert, and the whole sporting world, knew there had been no foul. Yet, like all fighters, Pat Glendon had agreed to abide by the decision of the referee. Pat abided, and accepted it as in keeping with the rest of his bad luck.

This was Pat Glendon. What bothered Stubener was whether or not Pat had written the letter. He carried it down town with him. What's become of Pat Glendon? Such was his greeting to all sports that morning. Nobody seemed to know. Some thought he must be dead, but none knew positively. The fight editor of a morning daily looked up the records and was able to state that his death had not been noted. It was from Tim Donovan, that he got a clue.

"Sure an' he ain't dead," said Donovan. "How could that be?—a man of his make that never boozed or blew himself? He made money, and what's more, he saved it and invested it. Didn't he have three saloons at the one time? An' wasn't he makin' slathers of money with them when he sold out? Now that I'm thinkin', that was the last time I laid eyes on him—when he sold them out. 'Twas all of twenty years and more ago. His wife had just died. I met him headin' for the Ferry. 'Where away, old sport?' says I. 'It's me for the woods,' says he. 'I've quit. Good-by, Tim, me boy.' And I've never seen him from that day to this. Of course he ain't dead."

"You say when his wife died—did he have any children?" Stubener queried.

"One, a little baby. He was luggin' it in his arms that very day."

"Was it a boy?"

"How should I be knowin'?"

It was then that Sam Stubener reached a decision, and that night found him in a Pullman speeding toward the wilds of Northern California.

II

Stubener was dropped off the overland at Deer Lick in the early morning, and he kicked his heels for an hour before the one saloon opened its doors. No, the saloonkeeper didn't know anything about Pat Glendon, had never heard of him, and if he was in that part of the country he must be out beyond somewhere. Neither had the one hanger-on ever heard of Pat Glendon. At the hotel the same ignorance obtained, and it was not until the storekeeper and postmaster opened up that Stubener struck the trail. Oh, yes, Pat Glendon lived out beyond. You took the stage at Alpine, which was forty miles and which was a logging camp. From Alpine, on horseback, you rode up Antelope Valley and crossed the divide to Bear Creek. Pat Glendon lived somewhere beyond that. The people of Alpine would know. Yes, there was a young Pat. The storekeeper had seen him. He had been in to Deer Lick two years back. Old Pat had not put in an appearance for five years. He bought his supplies at the store, and always paid by check, and he was a white-haired, strange old man. That was all the storekeeper knew, but the folks at Alpine could give him final directions.

It looked good to Stubener. Beyond doubt there was a young Pat Glendon, as well as an old one, living out beyond. That night the manager spent at the logging camp of Alpine, and early the following morning he rode a mountain cayuse up Antelope Valley. He rode over the divide and down Bear Creek. He rode all day, through the wildest, roughest country he had ever seen, and at sunset turned up Pinto Valley on a trail so stiff and narrow that more than once he elected to get off and walk.

It was eleven o'clock when he dismounted before a log cabin and was greeted by the baying of two huge deer-hounds. Then Pat Glendon opened the door, fell on his neck, and took him in.

"I knew ye'd come, Sam, me boy," said Pat, the while he limped about, building a fire, boiling coffee, and frying a big bear-steak. "The young un ain't home the night. We was gettin' short of meat, and he went out about sundown to pick up a deer. But I'll say no more. Wait till ye see him. He'll be home in the morn, and then you can try him out. There's the gloves. But wait till ye see him.

"As for me, I'm finished. Eighty-one come next January, an' pretty good for an ex-bruiser. But I never wasted meself, Sam, nor kept late hours an' burned the candle at all ends. I had a damned good candle, an' made the most of it, as you'll grant at lookin' at me. And I've taught the same to the young un. What do you think of a lad of twenty-two that's never had a drink in his life nor tasted tobacco? That's him. He's a giant, and he's lived natural all his days. Wait till he takes you out after deer. He'll break your heart travelin' light, him a carryin' the outfit and a big buck deer belike. He's a child of the open air, an' winter nor summer has he slept under a roof. The open for him, as I taught him. The one thing that worries me is how he'll take to sleepin' in houses, an' how he'll stand the tobacco smoke in the ring. 'Tis a terrible thing, that smoke, when you're fighting hard an' gaspin' for air. But no more, Sam, me boy. You're tired an' sure should be sleepin'. Wait till you see him, that's all. Wait till you see him."

But the garrulousness of age was on old Pat, and it was long before he permitted Stubener's eyes to close.

"He can run a deer down with his own legs, that young un," he broke out again. "'Tis the dandy trainin' for the lungs, the hunter's life. He don't know much of else, though, he's read a few books at times an' poetry stuff. He's just plain pure natural, as you'll see when you clap eyes on him. He's got the old Irish strong in him. Sometimes, the way he moons about, it's thinkin' strong I am that he believes in the fairies and such-like. He's a nature lover if ever there was one, an' he's afeard of cities. He's read about them, but the biggest he was ever in was Deer Lick. He misliked the many people, and his report was that they'd stand weedin' out. That was two years agone—the first and the last time he's seen a locomotive and a train of cars.

"Sometimes it's wrong I'm thinkin' I am, bringin' him up a natural. It's given him wind and stamina and the strength o' wild bulls. No city-grown man can have a look-in against him. I'm willin' to grant that Jeffries at his

18

best could 'a' worried the young un a bit, but only a bit. The young un could 'a' broke him like a straw. An' he don't look it. That's the everlasting wonder of it. He's only a fine-seeming young husky; but it's the quality of his muscle that's different. But wait till ye see him, that's all.

"A strange liking the boy has for posies, an' little meadows, a bit of pine with the moon beyond, windy sunsets, or the sun o' morns from the top of old Baldy. An' he has a hankerin' for the drawin' o' pitchers of things, an' of spouting about 'Lucifer or night' from the poetry books he got from the red-headed school teacher. But 'tis only his youngness. He'll settle down to the game once we get him started, but watch out for grouches when it first comes to livin' in a city for him.

"A good thing; he's woman-shy. They'll not bother him for years. He can't bring himself to understand the creatures, an' damn few of them has he seen at that. 'Twas the school teacher over at Samson's Flat that put the poetry stuff in his head. She was clean daffy over the young un, an' he never a-knowin'. A warm-haired girl she was—not a mountain girl, but from down in the flat-lands—an' as time went by she was fair desperate, an' the way she went after him was shameless. An' what d'ye think the boy did when he tumbled to it? He was scared as a jackrabbit. He took blankets an' ammunition an' hiked for tall timber. Not for a month did I lay eyes on him, an' then he sneaked in after dark and was gone in the morn. Nor would he as much as peep at her letters. 'Burn 'em,' he said. An' burn 'em I did. Twice she rode over on a cayuse all the way from Samson's Flat, an' I was sorry for the young creature. She was fair hungry for the boy, and she looked it in her face. An' at the end of three months she gave up school an' went back to her own country, an' then it was that the boy came home to the shack to live again.

"Women ha' ben the ruination of many a good fighter, but they won't be of him. He blushes like a girl if anything young in skirts looks at him a second time or too long the first one. An' they all look at him. But when he fights, when he fights!—God! it's the old savage Irish that flares in him, an' drives the fists of him. Not that he goes off his base. Don't walk away with that. At my best I was never as cool as he. I misdoubt 'twas the wrath of me that brought the accidents. But he's an iceberg. He's hot an' cold at the one time, a live wire in an ice-chest."

19

Stubener was dozing, when the old man's mumble aroused him. He listened drowsily.

"I made a man o' him, by God! I made a man o' him, with the two fists of him, an' the upstanding legs of him, an' the straight-seein' eyes. And I know the game in my head, an' I've kept up with the times and the modern changes. The crouch? Sure, he knows all the styles an' economies. He never moves two inches when an inch and a half will do the turn. And when he wants he can spring like a buck kangaroo. In-fightin'? Wait till you see. Better than his out-fightin', and he could sure 'a' sparred with Peter Jackson an' outfooted Corbett in his best. I tell you, I've taught'm it all, to the last trick, and he's improved on the teachin'. He's a fair genius at the game. An' he's had plenty of husky mountain men to try out on. I gave him the fancy work and they gave him the sloggin'. Nothing shy or delicate about them. Roarin' bulls an' big grizzly bears, that's what they are, when it comes to huggin' in a clinch or swingin' rough-like in the rushes. An' he plays with 'em. Man, d'ye hear me?—he plays with them, like you an' me would play with little puppy-dogs."

Another time Stubener awoke, to hear the old man mumbling:

"'Tis the funny think he don't take fightin' seriously. It's that easy to him he thinks it play. But wait till he's tapped a swift one. That's all, wait. An' you'll see'm throw on the juice in that cold storage plant of his an' turn loose the prettiest scientific wallopin' that ever you laid eyes on."

In the shivery gray of mountain dawn, Stubener was routed from his blankets by old Pat.

"He's comin' up the trail now," was the hoarse whisper. "Out with ye an' take your first peep at the biggest fightin' man the ring has ever seen, or will ever see in a thousand years again."

The manager peered through the open door, rubbing the sleep from his heavy eyes, and saw a young giant walk into the clearing. In one hand was a rifle, across his shoulders a heavy deer under which he moved as if it were weightless. He was dressed roughly in blue overalls and woolen shirt open at the throat. Coat he had none, and on his feet, instead of brogans, were moccasins. Stubener noted that his walk was smooth and catlike, without suggestion of his two hundred and twenty pounds of weight to which that of the deer was added. The fight manager was impressed from the first glimpse. Formidable the young fellow certainly was, but the manager sensed the strangeness and unusualness of him. He was a new type, something different from the run of fighters. He seemed a creature of the wild, more a night-roaming figure from some old fairy story or folk tale than a twentieth-century youth.

A thing Stubener quickly discovered was that young Pat was not much of a talker. He acknowledged old Pat's introduction with a grip of the hand but without speech, and silently set to work at building the fire and getting breakfast. To his father's direct questions he answered in monosyllables, as, for instance, when asked where he had picked up the deer.

"South Fork," was all he vouchsafed.

"Eleven miles across the mountains," the old man exposed pridefully to Stubener, "an' a trail that'd break your heart."

Breakfast consisted of black coffee, sourdough bread, and an immense quantity of bear-meat broiled over the coals. Of this the young fellow ate ravenously, and Stubener divined that both the Glendons were accustomed to an almost straight meat diet. Old Pat did all the talking, though it was not till the meal was ended that he broached the subject he had at heart.

"Pat, boy," he began, "you know who the gentleman is?"

Young Pat nodded, and cast a quick, comprehensive glance at the manager.

"Well, he'll be takin' you away with him and down to San Francisco."

"I'd sooner stay here, dad," was the answer.

Stubener felt a prick of disappointment. It was a wild goose chase after all. This was no fighter, eager and fretting to be at it. His huge brawn counted for nothing. It was nothing new. It was the big fellows that usually had the streak of fat.

21

But old Pat's Celtic wrath flared up, and his voice was harsh with command.

"You'll go down to the cities an' fight, me boy. That's what I've trained you for, an' you'll do it."

"All right," was the unexpected response, rumbled apathetically from the deep chest.

"And fight like hell," the old man added.

Again Stubener felt disappointment at the absence of flash and fire in the young man's eyes as he answered:

"All right. When do we start?"

"Oh, Sam, here, he'll be wantin' a little huntin' and to fish a bit, as well as to try you out with the gloves." He looked at Sam, who nodded. "Suppose you strip and give'm a taste of your quality."

An hour later, Sam Stubener had his eyes opened. An ex-fighter himself, a heavyweight at that, he was even a better judge of fighters, and never had he seen one strip to like advantage.

"See the softness of him," old Pat chanted. "'Tis the true stuff. Look at the slope of the shoulders, an' the lungs of him. Clean, all clean, to the last drop an' ounce of him. You're lookin' at a man, Sam, the like of which was never seen before. Not a muscle of him bound. No weight-lifter or Sandow exercise artist there. See the fat snakes of muscles a-crawlin' soft an' lazy-like. Wait till you see them flashin' like a strikin' rattler. He's good for forty rounds this blessed instant, or a hundred. Go to it! Time!"

They went to it, for three-minute rounds with a minute rests, and Sam Stubener was immediately undeceived. Here was no streak of fat, no apathy, only a lazy, good-natured play of gloves and tricks, with a brusk stiffness and harsh sharpness in the contacts that he knew belonged only to the trained and instinctive fighting man.

"Easy, now, easy," old Pat warned. "Sam's not the man he used to be."

This nettled Sam, as it was intended to do, and he played his most famous trick and favorite punch—a feint for a clinch and a right rip to the stomach. But, quickly as it was delivered, young Pat saw it, and, though it landed, his body was going away. The next time, his body did not go away. As the rip started, he moved forward and twisted his left hip to meet it. It was only a matter of several inches, yet it blocked the blow. And thereafter, try as he would, Stubener's glove got no farther than that hip.

Stubener had roughed it with big men in his time, and, in exhibition bouts, had creditably held his own. But there was no holding his own here. Young Pat played with him, and in the clinches made him feel as powerful as a baby, landing on him seemingly at will, locking and blocking with masterful accuracy, and scarcely noticing or acknowledging his existence. Half the time young Pat seemed to spend in gazing off and out at the landscape in a dreamy sort of way. And right here Stubener made another mistake. He took it for a trick of old Pat's training, tried to sneak in a short-arm jolt, found his arm in a lightning lock, and had both his ears cuffed for his pains.

"The instinct for a blow," the old man chortled. "'Tis not put on, I'm tellin' you. He is a wiz. He knows a blow without the lookin', when it starts an' where, the speed, an' space, an' niceness of it. An' 'tis nothing I ever showed him. 'Tis inspiration. He was so born."

Once, in a clinch, the fight manager heeled his glove on young Pat's mouth, and there was just a hint of viciousness in the manner of doing it. A moment later, in the next clinch, Sam received the heel of the other's glove on his own mouth. There was nothing snappy about it, but the pressure, stolidly lazy as it was, put his head back till the joints cracked and for the moment he thought his neck was broken. He slacked his body and dropped his arms in token that the bout was over, felt the instant release, and staggered clear.

"He'll—he'll do," he gasped, looking the admiration he lacked the breath to utter.

Old Pat's eyes were brightly moist with pride and triumph.

"An' what will you be thinkin' to happen when some of the gay an' ugly ones tries to rough it on him?" he asked.

"He'll kill them, sure," was Stubener's verdict.

"No; he's too cool for that. But he'll just hurt them some for their dirtiness."

"Let's draw up the contract," said the manager.

"Wait till you know the whole worth of him!" Old Pat answered. "'Tis strong terms I'll be makin' you come to. Go for a deer-hunt with the boy over the hills an' learn the lungs and the legs of him. Then we'll sign up iron-clad and regular."

Stubener was gone two days on that hunt, and he learned all and more than old Pat had promised, and came back a very weary and very humble man. The young fellow's innocence of the world had been startling to the case-hardened manager, but he had found him nobody's fool. Virgin though his mind was, untouched by all save a narrow mountain experience, nevertheless he had proved possession of a natural keenness and shrewdness far beyond the average. In a way he was a mystery to Sam, who could not understand his terrible equanimity of temper. Nothing ruffled him or worried him, and his patience was of an enduring primitiveness. He never swore, not even the futile and emasculated cuss-words of sissy-boys.

"I'd swear all right if I wanted to," he had explained, when challenged by his companion. "But I guess I've never come to needing it. When I do, I'll swear, I suppose."

Old Pat, resolutely adhering to his decision, said good-by at the cabin.

"It won't be long, Pat, boy, when I'll be readin' about you in the papers. I'd like to go along, but I'm afeard it's me for the mountains till the end."

And then, drawing the manager aside, the old man turned loose on him almost savagely.

"Remember what I've ben tellin' ye over an' over. The boy's clean an' he's honest. He knows nothing of the rottenness of the game. I kept it all away from him, I tell you. He don't know the meanin' of fake. He knows only the bravery, an' romance an' glory of fightin', and I've filled him up with tales of the old ring heroes, though little enough, God knows, it's set him afire. Man, man, I'm tellin' you that I clipped the fight columns from the newspapers to keep it 'way from him—him a-thinkin' I was wantin' them for me scrap book. He don't know a man ever lay down or threw a fight. So don't you get him in anything that ain't straight. Don't turn the boy's stomach. That's why I put in the null and void clause. The first rottenness and the contract's broke of itself. No snide division of stake-money; no secret arrangements with the movin' pitcher men for guaranteed distance. There's slathers o' money for the both of you. But play it square or you lose. Understand?

"And whatever you'll be doin' watch out for the women," was old Pat's parting admonishment, young Pat astride his horse and reining in dutifully to hear. "Women is death an' damnation, remember that. But when you do find the one, the only one, hang on to her. She'll be worth more than glory an' money. But first be sure, an' when you're sure, don't let her slip through your fingers. Grab her with the two hands of you and hang on. Hang on if all the world goes to smash an' smithereens. Pat, boy, a good woman is ... a good woman. 'Tis the first word and the last."

III

Once in San Francisco, Sam Stubener's troubles began. Not that young Pat had a nasty temper, or was grouchy as his father had feared. On the contrary, he was phenomenally sweet and mild. But he was homesick for his beloved mountains. Also, he was secretly appalled by the city, though he trod its roaring streets imperturbable as a red Indian.

"I came down here to fight," he announced, at the end of the first week.

"Where's Jim Hanford?"

Stubener whistled.

"A big champion like him wouldn't look at you," was his answer. "'Go and get a reputation,' is what he'd say."

"I can lick him."

"But the public doesn't know that. If you licked him you'd be champion of the world, and no champion ever became so with his first fight."

"I can."

"But the public doesn't know it, Pat. It wouldn't come to see you fight. And it's the crowd that brings the money and the big purses. That's why Jim Hanford wouldn't consider you for a second. There'd be nothing in it for him. Besides, he's getting three thousand a week right now in vaudeville, with a contract for twenty-five weeks. Do you think he'd chuck that for a go with a man no one ever heard of? You've got to do something first, make a record. You've got to begin on the little local dubs that nobody ever heard of—guys like Chub Collins, Rough-House Kelly, and the Flying Dutchman. When you've put them away, you're only started on the first round of the ladder. But after that you'll go up like a balloon."

"I'll meet those three named in the same ring one after the other," was Pat's decision. "Make the arrangements accordingly."

Stubener laughed.

"What's wrong? Don't you think I can put them away?"

"I know you can," Stubener assured him. "But it can't be arranged that way. You've got to take them one at a time. Besides, remember, I know the game and I'm managing you. This proposition has to be worked up, and I'm the boy that knows how. If we're lucky, you may get to the top in a couple of years and be the champion with a mint of money."

Pat sighed at the prospect, then brightened up.

"And after that I can retire and go back home to the old man," he said.

Stubener was about to reply, but checked himself. Strange as was this championship material, he felt confident that when the top was reached it would prove very similar to that of all the others who had gone before. Besides, two years was a long way off, and there was much to be done in the meantime.

When Pat fell to moping around his quarters, reading endless poetry books and novels drawn from the public library, Stubener sent him off to live on a Contra Costa ranch across the Bay, under the watchful eye of Spider Walsh. At the end of a week Spider whispered that the job was a cinch. His charge was away and over the hills from dawn till dark, whipping the streams for trout, shooting quail and rabbits, and pursuing the one lone and crafty buck famous for having survived a decade of hunters. It was the Spider who waxed lazy and fat, while his charge kept himself in condition.

As Stubener expected, his unknown was laughed at by the fight club managers. Were not the woods full of unknowns who were always breaking out with championship rashes? A preliminary, say of four rounds—yes, they would grant him that. But the main event—never. Stubener was resolved that young Pat should make his debut in nothing less than a main event, and, by the prestige of his own name he at last managed it. With much misgiving, the Mission Club agreed that Pat Glendon could go fifteen rounds with Rough-House Kelly for a purse of one hundred dollars. It was the custom of young fighters to assume the names of old ring heroes, so no one suspected that he was the son of the great Pat Glendon, while Stubener held his peace. It was a good press surprise package to spring later.

Came the night of the fight, after a month of waiting. Stubener's anxiety was keen. His professional reputation was staked that his man would make a showing, and he was astounded to see Pat, seated in his corner a bare five minutes, lose the healthy color from his cheeks, which turned a sickly yellow.

"Cheer up, boy," Stubener said, slapping him on the shoulder. "The first time in the ring is always strange, and Kelly has a way of letting his opponent wait for him on the chance of getting stage-fright."

"It isn't that," Pat answered. "It's the tobacco smoke. I'm not used to it, and it's making me fair sick."

His manager experienced the quick shock of relief. A man who turned sick from mental causes, even if he were a Samson, could never win to place in the prize ring. As for tobacco smoke, the youngster would have to get used to it, that was all.

Young Pat's entrance into the ring had been met with silence, but when Rough-House Kelly crawled through the ropes his greeting was uproarious. He did not belie his name. He was a ferocious-looking man, black and hairy, with huge, knotty muscles, weighing a full two hundred pounds. Pat looked across at him curiously, and received a savage scowl. After both had been introduced to the audience, they shook hands. And even as their gloves gripped, Kelly ground his teeth, convulsed his face with an expression of rage, and muttered:

"You've got yer nerve wid yeh." He flung Pat's hand roughly from his, and hissed, "I'll eat yeh up, ye pup!"

The audience laughed at the action, and it guessed hilariously at what Kelly must have said.

Back in his corner, and waiting the gong, Pat turned to Stubener.

"Why is he angry with me?" he asked.

"He ain't," Stubener answered. "That's his way, trying to scare you. It's just mouth-fighting."

"It isn't boxing," was Pat's comment; and Stubener, with a quick glance, noted that his eyes were as mildly blue as ever.

"Be careful," the manager warned, as the gong for the first round sounded and Pat stood up. "He's liable to come at you like a man-eater."

And like a man-eater Kelly did come at him, rushing across the ring in wild fury. Pat, who in his easy way had advanced only a couple of paces, gauged the other's momentum, side-stepped, and brought his stiff-arched right across to the jaw. Then he stood and looked on with a great curiosity. The fight was over. Kelly had fallen like a stricken bullock to the floor, and there he lay without movement while the referee, bending over him, shouted the ten seconds in his unheeding ear. When Kelly's seconds came to lift him, Pat was before them. Gathering the huge, inert bulk of the man in his arms, he carried him to his corner and deposited him on the stool and in the arms of his seconds.

Half a minute later, Kelly's head lifted and his eyes wavered open. He looked about him stupidly and then to one of his seconds.

"What happened?" he queried hoarsely. "Did the roof fall on me?"

IV

As a result of his fight with Kelly, though the general opinion was that he had won by a fluke, Pat was matched with Rufe Mason. This took place three weeks later, and the Sierra Club audience at Dreamland Rink failed to see what happened. Rufe Mason was a heavyweight, noted locally for his cleverness. When the gong for the first round sounded, both men met in the center of the ring. Neither rushed. Nor did they strike a blow. They felt around each other, their arms bent, their gloves so close together that they almost touched. This lasted for perhaps five seconds. Then it happened, and so quickly that not one in a hundred of the audience saw. Rufe Mason made a feint with his right. It was obviously not a real feint, but a feeler, a mere tentative threatening of a possible blow. It was at this instant that Pat loosed his punch. So close together were they that the distance the blow traveled was a scant eight inches. It was a short-arm left jolt, and it was accomplished by a twist of the left forearm and a thrust of the shoulder. It landed flush on the point of the chin and the astounded audience saw Rufe Mason's legs crumple under him as his body sank to the floor. But the referee had seen, and he promptly proceeded to count him out. Again Pat carried his opponent to his corner, and it was ten minutes before Rufe Mason, supported by his seconds, with sagging knees and rolling, glassy eyes, was able to move down the aisle through the stupefied and incredulous audience on the way to his dressing room.

"No wonder," he told a reporter, "that Rough-House Kelly thought the roof hit him."

After Chub Collins had been put out in the twelfth second of the first round of a fifteen-round contest, Stubener felt compelled to speak to Pat.

"Do you know what they're calling you now?" he asked.

Pat shook his head.

"One Punch Glendon."

Pat smiled politely. He was little interested in what he was called. He had certain work cut out which he must do ere he could win back to his mountains, and he was phlegmatically doing it, that was all.

"It won't do," his manager continued, with an ominous shake of the head. "You can't go on putting your men out so quickly. You must give them more time."

"I'm here to fight, ain't I?" Pat demanded in surprise.

Again Stubener shook his head.

"It's this way, Pat. You've got to be big and generous in the fighting game. Don't get all the other fighters sore. And it's not fair to the audience. They want a run for their money. Besides, no one will fight you. They'll all be scared out. And you can't draw crowds with ten-second fights. I leave it to you. Would you pay a dollar, or five, to see a ten-second fight?"

Pat was convinced, and he promised to give future audiences the requisite run for their money, though he stated that, personally, he preferred going fishing to witnessing a hundred rounds of fighting.

And still, Pat had got practically nowhere in the game. The local sports laughed when his name was mentioned. It called to mind funny fights and Rough-House Kelly's remark about the roof. Nobody knew how Pat could fight. They had never seen him. Where was his wind, his stamina, his ability to mix it with rough customers through long grueling contests? He had demonstrated nothing but the possession of a lucky punch and a depressing proclivity for flukes.

So it was that his fourth match was arranged with Pete Sosso, a Portuguese fighter from Butchertown, known only for the amazing tricks he played in the ring. Pat did not train for the fight. Instead he made a flying and sorrowful trip to the mountains to bury his father. Old Pat had known well the condition of his heart, and it had stopped suddenly on him.

Young Pat arrived back in San Francisco with so close a margin of time that he changed into his fighting togs directly from his traveling suit, and even then the audience was kept waiting ten minutes.

"Remember, give him a chance," Stubener cautioned him as he climbed through the ropes. "Play with him, but do it seriously. Let him go ten or twelve rounds, then get him."

Pat obeyed instructions, and, though it would have been easy enough to put Sosso out, so tricky was he that to stand up to him and not put him out kept his hands full. It was a pretty exhibition, and the audience was delighted. Sosso's whirlwind attacks, wild feints, retreats, and rushes, required all Pat's science to protect himself, and even then he did not escape unscathed.

Stubener praised him in the minute-rests, and all would have been well, had not Sosso, in the fourth round, played one of his most spectacular tricks. Pat, in a mix-up, had landed a hook to Sosso's jaw, when to his amazement, the latter dropped his hands and reeled backward, eyes rolling, legs bending and giving, in a high state of grogginess. Pat could not understand. It had not been a knock-out blow, and yet there was his man all ready to fall to the mat. Pat dropped his own hands and wonderingly watched his reeling opponent. Sosso staggered away, almost fell, recovered, and staggered obliquely and blindly forward again.

For the first and the last time in his fighting career, Pat was caught off his guard. He actually stepped aside to let the reeling man go by. Still reeling, Sosso suddenly loosed his right. Pat received it full on his jaw with an impact that rattled all his teeth. A great roar of delight went up from the audience. But Pat did not hear. He saw only Sosso before him, grinning and defiant, and not the least bit groggy. Pat was hurt by the blow, but vastly more outraged by the trick. All the wrath that his father ever had surged up in him. He shook his head as if to get rid of the shock of the blow and steadied himself before his man. It all occurred in the next second. With a feint that drew his opponent, Pat fetched his left to the solar plexus, almost at the same instant whipping his right across to the jaw. The latter blow landed on Sosso's mouth ere his falling body struck the floor. The club doctors worked half an hour to bring him to. After that they put eleven stitches in his mouth and packed him off in an ambulance.

"I'm sorry," Pat told his manager, "I'm afraid I lost my temper. I'll never do it again in the ring. Dad always cautioned me about it. He said it had made him lose more than one battle. I didn't know I could lose my temper that way, but now that I know I'll keep it in control."

And Stubener believed him. He was coming to the stage where he could believe anything about his young charge.

"You don't need to get angry," he said, "you're so thoroughly the master of your man at any stage."

"At any inch or second of the fight," Pat affirmed.

"And you can put them out any time you want."

"Sure I can. I don't want to boast. But I just seem to possess the ability. My eyes show me the opening that my skill knows how to make, and time and distance are second nature to me. Dad called it a gift, but I thought he was blarneying me. Now that I've been up against these men, I guess he was right. He said I had the mind and muscle correlation."

"At any inch or second of the fight," Stubener repeated musingly.

Pat nodded, and Stubener, absolutely believing him, caught a vision of a golden future that should have fetched old Pat out of his grave.

"Well, don't forget, we've got to give the crowd a run for its money," he said. "We'll fix it up between us how many rounds a fight should go. Now your next bout will be with the Flying Dutchman. Suppose you let it run the full fifteen and put him out in the last round. That will give you a chance to make a showing as well."

"All right, Sam," was the answer.

"It will be a test for you," Stubener warned. "You may fail to put him out in that last round."

"Watch me." Pat paused to put weight to his promise, and picked up a volume of Longfellow. "If I don't I'll never read poetry again, and that's going some."

"You bet it is," his manager proclaimed jubilantly, "though what you see in such stuff is beyond me."

Pat sighed, but did not reply. In all his life he had found but one person who cared for poetry, and that had been the red-haired school teacher who scared him off into the woods.

V

"Where are you going?" Stubener demanded in surprise, looking at his watch.

Pat, with his hand on the door-knob, paused and turned around.

"To the Academy of Sciences," he said. "There's a professor who's going to give a lecture there on Browning to-night, and Browning is the sort of writer you need assistance with. Sometimes I think I ought to go to night school."

"But great Scott, man!" exclaimed the horrified manager. "You're on with the Flying Dutchman to-night."

"I know it. But I won't enter the ring a moment before half past nine or quarter to ten. The lecture will be over at nine fifteen. If you want to make sure, come around and pick me up in your machine."

Stubener shrugged his shoulders helplessly.

"You've got no kick coming," Pat assured him. "Dad used to tell me a man's worst time was in the hours just before a fight, and that many a fight was lost by a man's breaking down right there, with nothing to do but think and be anxious. Well, you'll never need to worry about me that way. You ought to be glad I can go off to a lecture."

And later that night, in the course of watching fifteen splendid rounds, Stubener chuckled to himself more than once at the idea of what that audience of sports would think, did it know that this magnificent young prize-fighter had come to the ring directly from a Browning lecture.

The Flying Dutchman was a young Swede who possessed an unwonted willingness to fight and who was blessed with phenomenal endurance. He never rested, was always on the offensive, and rushed and fought from gong to gong. In the out-fighting his arms whirled about like flails, in the in-fighting he was forever shouldering or half-wrestling and starting blows whenever he could get a hand free. From start to finish he was a whirlwind, hence his name. His failing was lack of judgment in time and distance. Nevertheless he had won many fights by virtue of landing one in each dozen or so of the unending fusillades of punches he delivered. Pat, with strong upon him the caution that he must not put his opponent out, was kept busy. Nor, though he escaped vital damage, could he avoid entirely those eternal flying gloves. But it was good training, and in a mild way he enjoyed the contest.

"Could you get him now?" Stubener whispered in his ear during the minute rest at the end of the fifth round.

"Sure," was Pat's answer.

"You know he's never yet been knocked out by any one," Stubener warned a couple of rounds later.

"Then I'm afraid I'll have to break my knuckles," Pat smiled. "I know the punch I've got in me, and when I land it something's got to go. If he won't, my knuckles will."

"Do you think you could get him now?" Stubener asked at the end of the thirteenth round.

"Anytime, I tell you."

"Well, then, Pat, let him run to the fifteenth."

In the fourteenth round the Flying Dutchman exceeded himself. At the stroke of the gong he rushed clear across the ring to the opposite corner where Pat was leisurely getting to his feet. The house cheered, for it knew the Flying Dutchman had cut loose. Pat, catching the fun of it, whimsically decided to meet the terrific onslaught with a wholly passive defense and not to strike a blow. Nor did he strike a blow, nor feint a blow, during the three minutes of whirlwind that followed. He gave a rare exhibition of stalling, sometimes hugging his bowed face with his left arm, his abdomen with his right; at other times, changing as the point of attack changed, so that both gloves were held on either side his face, or both elbows and forearms guarded his midsection; and all the time moving about, clumsily shouldering, or half-falling forward against his opponent and clogging his efforts; himself never striking nor threatening to strike, the while rocking with the impacts of the storming blows that beat upon his various guards the devil's own tattoo.

Those close at the ringside saw and appreciated, but the rest of the audience, fooled, arose to its feet and roared its applause in the mistaken notion that Pat, helpless, was receiving a terrible beating. With the end of the round, the audience, dumbfounded, sank back into its seats as Pat walked steadily to his corner. It was not understandable. He should have been beaten to a pulp, and yet nothing had happened to him.

"Now are you going to get him?" Stubener queried anxiously.

"Inside ten seconds," was Pat's confident assertion. "Watch me."

There was no trick about it. When the gong struck and Pat bounded to his feet, he advertised it unmistakably that for the first time in the fight he was starting after his man. Not one onlooker misunderstood. The Flying Dutchman read the advertisement, too, and for the first time in his career, as they met in the center of the ring, visibly hesitated. For the fraction of a second they faced each other in position. Then the Flying Dutchman leaped forward upon his man, and Pat, with a timed right-cross, dropped him cold as he leaped.

It was after this battle that Pat Glendon started on his upward rush to fame. The sports and the sporting writers took him up. For the first time the Flying Dutchman had been knocked out. His conqueror had proved a wizard of defense. His previous victories had not been flukes. He had a kick in both his hands. Giant that he was, he would go far. The time was already past, the writers asserted, for him to waste himself on the third-raters and chopping blocks. Where were Ben Menzies, Rege Rede, Bill Tarwater, and Ernest Lawson? It was time for them to meet this young cub that had suddenly shown himself a fighter of quality. Where was his manager anyway, that he was not issuing the challenges?

And then fame came in a day; for Stubener divulged the secret that his man was none other than the son of Pat Glendon, Old Pat, the old-time ring hero. "Young" Pat Glendon, he was promptly christened, and sports and writers flocked about him to admire him, and back him, and write him up.

Beginning with Ben Menzies and finishing with Bill Tarwater, he challenged, fought, and knocked out the four second-raters. To do this, he was compelled to travel, the battles taking place in Goldfield, Denver, Texas, and New York. To accomplish it required months, for the bigger fights were not easily arranged, and the men themselves demanded more time for training.

The second year saw him running to cover and disposing of the half-dozen big fighters that clustered just beneath the top of the heavyweight ladder. On this top, firmly planted, stood "Big" Jim Hanford, the undefeated world champion. Here, on the top rungs, progress was slower, though Stubener was indefatigable in issuing challenges and in promoting sporting opinion to force the man to fight. Will King was disposed of in England, and Glendon pursued Tom Harrison half way around the world to defeat him on Boxing Day in Australia.

But the purses grew larger and larger. In place of a hundred dollars, such as his first battles had earned him, he was now receiving from twenty to thirty thousand dollars a fight, as well as equally large sums from the moving picture men. Stubener took his manager's percentage of all this, according to the terms of the contract old Pat had drawn up, and both he and Glendon, despite their heavy expenses, were waxing rich. This was due, more than anything else, to the clean lives they lived. They were not wasters.

Stubener was attracted to real estate, and his holdings in San Francisco, consisting of building flats and apartment houses, were bigger than Glendon ever dreamed. There was a secret syndicate of bettors, however, which could have made an accurate guess at the size of Stubener's holdings, while heavy bonus after heavy bonus, of which Glendon never heard, was paid over to his manager by the moving picture men.

Stubener's most serious task was in maintaining the innocence of his young gladiator. Nor did he find it difficult. Glendon, who had nothing to do with the business end, was little interested. Besides, wherever his travels took him, he spent his spare time in hunting and fishing. He rarely mingled with those of the sporting world, was notoriously shy and secluded, and preferred art galleries and books of verse to sporting gossip. Also, his trainers and sparring partners were rigorously instructed by the manager to keep their tongues away from the slightest hints of ring rottenness. In every way Stubener intervened between Glendon and the world. He was never even interviewed save in Stubener's presence.

Only once was Glendon approached. It was just prior to his battle with Henderson, and an offer of a hundred thousand was made to him to throw the fight. It was made hurriedly, in swift whispers, in a hotel corridor, and it was fortunate for the man that Pat controlled his temper and shouldered past him without reply. He brought the tale of it to Stubener, who said:

"It's only con, Pat. They were trying to josh you." He noted the blue eyes blaze. "And maybe worse than that. If they could have got you to fall for it, there might have been a big sensation in the papers that would have finished you. But I doubt it. Such things don't happen any more. It's a myth, that's what it is, that has come down from the middle history of the ring. There has been rottenness in the past, but no fighter or manager of reputation would dare anything of the sort to-day. Why, Pat, the men in the game are as clean and straight as those in professional baseball, than which there is nothing cleaner or straighter."

And all the while he talked, Stubener knew in his heart that the forthcoming fight with Henderson was not to be shorter than twelve rounds—this for the moving pictures—and not longer than the fourteenth round. And he knew, furthermore, so big were the stakes involved, that Henderson himself was pledged not to last beyond the fourteenth.

And Glendon, never approached again, dismissed the matter from his mind and went out to spend the afternoon in taking color photographs. The camera had become his latest hobby. Loving pictures, yet unable to paint, he had compromised by taking up photography. In his hand baggage was one grip packed with books on the subject, and he spent long hours in the dark room, realizing for himself the various processes. Never had there been a great fighter who was as aloof from the fighting world as he. Because he had little to

39

say with those he encountered, he was called sullen and unsocial, and out of this a newspaper reputation took form that was not an exaggeration so much as it was an entire misconception. Boiled down, his character in print was that of an ox-muscled and dumbly stupid brute, and one callow sporting writer dubbed him the "abysmal brute." The name stuck. The rest of the fraternity hailed it with delight, and thereafter Glendon's name never appeared in print unconnected with it. Often, in a headline or under a photograph, "The Abysmal Brute," capitalized and without quotation marks, appeared alone. All the world knew who was this brute. This made him draw into himself closer than ever, while it developed a bitter prejudice against newspaper folk.

Regarding fighting itself, his earlier mild interest grew stronger. The men he now fought were anything but dubs, and victory did not come so easily. They were picked men, experienced ring generals, and each battle was a problem. There were occasions when he found it impossible to put them out in any designated later round of a fight. Thus, with Sulzberger, the gigantic German, try as he would in the eighteenth round, he failed to get him, in the nineteenth it was the same story, and not till the twentieth did he manage to break through the baffling guard and drop him. Glendon's increasing enjoyment of the game was accompanied by severer and prolonged training. Never dissipating, spending much of his time on hunting trips in the hills, he was practically always in the pink of condition, and, unlike his father, no unfortunate accidents marred his career. He never broke a bone, nor injured so much as a knuckle. One thing that Stubener noted with secret glee was that his young fighter no longer talked of going permanently back to his mountains when he had won the championship away from Jim Hanford.

VI

The consummation of his career was rapidly approaching. The great champion had even publicly intimated his readiness to take on Glendon as soon as the latter had disposed of the three or four aspirants for the championship who intervened. In six months Pat managed to put away Kid McGrath and Philadelphia Jack McBride, and there remained only Nat Powers and Tom Cannam. And all would have been well had not a certain society girl gone adventuring into journalism, and had not Stubener agreed to an interview with the woman reporter of the San Francisco "Courier-Journal."

Her work was always published over the name of Maud Sangster, which, by the way, was her own name. The Sangsters were a notoriously wealthy family. The founder, old Jacob Sangster, had packed his blankets and worked as a farm-hand in the West. He had discovered an inexhaustible borax deposit in Nevada, and, from hauling it out by mule-teams, had built a railroad to do the freighting. Following that, he had poured the profits of borax into the purchase of hundreds and thousands of square miles of timber lands in California, Oregon, and Washington. Still later, he had combined politics with business, bought statesmen, judges, and machines, and become a captain of complicated industry. And after that he had died, full of honor and pessimism, leaving his name a muddy blot for future historians to smudge, and also leaving a matter of a couple of hundreds of millions for his four sons to squabble over. The legal, industrial, and political battles that followed, vexed and amused California for a generation, and culminated in deadly hatred and unspeaking terms between the four sons. The youngest, Theodore, in middle life experienced a change of heart, sold out his stock farms and racing stables, and plunged into a fight with all the corrupt powers of his native state, including most of its millionaires, in a quixotic attempt to purge it of the infamy which had been implanted by old Jacob Sangster.

Maud Sangster was Theodore's oldest daughter. The Sangster stock uniformly bred fighters among the men and beauties among the women.

Nor was Maud an exception. Also, she must have inherited some of the virus of adventure from the Sangster breed, for she had come to womanhood and done a multitude of things of which no woman in her position should have been guilty. A match in ten thousand, she remained unmarried. She had sojourned in Europe without bringing home a nobleman for spouse, and had declined a goodly portion of her own set at home. She had gone in for outdoor sports, won the tennis championship of the state, kept the society weeklies agog with her unconventionalities, walked from San Mateo to Santa Cruz against time on a wager, and once caused a sensation by playing polo in a men's team at a private Burlingame practice game. Incidentally, she had gone in for art, and maintained a studio in San Francisco's Latin Quarter.

All this had been of little moment until her father's reform attack became acute. Passionately independent, never yet having met the man to whom she could gladly submit, and bored by those who had aspired, she resented her father's interference with her way of life and put the climax on all her social misdeeds by leaving home and going to work on the "Courier-Journal." Beginning at twenty dollars a week, her salary had swiftly risen to fifty. Her work was principally musical, dramatic, and art criticism, though she was not above mere journalistic stunts if they promised to be sufficiently interesting. Thus she scooped the big interview with Morgan at a time when he was being futilely trailed by a dozen New York star journalists, went down to the bottom of the Golden Gate in a diver's suit, and flew with Rood, the bird man, when he broke all records of continuous flight by reaching as far as Riverside.

Now it must not be imagined that Maud Sangster was a hard-bitten Amazon. On the contrary, she was a gray-eyed, slender young woman, of three or four and twenty, of medium stature, and possessing uncommonly small hands and feet for an outdoor woman or any other kind of a woman. Also, far in excess of most outdoor women, she knew how to be daintily feminine.

It was on her own suggestion that she received the editor's commission to interview Pat Glendon. With the exception of having caught a glimpse, once, of Bob Fitzsimmons in evening dress at the Palace Grill, she had never seen a prizefighter in her life. Nor was she curious to see one—at least she had not been curious until Young Pat Glendon came to San Francisco to train for his fight with Nat Powers. Then his newspaper reputation had aroused her. The Abysmal Brute!—it certainly must be worth seeing. From what she read of him she gleaned that he was a man-monster, profoundly stupid and with the sullenness and ferocity of a jungle beast. True, his published photographs did not show all that, but they did show the hugeness of brawn that might be expected to go with it. And so, accompanied by a staff photographer, she went out to the training quarters at the Cliff House at the hour appointed by Stubener.

That real estate owner was having trouble. Pat was rebellious. He sat, one big leg dangling over the side of the arm chair and Shakespeare's Sonnets face downward on his knee, orating against the new woman.

"What do they want to come butting into the game for?" he demanded. "It's not their place. What do they know about it anyway? The men are bad enough as it is. I'm not a holy show. This woman's coming here to make me one. I never have stood for women around the training quarters, and I don't care if she is a reporter."

"But she's not an ordinary reporter," Stubener interposed. "You've heard of the Sangsters?—the millionaires?"

Pat nodded.

"Well, she's one of them. She's high society and all that stuff. She could be running with the Blingum crowd now if she wanted to instead of working for wages. Her old man's worth fifty millions if he's worth a cent."

"Then what's she working on a paper for?—keeping some poor devil out of a job."

"She and the old man fell out, had a tiff or something, about the time he started to clean up San Francisco. She quit. That's all—left home and got a job. And let me tell you one thing, Pat: she can everlastingly sling English. There isn't a pen-pusher on the Coast can touch her when she gets going."

Pat began to show interest, and Stubener hurried on.

"She writes poetry, too—the regular la-de-dah stuff, just like you. Only I guess hers is better, because she published a whole book of it once. And she writes up the shows. She interviews every big actor that hits this burg."

"I've seen her name in the papers," Pat commented.

"Sure you have. And you're honored, Pat, by her coming to interview you. It won't bother you any. I'll stick right by and give her most of the dope myself. You know I've always done that."

Pat looked his gratitude.

"And another thing, Pat: don't forget you've got to put up with this interviewing. It's part of your business. It's big advertising, and it comes free. We can't buy it. It interests people, draws the crowds, and it's crowds that pile up the gate receipts." He stopped and listened, then looked at his watch. "I think that's her now. I'll go and get her and bring her in. I'll tip it off to her to cut it short, you know, and it won't take long." He turned in the doorway. "And be decent, Pat. Don't shut up like a clam. Talk a bit to her when she asks you questions."

Pat put the Sonnets on the table, took up a newspaper, and was apparently deep in its contents when the two entered the room and he stood up. The meeting was a mutual shock. When blue eyes met gray, it was almost as if the man and the woman shouted triumphantly to each other, as if each had found something sought and unexpected. But this was for the instant only. Each had anticipated in the other something so totally different that the next moment the clear cry of recognition gave way to confusion. As is the way of women, she was the first to achieve control, and she did it without having given any outward sign that she had ever lost it. She advanced most of the distance across the floor to meet Glendon. As for him, he scarcely knew how he stumbled through the introduction. Here was a woman, a WOMAN. He had not known that such a creature could exist. The few women he had noticed had never prefigured this. He wondered what Old Pat's judgment would have been of her, if she was the sort he had recommended to hang on to with both his hands. He discovered that in some way he was holding her hand. He looked at it, curious and fascinated, marveling at its fragility.

She, on the other hand, had proceeded to obliterate the echoes of that first clear call. It had been a peculiar experience, that was all, this sudden outrush of her toward this strange man. For was not he the abysmal brute of the prize-ring, the great, fighting, stupid bulk of a male animal who hammered up his fellow males of the same stupid order? She smiled at the way he continued to hold her hand.

"I'll have it back, please, Mr. Glendon," she said. "I ... I really need it, you know."

He looked at her blankly, followed her gaze to her imprisoned hand, and dropped it in a rush of awkwardness that sent the blood in a manifest blush to his face.

She noted the blush, and the thought came to her that he did not seem quite the uncouth brute she had pictured. She could not conceive of a brute blushing at anything. And also, she found herself pleased with the fact that he lacked the easy glibness to murmur an apology. But the way he devoured her with his eyes was disconcerting. He stared at her as if in a trance, while his cheeks flushed even more redly.

Stubener by this time had fetched a chair for her, and Glendon automatically sank down into his.

"He's in fine shape, Miss Sangster, in fine shape," the manager was saying. "That's right, isn't it, Pat? Never felt better in your life?"

Glendon was bothered by this. His brows contracted in a troubled way, and he made no reply.

"I've wanted to meet you for a long time, Mr. Glendon," Miss Sangster said. "I never interviewed a pugilist before, so if I don't go about it expertly you'll forgive me, I am sure."

"Maybe you'd better start in by seeing him in action," was the manager's suggestion. "While he's getting into his fighting togs I can tell you a lot about him—fresh stuff, too. We'll call in Walsh, Pat, and go a couple of rounds."

"We'll do nothing of the sort," Glendon growled roughly, in just the way an abysmal brute should. "Go ahead with the interview."

The business went ahead unsatisfactorily. Stubener did most of the talking and suggesting, which was sufficient to irritate Maud Sangster, while Pat volunteered nothing. She studied his fine countenance, the eyes clear blue and wide apart, the well-modeled, almost aquiline, nose, the firm, chaste lips that were sweet in a masculine way in their curl at the corners and that gave no hint of any sullenness. It was a baffling personality, she concluded, if what the papers said of him was so. In vain she sought for earmarks of the brute. And in vain she attempted to establish contacts. For one thing, she knew too little about prize-fighters and the ring, and whenever she opened up a lead it was promptly snatched away by the information-oozing Stubener.

"It must be most interesting, this life of a pugilist," she said once, adding with a sigh, "I wish I knew more about it. Tell me: why do you fight?—Oh, aside from money reasons." (This latter to forestall Stubener). "Do you enjoy fighting? Are you stirred by it, by pitting yourself against other men? I hardly know how to express what I mean, so you must be patient with me."

Pat and Stubener began speaking together, but for once Pat bore his manager down.

"I didn't care for it at first—"

"You see, it was too dead easy for him," Stubener interrupted.

"But later," Pat went on, "when I encountered the better fighters, the real big clever ones, where I was more—"

"On your mettle?" she suggested.

"Yes; that's it, more on my mettle, I found I did care for it ... a great deal, in fact. But still, it's not so absorbing to me as it might be. You see, while each battle is a sort of problem which I must work out with my wits and muscle, yet to me the issue is never in doubt—"

"He's never had a fight go to a decision," Stubener proclaimed. "He's won every battle by the knock-out route."

"And it's this certainty of the outcome that robs it of what I imagine must be its finest thrills," Pat concluded.

"Maybe you'll get some of them thrills when you go up against Jim Hanford," said the manager.

Pat smiled, but did not speak.

"Tell me some more," she urged, "more about the way you feel when you are fighting."

And then Pat amazed his manager, Miss Sangster, and himself, by blurting out:

"It seems to me I don't want to talk with you on such things. It's as if there are things more important for you and me to talk about. I—"

He stopped abruptly, aware of what he was saying but unaware of why he was saying it.

"Yes," she cried eagerly. "That's it. That is what makes a good interview— the real personality, you know."

But Pat remained tongue-tied, and Stubener wandered away on a statistical comparison of his champion's weights, measurements, and expansions with those of Sandow, the Terrible Turk, Jeffries, and the other modern strong men. This was of little interest to Maud Sangster, and she showed that she was bored. Her eyes chanced to rest on the Sonnets. She picked the book up and glanced inquiringly at Stubener.

"That's Pat's," he said. "He goes in for that kind of stuff, and color photography, and art exhibits, and such things. But for heaven's sake don't publish anything about it. It would ruin his reputation."

She looked accusingly at Glendon, who immediately became awkward. To her it was delicious. A shy young man, with the body of a giant, who was one of the kings of bruisers, and who read poetry, and went to art exhibits, and experimented with color photography! Of a surety there was no abysmal brute here. His very shyness she divined now was due to sensitiveness and not stupidity. Shakespeare's Sonnets! This was a phase that would bear investigation. But Stubener stole the opportunity away and was back chanting his everlasting statistics.

A few minutes later, and most unwittingly, she opened up the biggest lead of all. That first sharp attraction toward him had begun to stir again after the discovery of the Sonnets. The magnificent frame of his, the handsome face, the chaste lips, the clear-looking eyes, the fine forehead which the short crop of blond hair did not hide, the aura of physical well-being and cleanness which he seemed to emanate—all this, and more that she sensed, drew her as she had never been drawn by any man, and yet through her mind kept running the nasty rumors that she had heard only the day before at the "Courier-Journal" office.

"You were right," she said. "There is something more important to talk about. There is something in my mind I want you to reconcile for me. Do you mind?"

Pat shook his head.

"If I am frank?—abominably frank? I've heard the men, sometimes, talking of particular fights and of the betting odds, and, while I gave no heed to it at the time, it seemed to me it was firmly agreed that there was a great deal of trickery and cheating connected with the sport. Now, when I look at you, for instance, I find it hard to understand how you can be a party to such cheating. I can understand your liking the sport for a sport, as well as for the money it brings you, but I can't understand—"

"There's nothing to understand," Stubener broke in, while Pat's lips were wreathed in a gentle, tolerant smile. "It's all fairy tales, this talk about faking, about fixed fights, and all that rot. There's nothing to it, Miss Sangster, I assure you. And now let me tell you about how I discovered Mr. Glendon. It was a letter I got from his father—"

But Maud Sangster refused to be side-tracked, and addressed herself to Pat.

"Listen. I remember one case particularly. It was some fight that took place several months ago—I forget the contestants. One of the editors of the "Courier-Journal" told me he intended to make a good winning. He didn't hope; he said he intended. He said he was on the inside and was betting on the number of rounds. He told me the fight would end in the nineteenth. This was the night before. And the next day he triumphantly called my attention to the fact that it had ended in that very round. I didn't think anything of it one way or the other. I was not interested in prize-fighting then. But I am now. At the time it seemed quite in accord with the vague conception I had about fighting. So you see, it isn't all fairy tales, is it?"

"I know that fight," Glendon said. "It was Owen and Murgweather. And it did end in the nineteenth round, Sam. And she said she heard that round named the day before. How do you account for it, Sam?"

"How do you account for a man picking a lucky lottery ticket?" the manager evaded, while getting his wits together to answer. "That's the very point. Men who study form and condition and seconds and rules and such things often pick the number of rounds, just as men have been known to pick hundred-to-one shots in the races. And don't forget one thing: for every man that wins, there's another that loses, there's another that didn't pick right. Miss Sangster, I assure you, on my honor, that faking and fixing in the fight game is … is non-existent."

"What is your opinion, Mr. Glendon?" she asked.

"The same as mine," Stubener snatched the answer. "He knows what I say is true, every word of it. He's never fought anything but a straight fight in his life. Isn't that right, Pat?"

"Yes; it's right," Pat affirmed, and the peculiar thing to Maud Sangster was that she was convinced he spoke the truth.

She brushed her forehead with her hand, as if to rid herself of the bepuzzlement that clouded her brain.

"Listen," she said. "Last night the same editor told me that your forthcoming fight was arranged to the very round in which it would end."

Stubener was verging on a panic, but Pat's speech saved him from replying.

"Then the editor lies," Pat's voice boomed now for the first time.

"He did not lie before, about that other fight," she challenged.

"What round did he say my fight with Nat Powers would end in?"

Before she could answer, the manager was into the thick of it.

"Oh, rats, Pat!" he cried. "Shut up. It's only the regular run of ring rumors. Let's get on with this interview."

He was ignored by Glendon, whose eyes, bent on hers, were no longer mildly blue, but harsh and imperative. She was sure now that she had stumbled on something tremendous, something that would explain all that had baffled her. At the same time she thrilled to the mastery of his voice and gaze. Here was a male man who would take hold of life and shake out of it what he wanted.

"What round did the editor say?" Glendon reiterated his demand.

"For the love of Mike, Pat, stop this foolishness," Stubener broke in.

"I wish you would give me a chance to answer," Maud Sangster said.

"I guess I'm able to talk with Miss Sangster," Glendon added. "You get out, Sam. Go off and take care of that photographer."

They looked at each other for a tense, silent moment, then the manager moved slowly to the door, opened it, and turned his head to listen.

"And now what round did he say?"

"I hope I haven't made a mistake," she said tremulously, "but I am very sure that he said the sixteenth round."

She saw surprise and anger leap into Glendon's face, and the anger and accusation in the glance he cast at his manager, and she knew the blow had driven home.

And there was reason for his anger. He knew he had talked it over with Stubener, and they had reached a decision to give the audience a good run for its money without unnecessarily prolonging the fight, and to end it in the sixteenth. And here was a woman, from a newspaper office, naming the very round.

Stubener, in the doorway, looked limp and pale, and it was evident he was holding himself together by an effort.

"I'll see you later," Pat told him. "Shut the door behind you."

The door closed, and the two were left alone. Glendon did not speak. The expression on his face was frankly one of trouble and perplexity.

"Well?" she asked.

He got up and towered above her, then sat down again, moistening his lips with his tongue.

"I'll tell you one thing," he finally said, "The fight won't end in the sixteenth round."

She did not speak, but her unconvinced and quizzical smile hurt him.

"You wait and see, Miss Sangster, and you'll see that editor man is mistaken."

"You mean the program is to be changed?" she queried audaciously.

He quivered to the cut of her words.

"I am not accustomed to lying," he said stiffly, "even to women."

"Neither have you to me, nor have you denied the program is to be changed. Perhaps, Mr. Glendon, I am stupid, but I fail to see the difference in what number the final round occurs so long as it is predetermined and known."

"I'll tell you that round, and not another soul shall know."

She shrugged her shoulders and smiled.

"It sounds to me very much like a racing tip. They are always given that way, you know. Furthermore, I am not quite stupid, and I know there is something wrong here. Why were you made angry by my naming the round? Why were you angry with your manager? Why did you send him from the room?"

For reply, Glendon walked over to the window, as if to look out, where he changed his mind and partly turned, and she knew, without seeing, that he was studying her face. He came back and sat down.

"You've said I haven't lied to you, Miss Sangster, and you were right. I haven't." He paused, groping painfully for a correct statement of the situation. "Now do you think you can believe what I am going to tell you? Will you take the word of a … prize-fighter?"

She nodded gravely, looking him straight in the eyes and certain that what he was about to tell was the truth.

"I've always fought straight and square. I've never touched a piece of dirty money in my life, nor attempted a dirty trick. Now I can go on from that. You've shaken me up pretty badly by what you told me. I don't know what to make of it. I can't pass a snap judgment on it. I don't know. But it looks bad. That's what troubles me. For see you, Stubener and I have talked this fight over, and it was understood between us that I would end the fight in the sixteenth round. Now you bring the same word. How did that editor know? Not from me. Stubener must have let it out … unless…." He stopped to debate the problem. "Unless that editor is a lucky guesser. I can't make up my mind about it. I'll have to keep my eyes open and wait and learn. Every word I've given you is straight, and there's my hand on it."

Again he towered out of his chair and over to her. Her small hand was gripped in his big one as she arose to meet him, and after a fair, straight look into the eyes between them, both glanced unconsciously at the clasped hands. She felt that she had never been more aware that she was a woman. The sex emphasis of those two hands—the soft and fragile feminine and the heavy, muscular masculine—was startling. Glendon was the first to speak.

"You could be hurt so easily," he said; and at the same time she felt the firmness of his grip almost caressingly relax.

She remembered the old Prussian king's love for giants, and laughed at the incongruity of the thought-association as she withdrew her hand.

"I am glad you came here to-day," he said, then hurried on awkwardly to make an explanation which the warm light of admiration in his eyes belied. "I mean because maybe you have opened my eyes to the crooked dealing that has been going on."

"You have surprised me," she urged. "It seemed to me that it is so generally understood that prize-fighting is full of crookedness, that I cannot understand how you, one of its chief exponents, could be ignorant of it. I thought as a matter of course that you would know all about it, and now you have convinced me that you never dreamed of it. You must be different from other fighters."

He nodded his head.

"That explains it, I guess. And that's what comes of keeping away from it—from the other fighters, and promoters, and sports. It was easy to pull the wool over my eyes. Yet it remains to be seen whether it has really been pulled over or not. You see, I am going to find out for myself."

"And change it?" she queried, rather breathlessly, convinced somehow that he could do anything he set out to accomplish.

"No; quit it," was his answer. "If it isn't straight I won't have anything more to do with it. And one thing is certain: this coming fight with Nat Powers won't end in the sixteenth round. If there is any truth in that editor's tip, they'll all be fooled. Instead of putting him out in the sixteenth, I'll let the fight run on into the twenties. You wait and see."

"And I'm not to tell the editor?"

She was on her feet now, preparing to go.

"Certainly not. If he is only guessing, let him take his chances. And if there's anything rotten about it he deserves to lose all he bets. This is to be a little secret between you and me. I'll tell you what I'll do. I'll name the round to you. I won't run it into the twenties. I'll stop Nat Powers in the eighteenth."

"And I'll not whisper it," she assured him.

"I'd like to ask you a favor," he said tentatively. "Maybe it's a big favor."

She showed her acquiescence in her face, as if it were already granted, and he went on:

"Of course, I know you won't use this faking in the interview. But I want more than that. I don't want you to publish anything at all."

She gave him a quick look with her searching gray eyes, then surprised herself by her answer.

"Certainly," she said. "It will not be published. I won't write a line of it."

"I knew it," he said simply.

For the moment she was disappointed by the lack of thanks, and the next moment she was glad that he had not thanked her. She sensed the different foundation he was building under this meeting of an hour with her, and she became daringly explorative.

"How did you know it?" she asked.

"I don't know." He shook his head. "I can't explain it. I knew it as a matter of course. Somehow it seems to me I know a lot about you and me."

"But why not publish the interview? As your manager says, it is good advertising."

"I know it," he answered slowly. "But I don't want to know you that way. I think it would hurt if you should publish it. I don't want to think that I knew you professionally. I'd like to remember our talk here as a talk between a man and a woman. I don't know whether you understand what I'm driving at. But it's the way I feel. I want to remember this just as a man and a woman."

As he spoke, in his eyes was all the expression with which a man looks at a woman. She felt the force and beat of him, and she felt strangely tongue-tied and awkward before this man who had been reputed tongue-tied and awkward. He could certainly talk straighter to the point and more convincingly than most men, and what struck her most forcibly was her own inborn certainty that it was mere naïve and simple frankness on his part and not a practised artfulness.

He saw her into her machine, and gave her another thrill when he said good-by. Once again their hands were clasped as he said:

"Some day I'll see you again. I want to see you again. Somehow I have a feeling that the last word has not been said between us."

And as the machine rolled away she was aware of a similar feeling. She had not seen the last of this very disquieting Pat Glendon, king of the bruisers and abysmal brute.

Back in the training quarters, Glendon encountered his perturbed manager.

"What did you fire me out for?" Stubener demanded. "We're finished. A hell of a mess you've made. You've never stood for meeting a reporter alone before, and now you'll see when that interview comes out."

Glendon, who had been regarding him with cool amusement, made as if to turn and pass on, and then changed his mind.

"It won't come out," he said.

Stubener looked up sharply.

"I asked her not to," Glendon explained.

Then Stubener exploded.

"As if she'd kill a juicy thing like that."

Glendon became very cold and his voice was harsh and grating.

"It won't be published. She told me so. And to doubt it is to call her a liar."

The Irish flame was in his eyes, and by that, and by the unconscious clenching of his passion-wrought hands, Stubener, who knew the strength of them, and of the man he faced, no longer dared to doubt.

VII

It did not take Stubener long to find out that Glendon intended extending the distance of the fight, though try as he would he could get no hint of the number of the round. He wasted no time, however, and privily clinched certain arrangements with Nat Powers and Nat Powers' manager. Powers had a faithful following of bettors, and the betting syndicate was not to be denied its harvest.

On the night of the fight, Maud Sangster was guilty of a more daring unconventionality than any she had yet committed, though no whisper of it leaked out to shock society. Under the protection of the editor, she occupied a ring-side seat. Her hair and most of her face were hidden under a slouch hat, while she wore a man's long overcoat that fell to her heels. Entering in the thick of the crowd, she was not noticed; nor did the newspaper men, in the press seats against the ring directly in front of her, recognize her.

As was the growing custom, there were no preliminary bouts, and she had barely gained her seat when roars of applause announced the arrival of Nat Powers. He came down the aisle in the midst of his seconds, and she was almost frightened by the formidable bulk of him. Yet he leaped the ropes as lightly as a man half his weight, and grinned acknowledgment to the tumultuous greeting that arose from all the house. He was not pretty. Two cauliflower ears attested his profession and its attendant brutality, while his broken nose had been so often spread over his face as to defy the surgeon's art to reconstruct it.

Another uproar heralded the arrival of Glendon, and she watched him eagerly as he went through the ropes to his corner. But it was not until the tedious time of announcements, introductions, and challenges was over, that the two men threw off their wraps and faced each other in ring costume. Concentrated upon them from overhead was the white glare of many electric lights—this for the benefit of the moving picture cameras; and she felt, as she looked at the two sharply contrasted men, that it was in Glendon that she saw the thoroughbred and in Powers the abysmal brute. Both looked their parts—Glendon, clean cut in face and form, softly and massively beautiful, Powers almost asymmetrically rugged and heavily matted with hair.

As they made their preliminary pose for the cameras, confronting each other in fighting attitudes, it chanced that Glendon's gaze dropped down through the ropes and rested on her face. Though he gave no sign, she knew, with a swift leap of the heart, that he had recognized her. The next moment the gong sounded, the announcer cried "Let her go!" and the battle was on.

It was a good fight. There was no blood, no marring, and both were clever. Half of the first round was spent in feeling each other out, but Maud Sangster found the play and feint and tap of the gloves sufficiently exciting. During some of the fiercer rallies in later stages of the fight, the editor was compelled to touch her arm to remind her who she was and where she was.

Powers fought easily and cleanly, as became the hero of half a hundred ring battles, and an admiring claque applauded his every cleverness. Yet he did not unduly exert himself save in occasional strenuous rallies that brought the audience yelling to its feet in the mistaken notion that he was getting his man.

It was at such a moment, when her unpractised eye could not inform her that Glendon was escaping serious damage, that the editor leaned to her and said:

"Young Pat will win all right. He's a comer, and they can't stop him. But he'll win in the sixteenth and not before."

"Or after?" she asked.

She almost laughed at the certitude of her companion's negative. She knew better.

Powers was noted for hunting his man from moment to moment and round to round, and Glendon was content to accede to this program. His defense was admirable, and he threw in just enough of offense to whet the edge of the audience's interest. Though he knew he was scheduled to lose,

Powers had had too long a ring experience to hesitate from knocking his man out if the opportunity offered. He had had the double cross worked too often on him to be chary in working it on others. If he got his chance he was prepared to knock his man out and let the syndicate go hang. Thanks to clever press publicity, the idea was prevalent that at last Young Glendon had met his master. In his heart, Powers, however, knew that it was himself who had encountered the better man. More than once, in the faster in-fighting, he received the weight of punches that he knew had been deliberately made no heavier.

On Glendon's part, there were times and times when a slip or error of judgment could have exposed him to one of his antagonist's sledge-hammer blows and lost him the fight. Yet his was that almost miraculous power of accurate timing and distancing, and his confidence was not shaken by the several close shaves he experienced. He had never lost a fight, never been knocked down, and he had always been so thoroughly the master of the man he faced, that such a possibility was unthinkable.

At the end of the fifteenth round, both men were in good condition, though Powers was breathing a trifle heavily and there were men in the ringside seats offering odds that he would "blow up."

It was just before the gong for the sixteenth round struck that Stubener, leaning over Glendon from behind in his corner, whispered:

"Are you going to get him now?"

Glendon, with a back toss of his head, shook it and laughed mockingly up into his manager's anxious face.

With the stroke of the gong for the sixteenth round, Glendon was surprised to see Powers cut loose. From the first second it was a tornado of fighting, and Glendon was hard put to escape serious damage. He blocked, clinched, ducked, sidestepped, was rushed backward against the ropes and was met by fresh rushes when he surged out to center. Several times Powers left inviting openings, but Glendon refused to loose the lightning-bolt of a blow that would drop his man. He was reserving that blow for two rounds later. Not in the whole fight had he ever exerted his full strength, nor struck with the force that was in him.

For two minutes, without the slightest let-up, Powers went at him hammer and tongs. In another minute the round would be over and the betting syndicate hard hit. But that minute was not to be. They had just come together in the center of the ring. It was as ordinary a clinch as any in the fight, save that Powers was struggling and roughing it every instant. Glendon whipped his left over in a crisp but easy jolt to the side of the face. It was like any of a score of similar jolts he had already delivered in the course of the fight. To his amazement he felt Powers go limp in his arms and begin sinking to the floor on sagging, spraddling legs that refused to bear his weight. He struck the floor with a thump, rolled half over on his side, and lay with closed eyes and motionless. The referee, bending above him, was shouting the count.

At the cry of "Nine!" Powers quivered as if making a vain effort to rise.

"Ten!—and out!" cried the referee.

He caught Glendon's hand and raised it aloft to the roaring audience in token that he was the winner.

For the first time in the ring, Glendon was dazed. It had not been a knockout blow. He could stake his life on that. It had not been to the jaw but to the side of the face, and he knew it had gone there and nowhere else. Yet the man was out, had been counted out, and he had faked it beautifully. That final thump on the floor had been a convincing masterpiece. To the audience it was indubitably a knockout, and the moving picture machines would perpetuate the lie. The editor had called the turn after all, and a crooked turn it was.

Glendon shot a swift glance through the ropes to the face of Maud Sangster. She was looking straight at him, but her eyes were bleak and hard, and there was neither recognition nor expression in them. Even as he looked, she turned away unconcernedly and said something to the man beside her.

Powers' seconds were carrying him to his corner, a seeming limp wreck of a man. Glendon's seconds were advancing upon him to congratulate him and to remove his gloves. But Stubener was ahead of them. His face was beaming as he caught Glendon's right glove in both his hands and cried:

"Good boy, Pat. I knew you'd do it."

Glendon pulled his glove away. And for the first time in the years they had been together, his manager heard him swear.

"You go to hell," he said, and turned to hold out his hands for his seconds to pull off the gloves.

VIII

That night, after receiving the editor's final dictum that there was not a square fighter in the game, Maud Sangster cried quietly for a moment on the edge of her bed, grew angry, and went to sleep hugely disgusted with herself, prize-fighters, and the world in general.

The next afternoon she began work on an interview with Henry Addison that was destined never to be finished. It was in the private room that was accorded her at the "Courier-Journal" office that the thing happened. She had paused in her writing to glance at a headline in the afternoon paper announcing that Glendon was matched with Tom Cannam, when one of the door-boys brought in a card. It was Glendon's.

"Tell him I can't be seen," she told the boy.

In a minute he was back.

"He says he's coming in anyway, but he'd rather have your permission."

"Did you tell him I was busy?" she asked.

"Yes'm, but he said he was coming just the same."

She made no answer, and the boy, his eyes shining with admiration for the importunate visitor, rattled on.

"I know'm. He's a awful big guy. If he started roughhousing he could clean the whole office out. He's young Glendon, who won the fight last night."

"Very well, then. Bring him in. We don't want the office cleaned out, you know."

No greetings were exchanged when Glendon entered. She was as cold and inhospitable as a gray day, and neither invited him to a chair nor recognized him with her eyes, sitting half turned away from him at her desk and waiting for him to state his business. He gave no sign of how this cavalier treatment affected him, but plunged directly into his subject.

"I want to talk to you," he said shortly. "That fight. It did end in that round."

She shrugged her shoulders.

"I knew it would."

"You didn't," he retorted. "You didn't. I didn't."

She turned and looked at him with quiet affectation of boredom.

"What is the use?" she asked. "Prize-fighting is prize-fighting, and we all know what it means. The fight did end in the round I told you it would."

"It did," he agreed. "But you didn't know it would. In all the world you and I were at least two that knew Powers wouldn't be knocked out in the sixteenth."

She remained silent.

"I say you knew he wouldn't." He spoke peremptorily, and, when she still declined to speak, stepped nearer to her. "Answer me," he commanded.

She nodded her head.

"But he was," she insisted.

"He wasn't. He wasn't knocked out at all. Do you get that? I am going to tell you about it, and you are going to listen. I didn't lie to you. Do you get that? I didn't lie to you. I was a fool, and they fooled me, and you along with me. You thought you saw him knocked out. Yet the blow I struck was not heavy enough. It didn't hit him in the right place either. He made believe it did. He faked that knockout."

He paused and looked at her expectantly. And somehow, with a leap and thrill, she knew that she believed him, and she felt pervaded by a warm happiness at the reinstatement of this man who meant nothing to her and whom she had seen but twice in her life.

"Well?" he demanded, and she thrilled anew at the compellingness of him.

She stood up, and her hand went out to his.

"I believe you," she said. "And I am glad, most glad."

It was a longer grip than she had anticipated. He looked at her with eyes that burned and to which her own unconsciously answered back. Never was there such a man, was her thought. Her eyes dropped first, and his followed, so that, as before, both gazed at the clasped hands. He made a movement of his whole body toward her, impulsive and involuntary, as if to gather her to him, then checked himself abruptly, with an unmistakable effort. She saw it, and felt the pull of his hand as it started to draw her to him. And to her amazement she felt the desire to yield, the desire almost overwhelmingly to be drawn into the strong circle of those arms. And had he compelled, she knew that she would not have refrained. She was almost dizzy, when he checked himself and with a closing of his fingers that half crushed hers, dropped her hand, almost flung it from him.

"God!" he breathed. "You were made for me."

He turned partly away from her, sweeping his hand to his forehead. She knew she would hate him forever if he dared one stammered word of apology or explanation. But he seemed to have the way always of doing the right thing where she was concerned. She sank into her chair, and he into another, first drawing it around so as to face her across the corner of the desk.

"I spent last night in a Turkish bath," he said. "I sent for an old broken-down bruiser. He was a friend of my father in the old days. I knew there couldn't be a thing about the ring he didn't know, and I made him talk. The funny thing was that it was all I could do to convince him that I didn't know the things I asked him about. He called me the babe in the woods. I guess he was right. I was raised in the woods, and woods is about all I know.

"Well, I received an education from that old man last night. The ring is rottener than you told me. It seems everybody connected with it is crooked. The very supervisors that grant the fight permits graft off of the promoters; and the promoters, managers, and fighters graft off of each other and off the public. It's down to a system, in one way, and on the other hand they're always—do you know what the double cross is?" (She nodded.) "Well, they don't seem to miss a chance to give each other the double cross.

"The stuff that old man told me took my breath away. And here I've been in the thick of it for several years and knew nothing of it. I was a real babe in the woods. And yet I can see how I've been fooled. I was so made that nobody could stop me. I was bound to win, and, thanks to Stubener, everything crooked was kept away from me. This morning I cornered Spider Walsh and made him talk. He was my first trainer, you know, and he followed Stubener's instructions. They kept me in ignorance. Besides, I didn't herd with the sporting crowd. I spent my time hunting and fishing and monkeying with cameras and such things. Do you know what Walsh and Stubener called me between themselves?—the Virgin. I only learned it this morning from Walsh, and it was like pulling teeth. And they were right. I was a little innocent lamb.

"And Stubener was using me for crookedness, too, only I didn't know it. I can look back now and see how it was worked. But you see, I wasn't interested enough in the game to be suspicious. I was born with a good body and a cool head, I was raised in the open, and I was taught by my father, who knew more about fighting than any man living or dead. It was too easy. The ring didn't absorb me. There was never any doubt of the outcome. But I'm done with it now."

She pointed to the headline announcing his match with Tom Cannam.

"That's Stubener's work," he explained. "It was programmed months ago. But I don't care. I'm heading for the mountains. I've quit."

She glanced at the unfinished interview on the desk and sighed.

"How lordly men are," she said. "Masters of destiny. They do as they please—"

"From what I've heard," he interrupted, "you've done pretty much as you please. It's one of the things I like about you. And what has struck me hard from the first was the way you and I understand each other."

He broke off and looked at her with burning eyes.

"Well, the ring did one thing for me," he went on. "It made me acquainted with you. And when you find the one woman, there's just one thing to do. Take her in your two hands and don't let go. Come on, let us start for the mountains."

It had come with the suddenness of a thunder-clap, and yet she felt that she had been expecting it. Her heart was beating up and almost choking her in a strangely delicious way. Here at least was the primitive and the simple with a vengeance. Then, too, it seemed a dream. Such things did not take place in modern newspaper offices. Love could not be made in such fashion; it only so occurred on the stage and in novels.

He had arisen, and was holding out both hands to her.

"I don't dare," she said in a whisper, half to herself. "I don't dare."

And thereat she was stung by the quick contempt that flashed in his eyes but that swiftly changed to open incredulity.

"You'd dare anything you wanted," he was saying. "I know that. It's not a case of dare, but of want. Do you want?"

She had arisen, and was now swaying as if in a dream. It flashed into her mind to wonder if it were hypnotism. She wanted to glance about her at the familiar objects of the room in order to identify herself with reality, but she could not take her eyes from his. Nor did she speak.

He had stepped beside her. His hand was on her arm, and she leaned toward him involuntarily. It was all part of the dream, and it was no longer hers to question anything. It was the great dare. He was right. She could dare what she wanted, and she did want. He was helping her into her jacket. She was thrusting the hat-pins through her hair. And even as she realized it, she found herself walking beside him through the opened door. The "Flight of the Duchess" and "The Statue and the Bust," darted through her mind. Then she remembered "Waring."

"'What's become of Waring?'" she murmured.

"'Land travel or sea-faring?'" he murmured back.

And to her this kindred sufficient note was a vindication of her madness.

At the entrance of the building he raised his hand to call a taxi, but was stopped by her touch on his arm.

"Where are we going?" she breathed.

"To the Ferry. We've just time to catch that Sacramento train."

"But I can't go this way," she protested. "I ... I haven't even a change of handkerchiefs."

He held up his hand again before replying.

"You can shop in Sacramento. We'll get married there and catch the night overland north. I'll arrange everything by telegraph from the train."

As the cab drew to the curb, she looked quickly about her at the familiar street and the familiar throng, then, with almost a flurry of alarm, into Glendon's face.

"I don't know a thing about you," she said.

"We know everything about each other," was his answer.

She felt the support and urge of his arms, and lifted her foot to the step. The next moment the door had closed, he was beside her, and the cab was heading down Market Street. He passed his arm around her, drew her close, and kissed her. When next she glimpsed his face she was certain that it was dyed with a faint blush.

"I ... I've heard there was an art in kissing," he stammered. "I don't know anything about it myself, but I'll learn. You see, you're the first woman I ever kissed."

IX

Where a jagged peak of rock thrust above the vast virgin forest, reclined a man and a woman. Beneath them, on the edge of the trees, were tethered two horses. Behind each saddle were a pair of small saddle-bags. The trees were monotonously huge. Towering hundreds of feet into the air, they ran from eight to ten and twelve feet in diameter. Many were much larger. All morning they had toiled up the divide through this unbroken forest, and this peak of rock had been the first spot where they could get out of the forest in order to see the forest.

Beneath them and away, far as they could see, lay range upon range of haze-empurpled mountains. There was no end to these ranges. They rose one behind another to the dim, distant skyline, where they faded away with a vague promise of unending extension beyond. There were no clearings in the forest; north, south, east, and west, untouched, unbroken, it covered the land with its mighty growth.

They lay, feasting their eyes on the sight, her hand clasped in one of his; for this was their honeymoon, and these were the redwoods of Mendocino. Across from Shasta they had come, with horses and saddle-bags, and down through the wilds of the coast counties, and they had no plan except to continue until some other plan entered their heads. They were roughly dressed, she in travel-stained khaki, he in overalls and woolen shirt. The latter was open at the sunburned neck, and in his hugeness he seemed a fit dweller among the forest giants, while for her, as a dweller with him, there were no signs of aught else but happiness.

"Well, Big Man," she said, propping herself up on an elbow to gaze at him, "it is more wonderful than you promised. And we are going through it together."

"And there's a lot of the rest of the world we'll go through together," he answered, shifting his position so as to get her hand in both of his.

"But not till we've finished with this," she urged. "I seem never to grow tired of the big woods … and of you."

He slid effortlessly into a sitting posture and gathered her into his arms.

"Oh, you lover," she whispered. "And I had given up hope of finding such a one."

"And I never hoped at all. I must just have known all the time that I was going to find you. Glad?"

Her answer was a soft pressure where her hand rested on his neck, and for long minutes they looked out over the great woods and dreamed.

"You remember I told you how I ran away from the red-haired school teacher? That was the first time I saw this country. I was on foot, but forty or fifty miles a day was play for me. I was a regular Indian. I wasn't thinking about you then. Game was pretty scarce in the redwoods, but there was plenty of fine trout. That was when I camped on these rocks. I didn't dream that some day I'd be back with you, YOU."

"And be a champion of the ring, too," she suggested.

"No; I didn't think about that at all. Dad had always told me I was going to be, and I took it for granted. You see, he was very wise. He was a great man."

"But he didn't see you leaving the ring."

"I don't know. He was so careful in hiding its crookedness from me, that I think he feared it. I've told you about the contract with Stubener. Dad put in that clause about crookedness. The first crooked thing my manager did was to break the contract."

"And yet you are going to fight this Tom Cannam. Is it worth while?"

He looked at her quickly.

"Don't you want me to?"

"Dear lover, I want you to do whatever you want."

So she said, and to herself, her words still ringing in her ears, she marveled that she, not least among the stubbornly independent of the breed of Sangster, should utter them. Yet she knew they were true, and she was glad.

"It will be fun," he said.

"But I don't understand all the gleeful details."

"I haven't worked them out yet. You might help me. In the first place I'm going to double-cross Stubener and the betting syndicate. It will be part of the joke. I am going to put Cannam out in the first round. For the first time I shall be really angry when I fight. Poor Tom Cannam, who's as crooked as the rest, will be the chief sacrifice. You see, I intend to make a speech in the ring. It's unusual, but it will be a success, for I am going to tell the audience all the inside workings of the game. It's a good game, too, but they're running it on business principles, and that's what spoils it. But there, I'm giving the speech to you instead of at the ring."

"I wish I could be there to hear," she said.

He looked at her and debated.

"I'd like to have you. But it's sure to be a rough time. There is no telling what may happen when I start my program. But I'll come straight to you as soon as it's over. And it will be the last appearance of Young Glendon in the ring, in any ring."

"But, dear, you've never made a speech in your life," she objected. "You might fail."

He shook his head positively.

"I'm Irish," he announced, "and what Irishman was there who couldn't speak?" He paused to laugh merrily. "Stubener thinks I'm crazy. Says a man can't train on matrimony. A lot he knows about matrimony, or me, or you, or anything except real estate and fixed fights. But I'll show him that night, and poor Tom, too. I really feel sorry for Tom."

"My dear abysmal brute is going to behave most abysmally and brutally, I fear," she murmured.

He laughed.

"I'm going to make a noble attempt at it. Positively my last appearance, you know. And then it will be you, YOU. But if you don't want that last appearance, say the word."

"Of course I want it, Big Man. I want my Big Man for himself, and to be himself he must be himself. If you want this, I want it for you, and for myself, too. Suppose I said I wanted to go on the stage, or to the South Seas or the North Pole?"

He answered slowly, almost solemnly.

"Then I'd say go ahead. Because you are you and must be yourself and do whatever you want. I love you because you are you."

"And we're both a silly pair of lovers," she said, when his embrace had relaxed.

"Isn't it great!" he cried.

He stood up, measured the sun with his eye, and extended his hand out over the big woods that covered the serried, purple ranges.

"We've got to sleep out there somewhere. It's thirty miles to the nearest camp."

X

Who, of all the sports present, will ever forget the memorable night at the Golden Gate Arena, when Young Glendon put Tom Cannam to sleep and an even greater one than Tom Cannam, kept the great audience on the ragged edge of riot for an hour, caused the subsequent graft investigation of the supervisors and the indictments of the contractors and the building commissioners, and pretty generally disrupted the whole fight game. It was a complete surprise. Not even Stubener had the slightest apprehension of what was coming. It was true that his man had been insubordinate after the Nat Powers affair, and had run off and got married; but all that was over. Young Pat had done the expected, swallowed the inevitable crookedness of the ring, and come back into it again.

The Golden Gate Arena was new. This was its first fight, and it was the biggest building of the kind San Francisco had ever erected. It seated twenty-five thousand, and every seat was occupied. Sports had traveled from all the world to be present, and they had paid fifty dollars for their ring-side seats. The cheapest seat in the house had sold for five dollars.

The old familiar roar of applause went up when Billy Morgan, the veteran announcer, climbed through the ropes and bared his gray head. As he opened his mouth to speak, a heavy crash came from a near section where several tiers of low seats had collapsed. The crowd broke into loud laughter and shouted jocular regrets and advice to the victims, none of whom had been hurt. The crash of the seats and the hilarious uproar caused the captain of police in charge to look at one of his lieutenants and lift his brows in token that they would have their hands full and a lively night.

One by one, welcomed by uproarious applause, seven doughty old ring heroes climbed through the ropes to be introduced. They were all ex-heavyweight champions of the world. Billy Morgan accompanied each presentation to the audience with an appropriate phrase. One was hailed as "Honest John" and "Old Reliable," another was "the squarest two-fisted fighter the ring ever saw." And of others: "the hero of a hundred battles and never threw one and never lay down"; "the gamest of the old guard"; "the only one who ever came back"; "the greatest warrior of them all"; and "the hardest nut in the ring to crack."

All this took time. A speech was insisted on from each of them, and they mumbled and muttered in reply with proud blushes and awkward shamblings. The longest speech was from "Old Reliable" and lasted nearly a minute. Then they had to be photographed. The ring filled up with celebrities, with champion wrestlers, famous conditioners, and veteran time-keepers and referees. Light-weights and middle-weights swarmed. Everybody seemed to be challenging everybody. Nat Powers was there, demanding a return match from Young Glendon, and so were all the other shining lights whom Glendon had snuffed out. Also, they all challenged Jim Hanford, who, in turn, had to make his statement, which was to the effect that he would accord the next fight to the winner of the one that was about to take place. The audience immediately proceeded to name the winner, half of it wildly crying "Glendon," and the other half "Powers." In the midst of the pandemonium another tier of seats went down, and half a dozen rows were on between cheated ticket holders and the stewards who had been reaping a fat harvest. The captain despatched a message to headquarters for additional police details.

The crowd was feeling good. When Cannam and Glendon made their ring entrances the Arena resembled a national political convention. Each was cheered for a solid five minutes. The ring was now cleared. Glendon sat in his corner surrounded by his seconds. As usual, Stubener was at his back. Cannam was introduced first, and after he had scraped and ducked his head, he was compelled to respond to the cries for a speech. He stammered and halted, but managed to grind out several ideas.

"I'm proud to be here to-night," he said, and found space to capture another thought while the applause was thundering. "I've fought square. I've fought square all my life. Nobody can deny that. And I'm going to do my best to-night."

There were loud cries of: "That's right, Tom!" "We know that!" "Good boy, Tom!" "You're the boy to fetch the bacon home!"

72

Then came Glendon's turn. From him, likewise, a speech was demanded, though for principals to give speeches was an unprecedented thing in the prize-ring. Billy Morgan held up his hand for silence, and in a clear, powerful voice Glendon began.

"Everybody has told you they were proud to be here to-night," he said. "I am not" The audience was startled, and he paused long enough to let it sink home, "I am not proud of my company. You wanted a speech. I'll give you a real one. This is my last fight. After to-night I leave the ring for good. Why? I have already told you. I don't like my company. The prize-ring is so crooked that no man engaged in it can hide behind a corkscrew. It is rotten to the core, from the little professional clubs right up to this affair to-night."

The low rumble of astonishment that had been rising at this point burst into a roar. There were loud boos and hisses, and many began crying: "Go on with the fight!" "We want the fight!" "Why don't you fight?" Glendon, waiting, noted that the principal disturbers near the ring were promoters and managers and fighters. In vain did he strive to make himself heard. The audience was divided, half crying out, "Fight!" and the other half, "Speech! Speech!"

Ten minutes of hopeless madness prevailed. Stubener, the referee, the owner of the Arena, and the promoter of the fight, pleaded with Glendon to go on with the fight. When he refused, the referee declared that he would award the fight in forfeit to Cannam if Glendon did not fight.

"You can't do it," the latter retorted. "I'll sue you in all the courts if you try that on, and I'll not promise you that you'll survive this crowd if you cheat it out of the fight. Besides, I'm going to fight. But before I do I'm going to finish my speech."

"But it's against the rules," protested the referee.

"It's nothing of the sort. There's not a word in the rules against ring-side speeches. Every big fighter here to-night has made a speech."

"Only a few words," shouted the promoter in Glendon's ear. "But you're giving a lecture."

"There's nothing in the rules against lectures," Glendon answered. "And now you fellows get out of the ring or I'll throw you out."

The promoter, apoplectic and struggling, was dropped over the ropes by his coat-collar. He was a large man, but so easily had Glendon done it with one hand that the audience went wild with delight. The cries for a speech increased in volume. Stubener and the owner beat a wise retreat. Glendon held up his hands to be heard, whereupon those that shouted for the fight redoubled their efforts. Two or three tiers of seats crashed down, and numbers who had thus lost their places, added to the turmoil by making a concerted rush to squeeze in on the still intact seats, while those behind, blocked from sight of the ring, yelled and raved for them to sit down.

Glendon walked to the ropes and spoke to the police captain. He was compelled to bend over and shout in his ear.

"If I don't give this speech," he said, "this crowd will wreck the place. If they break loose you can never hold them, you know that. Now you've got to help. You keep the ring clear and I'll silence the crowd."

He went back to the center of the ring and again held up his hands.

"You want that speech?" he shouted in a tremendous voice.

Hundreds near the ring heard him and cried "Yes!"

"Then let every man who wants to hear shut up the noise-maker next to him!"

The advice was taken, so that when he repeated it, his voice penetrated farther. Again and again he shouted it, and slowly, zone by zone, the silence pressed outward from the ring, accompanied by a muffled undertone of smacks and thuds and scuffles as the obstreperous were subdued by their neighbors. Almost had all confusion been smothered, when a tier of seats near the ring went down. This was greeted with fresh roars of laughter, which of itself died away, so that a lone voice, far back, was heard distinctly as it piped: "Go on, Glendon! We're with you!"

Glendon had the Celt's intuitive knowledge of the psychology of the crowd. He knew that what had been a vast disorderly mob five minutes before was now tightly in hand, and for added effect he deliberately delayed. Yet the delay was just long enough and not a second too long. For thirty seconds the silence was complete, and the effect produced was one of awe. Then, just as the first faint hints of restlessness came to his ears, he began to speak:

"When I finish this speech," he said, "I am going to fight. I promise you it will be a real fight, one of the few real fights you have ever seen. I am going to get my man in the shortest possible time. Billy Morgan, in making his final announcement, will tell you that it is to be a forty-five-round contest. Let me tell you that it will be nearer forty-five seconds.

"When I was interrupted I was telling you that the ring was rotten. It is—from top to bottom. It is run on business principles, and you all know what business principles are. Enough said. You are the suckers, every last one of you that is not making anything out of it. Why are the seats falling down to-night? Graft. Like the fight game, they were built on business principles."

He now held the audience stronger than ever, and knew it.

"There are three men squeezed on two seats. I can see that everywhere. What does it mean? Graft. The stewards don't get any wages. They are supposed to graft. Business principles again. You pay. Of course you pay. How are the fight permits obtained? Graft. And now let me ask you: if the men who build the seats graft, if the stewards graft, if the authorities graft, why shouldn't those higher up in the fight game graft? They do. And you pay.

"And let me tell you it is not the fault of the fighters. They don't run the game. The promoters and managers run it; they're the business men. The fighters are only fighters. They begin honestly enough, but the managers and promoters make them give in or kick them out. There have been straight fighters. And there are now a few, but they don't earn much as a rule. I guess there have been straight managers. Mine is about the best of the boiling. But just ask him how much he's got salted down in real estate and apartment houses."

Here the uproar began to drown his voice.

"Let every man who wants to hear shut up the man alongside of him!" Glendon instructed.

Again, like the murmur of a surf, there was a rustling of smacks, and thuds, and scuffles, and the house quieted down.

"Why does every fighter work overtime insisting that he's always fought square? Why are they called Honest Johns, and Honest Bills, and Honest Blacksmiths, and all the rest? Doesn't it ever strike you that they seem to be afraid of something? When a man comes to you shouting he is honest, you get suspicious. But when a prize-fighter passes the same dope out to you, you swallow it down.

"May the best man win! How often have you heard Billy Morgan say that! Let me tell you that the best man doesn't win so often, and when he does it's usually arranged for him. Most of the grudge fights you've heard or seen were arranged, too. It's a program. The whole thing is programmed. Do you think the promoters and managers are in it for their health? They're not. They're business men.

"Tom, Dick, and Harry are three fighters. Dick is the best man. In two fights he could prove it. But what happens? Tom licks Harry. Dick licks Tom. Harry licks Dick. Nothing proved. Then come the return matches. Harry licks Tom. Tom licks Dick. Dick licks Harry. Nothing proved. Then they try again. Dick is kicking. Says he wants to get along in the game. So Dick licks Tom, and Dick licks Harry. Eight fights to prove Dick the best man, when two could have done it. All arranged. A regular program. And you pay for it, and when your seats don't break down you get robbed of them by the stewards.

"It's a good game, too, if it were only square. The fighters would be square if they had a chance. But the graft is too big. When a handful of men can divide up three-quarters of a million dollars on three fights—"

A wild outburst compelled him to stop. Out of the medley of cries from all over the house, he could distinguish such as "What million dollars?"

"What three fights?" "Tell us!" "Go on!" Likewise there were boos and hisses, and cries of "Muckraker! Muckraker!"

"Do you want to hear?" Glendon shouted. "Then keep order!"

Once more he compelled the impressive half minute of silence.

"What is Jim Hanford planning? What is the program his crowd and mine are framing up? They know I've got him. He knows I've got him. I can whip him in one fight. But he's the champion of the world. If I don't give in to the program, they'll never give me a chance to fight him. The program calls for three fights. I am to win the first fight. It will be pulled off in Nevada if San Francisco won't stand for it. We are to make it a good fight. To make it good, each of us will put up a side bet of twenty thousand. It will be real money, but it won't be a real bet. Each gets his own slipped back to him. The same way with the purse. We'll divide it evenly, though the public division will be thirty-five and sixty-five. The purse, the moving picture royalties, the advertisements, and all the rest of the drags won't be a cent less than two hundred and fifty thousand. We'll divide it, and go to work on the return match. Hanford will win that, and we divide again. Then comes the third fight; I win as I have every right to; and we have taken three-quarters of a million out of the pockets of the fighting public. That's the program, but the money is dirty. And that's why I am quitting the ring to-night—"

It was at this moment that Jim Hanford, kicking a clinging policeman back among the seat-holders, heaved his huge frame through the ropes, bellowing:

"It's a lie!"

He rushed like an infuriated bull at Glendon, who sprang back, and then, instead of meeting the rush, ducked cleanly away. Unable to check himself, the big man fetched up against the ropes. Flung back by the spring of them, he was turning to make another rush, when Glendon landed him. Glendon, cool, clear-seeing, distanced his man perfectly to the jaw and struck the first full-strength blow of his career. All his strength, and his reserve of strength, went into that one smashing muscular explosion.

Hanford was dead in the air—in so far as unconsciousness may resemble death. So far as he was concerned, he ceased at the moment of contact with Glendon's fist. His feet left the floor and he was in the air until he struck the topmost rope. His inert body sprawled across it, sagged at the middle, and fell through the ropes and down out of the ring upon the heads of the men in the press seats.

The audience broke loose. It had already seen more than it had paid to see, for the great Jim Hanford, the world champion, had been knocked out. It was unofficial, but it had been with a single punch. Never had there been such a night in fistiana. Glendon looked ruefully at his damaged knuckles, cast a glance through the ropes to where Hanford was groggily coming to, and held up his hands. He had clinched his right to be heard, and the audience grew still.

"When I began to fight," he said, "they called me 'One-Punch Glendon.' You saw that punch a moment ago. I always had that punch. I went after my men and got them on the jump, though I was careful not to hit with all my might. Then I was educated. My manager told me it wasn't fair to the crowd. He advised me to make long fights so that the crowd could get a run for its money. I was a fool, a mutt. I was a green lad from the mountains. So help me God, I swallowed it as the truth. My manager used to talk over with me what round I would put my man out in. Then he tipped it off to the betting syndicate, and the betting syndicate went to it. Of course you paid. But I am glad for one thing. I never touched a cent of the money. They didn't dare offer it to me, because they knew it would give the game away.

"You remember my fight with Nat Powers. I never knocked him out. I had got suspicious. So the gang framed it up with him. I didn't know. I intended to let him go a couple of rounds over the sixteenth. That last punch in the sixteenth didn't shake him. But he faked the knock-out just the same and fooled all of you."

"How about to-night?" a voice called out. "Is it a frame-up?"

"It is," was Glendon's answer. "How's the syndicate betting? That Cannam will last to the fourteenth."

Howls and hoots went up. For the last time Glendon held up his hand for silence.

"I'm almost done now. But I want to tell you one thing. The syndicate gets landed to-night. This is to be a square fight. Tom Cannam won't last till the fourteenth round. He won't last the first round."

Cannam sprang to his feet in his corner and cried out in a fury:

"You can't do it. The man don't live who can get me in one round!"

Glendon ignored him and went on.

"Once now in my life I have struck with all my strength. You saw that a moment ago when I caught Hanford. To-night, for the second time, I am going to hit with all my strength—that is, if Cannam doesn't jump through the ropes right now and get away. And now I'm ready."

He went to his corner and held out his hands for his gloves. In the opposite corner Cannam raged while his seconds tried vainly to calm him. At last Billy Morgan managed to make the final announcement.

"This will be a forty-five round contest," he shouted. "Marquis of Queensbury Rules! And may the best man win! Let her go!"

The gong struck. The two men advanced. Glendon's right hand was extended for the customary shake, but Cannam, with an angry toss of the head, refused to take it. To the general surprise, he did not rush. Angry though he was, he fought carefully, his touched pride impelling him to bend every effort to last out the round. Several times he struck, but he struck cautiously, never relaxing his defense. Glendon hunted him about the ring, ever advancing with the remorseless tap-tap of his left foot. Yet he struck no blows, nor attempted to strike. He even dropped his hands to his sides and hunted the other defenselessly in an effort to draw him out. Cannam grinned defiantly, but declined to take advantage of the proffered opening.

Two minutes passed, and then a change came over Glendon. By every muscle, by every line of his face, he advertised that the moment had come for him to get his man. Acting it was, and it was well acted. He seemed to have become a thing of steel, as hard and pitiless as steel. The effect was apparent on Cannam, who redoubled his caution. Glendon quickly worked him into a corner and herded and held him there. Still he struck no blow, nor attempted to strike, and the suspense on Cannam's part grew painful. In vain he tried to work out of the corner, while he could not summon resolution to rush upon his opponent in an attempt to gain the respite of a clinch.

Then it came—a swift series of simple feints that were muscle flashes. Cannam was dazzled. So was the audience. No two of the onlookers could agree afterward as to what took place. Cannam ducked one feint and at the same time threw up his face guard to meet another feint for his jaw. He also attempted to change position with his legs. Ring-side witnesses swore that they saw Glendon start the blow from his right hip and leap forward like a tiger to add the weight of his body to it. Be that as it may, the blow caught Cannam on the point of the chin at the moment of his shift of position. And like Hanford, he was unconscious in the air before he struck the ropes and fell through on the heads of the reporters.

Of what happened afterward that night in the Golden Gate Arena, columns in the newspapers were unable adequately to describe. The police kept the ring clear, but they could not save the Arena. It was not a riot. It was an orgy. Not a seat was left standing. All over the great hall, by main strength, crowding and jostling to lay hands on beams and boards, the crowd uprooted and over-turned. Prize-fighters sought protection of the police, but there were not enough police to escort them out, and fighters, managers, and promoters were beaten and battered. Jim Hanford alone was spared. His jaw, prodigiously swollen, earned him this mercy. Outside, when finally driven from the building, the crowd fell upon a new seven-thousand-dollar motor car belonging to a well-known fight promoter and reduced it to scrapiron and kindling wood.

Glendon, unable to dress amid the wreckage of dressing rooms, gained his automobile, still in his ring costume and wrapped in a bath robe, but failed to escape. By weight of numbers the crowd caught and held his machine.

The police were too busy to rescue him, and in the end a compromise was effected, whereby the car was permitted to proceed at a walk escorted by five thousand cheering madmen.

It was midnight when this storm swept past Union Square and down upon the St. Francis. Cries for a speech went up, and though at the hotel entrance, Glendon was good-naturedly restrained from escaping. He even tried leaping out upon the heads of the enthusiasts, but his feet never touched the pavement. On heads and shoulders, clutched at and uplifted by every hand that could touch his body, he went back through the air to the machine. Then he gave his speech, and Maud Glendon, looking down from an upper window at her young Hercules towering on the seat of the automobile, knew, as she always knew, that he meant it when he repeated that he had fought his last fight and retired from the ring forever.

The End

THE FAITH OF MEN

A RELIC OF THE PLIOCENE

I wash my hands of him at the start. I cannot father his tales, nor will I be responsible for them. I make these preliminary reservations, observe, as a guard upon my own integrity. I possess a certain definite position in a small way, also a wife; and for the good name of the community that honours my existence with its approval, and for the sake of her posterity and mine, I cannot take the chances I once did, nor foster probabilities with the careless improvidence of youth. So, I repeat, I wash my hands of him, this Nimrod, this mighty hunter, this homely, blue-eyed, freckle-faced Thomas Stevens.

Having been honest to myself, and to whatever prospective olive branches my wife may be pleased to tender me, I can now afford to be generous. I shall not criticize the tales told me by Thomas Stevens, and, further, I shall withhold my judgment. If it be asked why, I can only add that judgment I have none. Long have I pondered, weighed, and balanced, but never have my conclusions been twice the same—forsooth! because Thomas Stevens is a greater man than I. If he have told truths, well and good; if untruths, still well and good. For who can prove? or who disprove? I eliminate myself from the proposition, while those of little faith may do as I have done—go find the same Thomas Stevens, and discuss to his face the various matters which, if fortune serve, I shall relate. As to where he may be found? The directions are simple: anywhere between 53 north latitude and the Pole, on the one hand; and, on the other, the likeliest hunting grounds that lie between the east coast of Siberia and farthermost Labrador. That he is there, somewhere, within that clearly defined territory, I pledge the word of an honourable man whose expectations entail straight speaking and right living.

Thomas Stevens may have toyed prodigiously with truth, but when we first met (it were well to mark this point), he wandered into my camp when I thought myself a thousand miles beyond the outermost post of civilization. At the sight of his human face, the first in weary months, I could have sprung forward and folded him in my arms (and I am not by any means a demonstrative man); but to him his visit seemed the most casual thing under the sun. He just strolled into the light of my camp, passed the time of day after the custom of men on beaten trails, threw my snowshoes the one way and a couple of dogs the other, and so made room for himself by the fire. Said he'd just dropped in to borrow a pinch of soda and to see if I had any decent tobacco. He plucked forth an ancient pipe, loaded it with painstaking care, and, without as much as by your leave, whacked half the tobacco of my pouch into his. Yes, the stuff was fairly good. He sighed with the contentment of the just, and literally absorbed the smoke from the crisping yellow flakes, and it did my smoker's heart good to behold him.

Hunter? Trapper? Prospector? He shrugged his shoulders No; just sort of knocking round a bit. Had come up from the Great Slave some time since, and was thinking of trapsing over into the Yukon country. The factor of Koshim had spoken about the discoveries on the Klondike, and he was of a mind to run over for a peep. I noticed that he spoke of the Klondike in the archaic vernacular, calling it the Reindeer River—a conceited custom that the Old Timers employ against the *che-chaquas* and all tenderfeet in general. But he did it so naively and as such a matter of course, that there was no sting, and I forgave him. He also had it in view, he said, before he crossed the divide into the Yukon, to make a little run up Fort o' Good Hope way.

Now Fort o' Good Hope is a far journey to the north, over and beyond the Circle, in a place where the feet of few men have trod; and when a nondescript ragamuffin comes in out of the night, from nowhere in particular, to sit by one's fire and discourse on such in terms of "trapsing" and "a little run," it is fair time to rouse up and shake off the dream. Wherefore I looked about me; saw the fly and, underneath, the pine boughs spread for the sleeping furs; saw the grub sacks, the camera, the frosty breaths of the dogs circling on the edge of the light; and, above, a great streamer of the aurora, bridging the zenith from south-east to north-west. I shivered. There is a magic in the Northland night, that steals in on one like fevers from malarial marshes. You are clutched and downed before you are aware. Then I looked to the snowshoes, lying prone and crossed where he had flung them. Also I had an eye to my tobacco pouch. Half, at least, of its goodly store had vamosed. That settled it. Fancy had not tricked me after all.

Crazed with suffering, I thought, looking steadfastly at the man—one of those wild stampeders, strayed far from his bearings and wandering like a lost soul through great vastnesses and unknown deeps. Oh, well, let his moods slip on, until, mayhap, he gathers his tangled wits together. Who knows?—the mere sound of a fellow-creature's voice may bring all straight again.

So I led him on in talk, and soon I marvelled, for he talked of game and the ways thereof. He had killed the Siberian wolf of westernmost Alaska, and the chamois in the secret Rockies. He averred he knew the haunts where the last buffalo still roamed; that he had hung on the flanks of the caribou when they ran by the hundred thousand, and slept in the Great Barrens on the musk-ox's winter trail.

And I shifted my judgment accordingly (the first revision, but by no account the last), and deemed him a monumental effigy of truth. Why it was I know not, but the spirit moved me to repeat a tale told to me by a man who had dwelt in the land too long to know better. It was of the great bear that hugs the steep slopes of St Elias, never descending to the levels of the gentler inclines. Now God so constituted this creature for its hillside habitat that the legs of one side are all of a foot longer than those of the other. This is mighty convenient, as will be reality admitted. So I hunted this rare beast in my own name, told it in the first person, present tense, painted the requisite locale, gave it the necessary garnishings and touches of verisimilitude, and looked to see the man stunned by the recital.

Not he. Had he doubted, I could have forgiven him. Had he objected, denying the dangers of such a hunt by virtue of the animal's inability to turn about and go the other way—had he done this, I say, I could have taken him by the hand for the true sportsman that he was. Not he. He sniffed, looked on me, and sniffed again; then gave my tobacco due praise, thrust one foot into my lap, and bade me examine the gear. It was a *mucluc* of the Innuit pattern, sewed together with sinew threads, and devoid of beads or furbelows. But it was the skin itself that was remarkable. In that it was all of half an inch thick, it reminded me of walrus-hide; but there the resemblance ceased, for no walrus ever bore so marvellous a growth of hair. On the side and ankles this hair was well-nigh worn away, what of friction with underbrush and snow; but around the top and down the more sheltered back it was coarse, dirty black, and very thick. I parted it with difficulty and looked beneath for the fine fur that is common with northern animals, but found it in this case to be absent. This, however, was compensated for by the length. Indeed, the tufts that had survived wear and tear measured all of seven or eight inches.

I looked up into the man's face, and he pulled his foot down and asked, "Find hide like that on your St Elias bear?"

I shook my head. "Nor on any other creature of land or sea," I answered candidly. The thickness of it, and the length of the hair, puzzled me.

"That," he said, and said without the slightest hint of impressiveness, "that came from a mammoth."

"Nonsense!" I exclaimed, for I could not forbear the protest of my unbelief. "The mammoth, my dear sir, long ago vanished from the earth. We know it once existed by the fossil remains that we have unearthed, and by a frozen carcase that the Siberian sun saw fit to melt from out the bosom of a glacier; but we also know that no living specimen exists. Our explorers—"

At this word he broke in impatiently. "Your explorers? Pish! A weakly breed. Let us hear no more of them. But tell me, O man, what you may know of the mammoth and his ways."

Beyond contradiction, this was leading to a yarn; so I baited my hook by ransacking my memory for whatever data I possessed on the subject in hand. To begin with, I emphasized that the animal was prehistoric, and marshalled all my facts in support of this. I mentioned the Siberian sand-bars that abounded with ancient mammoth bones; spoke of the large quantities of fossil ivory purchased from the Innuits by the Alaska Commercial Company; and acknowledged having myself mined six- and eight-foot tusks from the pay gravel of the Klondike creeks. "All fossils," I concluded, "found in the midst of *débris* deposited through countless ages."

"I remember when I was a kid," Thomas Stevens sniffed (he had a most confounded way of sniffing), "that I saw a petrified water-melon. Hence, though mistaken persons sometimes delude themselves into thinking that they are really raising or eating them, there are no such things as extant water-melons?"

"But the question of food," I objected, ignoring his point, which was puerile and without bearing. "The soil must bring forth vegetable life in lavish abundance to support so monstrous creations. Nowhere in the North is the soil so prolific. Ergo, the mammoth cannot exist."

"I pardon your ignorance concerning many matters of this Northland, for you are a young man and have travelled little; but, at the same time, I am inclined to agree with you on one thing. The mammoth no longer exists. How do I know? I killed the last one with my own right arm."

Thus spake Nimrod, the mighty Hunter. I threw a stick of firewood at the dogs and bade them quit their unholy howling, and waited. Undoubtedly this liar of singular felicity would open his mouth and requite me for my St. Elias bear.

"It was this way," he at last began, after the appropriate silence had intervened. "I was in camp one day—"

"Where?" I interrupted.

He waved his hand vaguely in the direction of the north-east, where stretched a *terra incognita* into which vastness few men have strayed and fewer emerged. "I was in camp one day with Klooch. Klooch was as handsome a little *kamooks* as ever whined betwixt the traces or shoved nose into a camp kettle. Her father was a full-blood Malemute from Russian Pastilik on Bering Sea, and I bred her, and with understanding, out of a clean-legged bitch of the Hudson Bay stock. I tell you, O man, she was a corker combination. And now, on this day I have in mind, she was brought to pup through a pure wild wolf of the woods—grey, and long of limb, with big lungs and no end of staying powers. Say! Was there ever the like? It was a new breed of dog I had started, and I could look forward to big things.

"As I have said, she was brought neatly to pup, and safely delivered. I was squatting on my hams over the litter—seven sturdy, blind little beggars—

when from behind came a bray of trumpets and crash of brass. There was a rush, like the wind-squall that kicks the heels of the rain, and I was midway to my feet when knocked flat on my face. At the same instant I heard Klooch sigh, very much as a man does when you've planted your fist in his belly. You can stake your sack I lay quiet, but I twisted my head around and saw a huge bulk swaying above me. Then the blue sky flashed into view and I got to my feet. A hairy mountain of flesh was just disappearing in the underbrush on the edge of the open. I caught a rear-end glimpse, with a stiff tail, as big in girth as my body, standing out straight behind. The next second only a tremendous hole remained in the thicket, though I could still hear the sounds as of a tornado dying quickly away, underbrush ripping and tearing, and trees snapping and crashing.

"I cast about for my rifle. It had been lying on the ground with the muzzle against a log; but now the stock was smashed, the barrel out of line, and the working-gear in a thousand bits. Then I looked for the slut, and—and what do you suppose?"

I shook my head.

"May my soul burn in a thousand hells if there was anything left of her! Klooch, the seven sturdy, blind little beggars—gone, all gone. Where she had stretched was a slimy, bloody depression in the soft earth, all of a yard in diameter, and around the edges a few scattered hairs."

I measured three feet on the snow, threw about it a circle, and glanced at Nimrod.

"The beast was thirty long and twenty high," he answered, "and its tusks scaled over six times three feet. I couldn't believe, myself, at the time, for all that it had just happened. But if my senses had played me, there was the broken gun and the hole in the brush. And there was—or, rather, there was not—Klooch and the pups. O man, it makes me hot all over now when I think of it Klooch! Another Eve! The mother of a new race! And a rampaging, ranting, old bull mammoth, like a second flood, wiping them, root and branch, off the face of the earth! Do you wonder that the blood-soaked earth cried out to high God? Or that I grabbed the hand-axe and took the trail?"

"The hand-axe?" I exclaimed, startled out of myself by the picture. "The hand-axe, and a big bull mammoth, thirty feet long, twenty feet—"

Nimrod joined me in my merriment, chuckling gleefully. "Wouldn't it kill you?" he cried. "Wasn't it a beaver's dream? Many's the time I've laughed about it since, but at the time it was no laughing matter, I was that danged mad, what of the gun and Klooch. Think of it, O man! A brand-new, unclassified, uncopyrighted breed, and wiped out before ever it opened its eyes or took out its intention papers! Well, so be it. Life's full of disappointments, and rightly so. Meat is best after a famine, and a bed soft after a hard trail.

"As I was saying, I took out after the beast with the hand-axe, and hung to its heels down the valley; but when he circled back toward the head, I was left winded at the lower end. Speaking of grub, I might as well stop long enough to explain a couple of points. Up thereabouts, in the midst of the mountains, is an almighty curious formation. There is no end of little valleys, each like the other much as peas in a pod, and all neatly tucked away with straight, rocky walls rising on all sides. And at the lower ends are always small openings where the drainage or glaciers must have broken out. The only way in is through these mouths, and they are all small, and some smaller than others. As to grub—you've slushed around on the rain-soaked islands of the Alaskan coast down Sitka way, most likely, seeing as you're a traveller. And you know how stuff grows there—big, and juicy, and jungly. Well, that's the way it was with those valleys. Thick, rich soil, with ferns and grasses and such things in patches higher than your head. Rain three days out of four during the summer months; and food in them for a thousand mammoths, to say nothing of small game for man.

"But to get back. Down at the lower end of the valley I got winded and gave over. I began to speculate, for when my wind left me my dander got hotter and hotter, and I knew I'd never know peace of mind till I dined on roasted mammoth-foot. And I knew, also, that that stood for *skookum mamook pukapuk*—excuse Chinook, I mean there was a big fight coming. Now the mouth of my valley was very narrow, and the walls steep. High up on one side was one of those big pivot rocks, or balancing rocks, as some call them, weighing all of a couple of hundred tons. Just the thing. I hit back for camp, keeping an eye open so the bull couldn't slip past, and got my ammunition. It wasn't worth anything with the rifle smashed; so I opened the shells, planted the powder under the rock, and touched it off with slow fuse. Wasn't much of a charge, but the old boulder tilted up lazily and dropped down into place, with just space enough to let the creek drain nicely. Now I had him."

"But how did you have him?" I queried. "Who ever heard of a man killing a mammoth with a hand-axe? And, for that matter, with anything else?"

"O man, have I not told you I was mad?" Nimrod replied, with a slight manifestation of sensitiveness. "Mad clean through, what of Klooch and the gun. Also, was I not a hunter? And was this not new and most unusual game? A hand-axe? Pish! I did not need it. Listen, and you shall hear of a hunt, such as might have happened in the youth of the world when cavemen rounded up the kill with hand-axe of stone. Such would have served me as well. Now is it not a fact that man can outwalk the dog or horse? That he can wear them out with the intelligence of his endurance?"

I nodded.

"Well?"

The light broke in on me, and I bade him continue.

"My valley was perhaps five miles around. The mouth was closed. There was no way to get out. A timid beast was that bull mammoth, and I had him at my mercy. I got on his heels again hollered like a fiend, pelted him with cobbles, and raced him around the valley three times before I knocked off for supper. Don't you see? A race-course! A man and a mammoth! A hippodrome, with sun, moon, and stars to referee!

"It took me two months to do it, but I did it. And that's no beaver dream. Round and round I ran him, me travelling on the inner circle, eating jerked meat and salmon berries on the run, and snatching winks of sleep between. Of course, he'd get desperate at times and turn. Then I'd head for soft ground where the creek spread out, and lay anathema upon him and his ancestry, and dare him to come on. But he was too wise to bog in a mud puddle. Once he pinned me in against the walls, and I crawled back into a deep crevice and waited. Whenever he felt for me with his trunk, I'd belt him with the hand-axe till he pulled out, shrieking fit to split my ear drums, he was that mad. He knew he had me and didn't have me, and it near drove him wild. But he was no man's fool. He knew he was safe as long as I stayed in the crevice, and he made up his mind to keep me there. And he was dead right, only he hadn't figured on the commissary. There was neither grub nor water around that spot, so on the face of it he couldn't keep up the siege. He'd stand before the opening for hours, keeping an eye on me and flapping mosquitoes away with his big blanket ears. Then the thirst would come on him and he'd ramp round and roar till the earth shook, calling me every name he could lay tongue to. This was to frighten me, of course; and when he thought I was sufficiently impressed, he'd back away softly and try to make a sneak for the creek. Sometimes I'd let him get almost there—only a couple of hundred yards away it was—when out I'd pop and back he'd come, lumbering along like the old landslide he was. After I'd done this a few times, and he'd figured it out, he changed his tactics. Grasped the time element, you see. Without a word of warning, away he'd go, tearing for the water like mad, scheming to get there and back before I ran away. Finally, after cursing me most horribly, he raised the siege and deliberately stalked off to the water-hole.

"That was the only time he penned me,—three days of it,—but after that the hippodrome never stopped. Round, and round, and round, like a six days' go-as-I-please, for he never pleased. My clothes went to rags and tatters, but I never stopped to mend, till at last I ran naked as a son of earth, with nothing but the old hand-axe in one hand and a cobble in the other. In fact, I never stopped, save for peeps of sleep in the crannies and ledges of the cliffs. As for the bull, he got perceptibly thinner and thinner—must have lost several tons at least—and as nervous as a schoolmarm on the wrong side of matrimony. When I'd come up with him and yell, or lain him with a rock at long range, he'd jump like a skittish colt and tremble all over. Then he'd pull out on the run, tail and trunk waving stiff, head over one shoulder and wicked eyes blazing, and the way he'd swear at me was something dreadful. A most immoral beast he was, a murderer, and a blasphemer.

"But towards the end he quit all this, and fell to whimpering and crying like a baby. His spirit broke and he became a quivering jelly-mountain of misery. He'd get attacks of palpitation of the heart, and stagger around like a drunken man, and fall down and bark his shins. And then he'd cry, but always on the run. O man, the gods themselves would have wept with him, and you yourself or any other man. It was pitiful, and there was so I much of it, but I only hardened my heart and hit up the pace. At last I wore him clean out, and he lay down, broken-winded, broken-hearted, hungry, and thirsty. When I found he wouldn't budge, I hamstrung him, and spent the better part of the day wading into him with the hand-axe, he a-sniffing and sobbing till I worked in far enough to shut him off. Thirty feet long he was, and twenty high, and a man could sling a hammock between his tusks and sleep comfortably. Barring the fact that I had run most of the juices out of him, he was fair eating, and his four feet, alone, roasted whole, would have lasted a man a twelvemonth. I spent the winter there myself."

"And where is this valley?" I asked

He waved his hand in the direction of the north-east, and said: "Your tobacco is very good. I carry a fair share of it in my pouch, but I shall carry the recollection of it until I die. In token of my appreciation, and in return for the moccasins on your own feet, I will present to you these *muclucs*. They commemorate Klooch and the seven blind little beggars. They are also souvenirs of an unparalleled event in history, namely, the destruction of the oldest breed of animal on earth, and the youngest. And their chief virtue lies in that they will never wear out."

Having effected the exchange, he knocked the ashes from his pipe, gripped my hand good-night, and wandered off through the snow. Concerning this tale, for which I have already disclaimed responsibility, I would recommend those of little faith to make a visit to the Smithsonian Institute. If they bring the requisite credentials and do not come in vacation time, they will undoubtedly gain an audience with Professor Dolvidson. The *muclucs* are in his possession, and he will verify, not the manner in which they were obtained, but the material of which they are composed. When he states that they are made from the skin of the mammoth, the scientific world accepts his verdict. What more would you have?

94

A HYPERBOREAN BREW

[The story of a scheming white man among the strange people who live on the rim of the Arctic sea]

Thomas Stevens's veracity may have been indeterminate as x, and his imagination the imagination of ordinary men increased to the nth power, but this, at least, must be said: never did he deliver himself of word nor deed that could be branded as a lie outright. . . He may have played with probability, and verged on the extremest edge of possibility, but in his tales the machinery never creaked. That he knew the Northland like a book, not a soul can deny. That he was a great traveller, and had set foot on countless unknown trails, many evidences affirm. Outside of my own personal knowledge, I knew men that had met him everywhere, but principally on the confines of Nowhere. There was Johnson, the ex-Hudson Bay Company factor, who had housed him in a Labrador factory until his dogs rested up a bit, and he was able to strike out again. There was McMahon, agent for the Alaska Commercial Company, who had run across him in Dutch Harbour, and later on, among the outlying islands of the Aleutian group. It was indisputable that he had guided one of the earlier United States surveys, and history states positively that in a similar capacity he served the Western Union when it attempted to put through its trans-Alaskan and Siberian telegraph to Europe. Further, there was Joe Lamson, the whaling captain, who, when ice-bound off the mouth of the Mackenzie, had had him come aboard after tobacco. This last touch proves Thomas Stevens's identity conclusively. His quest for tobacco was perennial and untiring. Ere we became fairly acquainted, I learned to greet him with one hand, and pass the pouch with the other. But the night I met him in John O'Brien's Dawson saloon, his head was wreathed in a nimbus of fifty-cent cigar smoke, and instead of my pouch he demanded my sack. We were standing by a faro table, and forthwith he tossed it upon the "high card." "Fifty," he said, and the game-keeper nodded. The "high card" turned, and he handed back my sack, called for a "tab," and drew me over to the scales, where the weigher nonchalantly cashed him out fifty dollars in dust.

"And now we'll drink," he said; and later, at the bar, when he lowered his glass: "Reminds me of a little brew I had up Tattarat way. No, you have no knowledge of the place, nor is it down on the charts. But it's up by the rim of the Arctic Sea, not so many hundred miles from the American line, and all of half a thousand God-forsaken souls live there, giving and taking in marriage, and starving and dying in-between-whiles. Explorers have overlooked them, and you will not find them in the census of 1890. A whale-ship was pinched there once, but the men, who had made shore over the ice, pulled out for the south and were never heard of.

"But it was a great brew we had, Moosu and I," he added a moment later, with just the slightest suspicion of a sigh.

I knew there were big deeds and wild doings behind that sigh, so I haled him into a corner, between a roulette outfit and a poker layout, and waited for his tongue to thaw.

"Had one objection to Moosu," he began, cocking his head meditatively— "one objection, and only one. He was an Indian from over on the edge of the Chippewyan country, but the trouble was, he'd picked up a smattering of the Scriptures. Been campmate a season with a renegade French Canadian who'd studied for the church. Moosu'd never seen applied Christianity, and his head was crammed with miracles, battles, and dispensations, and what not he didn't understand. Otherwise he was a good sort, and a handy man on trail or over a fire.

"We'd had a hard time together and were badly knocked out when we plumped upon Tattarat. Lost outfits and dogs crossing a divide in a fall blizzard, and our bellies clove to our backs and our clothes were in rags when we crawled into the village. They weren't much surprised at seeing us— because of the whalemen—and gave us the meanest shack in the village to live in, and the worst of their leavings to live on. What struck me at the time as strange was that they left us strictly alone. But Moosu explained it.

"'Shaman *sick tumtum*,' he said, meaning the shaman, or medicine man, was jealous, and had advised the people to have nothing to do with us. From the little he'd seen of the whalemen, he'd learned that mine was a stronger race, and a wiser; so he'd only behaved as shamans have always behaved the world over. And before I get done, you'll see how near right he was.

"'These people have a law,' said Mosu: 'whoso eats of meat must hunt. We be awkward, you and I, O master, in the weapons of this country; nor can we string bows nor fling spears after the manner approved. Wherefore the shaman and Tummasook, who is chief, have put their heads together, and it has been decreed that we work with the women and children in dragging in the meat and tending the wants of the hunters.'

"'And this is very wrong,' I made to answer; 'for we be better men, Moosu, than these people who walk in darkness. Further, we should rest and grow strong, for the way south is long, and on that trail the weak cannot prosper.'"

"'But we have nothing,' he objected, looking about him at the rotten timbers of the igloo, the stench of the ancient walrus meat that had been our supper disgusting his nostrils. 'And on this fare we cannot thrive. We have nothing save the bottle of "pain-killer," which will not fill emptiness, so we must bend to the yoke of the unbeliever and become hewers of wood and drawers of water. And there be good things in this place, the which we may not have. Ah, master, never has my nose lied to me, and I have followed it to secret caches and among the fur-bales of the igloos. Good provender did these people extort from the poor whalemen, and this provender has wandered into few hands. The woman Ipsukuk, who dwelleth in the far end of the village next she igloo of the chief, possesseth much flour and sugar, and even have my eyes told me of molasses smeared on her face. And in the igloo of Tummasook, the chief, there be tea—have I not seen the old pig guzzling? And the shaman owneth a caddy of "Star" and two buckets of prime smoking. And what have we? Nothing! Nothing!'

"But I was stunned by the word he brought of the tobacco, and made no answer.

"And Moosu, what of his own desire, broke silence: 'And there be Tukeliketa, daughter of a big hunter and wealthy man. A likely girl. Indeed, a very nice girl.'

"I figured hard during the night while Moosu snored, for I could not bear the thought of the tobacco so near which I could not smoke. True, as he had said, we had nothing. But the way became clear to me, and in the morning I said to him: 'Go thou cunningly abroad, after thy fashion, and procure me some sort of bone, crooked like a gooseneck, and hollow. Also, walk humbly, but have eyes awake to the lay of pots and pans and cooking contrivances. And remember, mine is the white man's wisdom, and do what I have bid you, with sureness and despatch.'

"While he was away I placed the whale-oil cooking lamp in the middle of the igloo, and moved the mangy sleeping furs back that I might have room. Then I took apart his gun and put the barrel by handy, and afterwards braided many wicks from the cotton that the women gather wild in the summer. When he came back, it was with the bone I had commanded, and with news that in the igloo of Tummasook there was a five-gallon kerosene can and a big copper kettle. So I said he had done well and we would tarry through the day. And when midnight was near I made harangue to him.

"'This chief, this Tummasook, hath a copper kettle, likewise a kerosene can.' I put a rock, smooth and wave-washed, in Moosu's hand. 'The camp is hushed and the stars are winking. Go thou, creep into the chief's igloo softly, and smite him thus upon the belly, and hard. And let the meat and good grub of the days to come put strength into thine arm. There will be uproar and outcry, and the village will come hot afoot. But be thou unafraid. Veil thy movements and lose thy form in the obscurity of the night and the confusion of men. And when the woman Ipsukuk is anigh thee,—she who smeareth her face with molasses,—do thou smite her likewise, and whosoever else that possesseth flour and cometh to thy hand. Then do thou lift thy voice in pain and double up with clasped hands, and make outcry in token that thou, too, hast felt the visitation of the night. And in this way shall we achieve honour and great possessions, and the caddy of "Star" and the prime smoking, and thy Tukeliketa, who is a likely maiden.'

"When he had departed on this errand, I bided patiently in the shack, and the tobacco seemed very near. Then there was a cry of affright in the night, that became an uproar and assailed the sky. I seized the 'pain-killer' and ran forth. There was much noise, and a wailing among the women, and fear sat heavily on all. Tummasook and the woman Ipsukuk rolled on the ground in pain, and with them there were divers others, also Moosu. I thrust aside those that cluttered the way of my feet, and put the mouth of the bottle to Moosu's lips. And straightway he became well and ceased his howling. Whereat there was a great clamour for the bottle from the others so stricken. But I made harangue, and ere they tasted and were made well I had mulcted Tummasook of his copper kettle and kerosene can, and the woman Ipsukuk of her sugar and molasses, and the other sick ones of goodly measures of flour. The shaman glowered wickedly at the people around my knees, though he poorly concealed the wonder that lay beneath. But I held my head high, and Moosu groaned beneath the loot as he followed my heels to the shack.

"There I set to work. In Tummasook's copper kettle I mixed three quarts of wheat flour with five of molasses, and to this I added of water twenty quarts. Then I placed the kettle near the lamp, that it might sour in the warmth and grow strong. Moosu understood, and said my wisdom passed understanding and was greater than Solomon's, who he had heard was a wise man of old time. The kerosene can I set over the lamp, and to its nose I affixed a snout, and into the snout the bone that was like a gooseneck. I sent Moosu without to pound ice, while I connected the barrel of his gun with the gooseneck, and midway on the barrel I piled the ice he had pounded. And at the far end of the gun-barrel, beyond the pan of ice, I placed a small iron pot. When the brew was strong enough (and it was two days ere it could stand on its own legs), I filled the kerosene can with it, and lighted the wicks I had braided.

"Now that all was ready, I spoke to Moosu. 'Go forth,' I said, 'to the chief men of the village, and give them greeting, and bid them come into my igloo and sleep the night away with me and the gods.'

"The brew was singing merrily when they began shoving aside the skin flap and crawling in, and I was heaping cracked ice on the gun-barrel. Out of the priming hole at the far end, drip, drip, drip into the iron pot fell the liquor—*hooch*, you know. But they'd never seen the like, and giggled nervously when I made harangue about its virtues. As I talked I noted the jealousy in the shaman's eye, so when I had done, I placed him side by side with Tummasook and the woman Ipsukuk. Then I gave them to drink, and their eyes watered and their stomachs warmed, till from being afraid they reached greedily for more; and when I had them well started, I turned to the others. Tummasook made a brag about how he had once killed a polar bear, and in the vigour of his pantomime nearly slew his mother's brother. But nobody heeded. The woman Ipsukuk fell to weeping for a son lost long years agone in the ice, and the shaman made incantation and prophecy. So it went, and before morning they were all on the floor, sleeping soundly with the gods.

"The story tells itself, does it not? The news of the magic potion spread. It was too marvellous for utterance. Tongues could tell but a tithe of the miracles it performed. It eased pain, gave surcease to sorrow, brought back old memories, dead faces, and forgotten dreams. It was a fire that ate through all the blood, and, burning, burned not. It stoutened the heart, stiffened the back, and made men more than men. It revealed the future, and gave visions and prophecy. It brimmed with wisdom and unfolded secrets. There was no end of the things it could do, and soon there was a clamouring on all hands to sleep with the gods. They brought their warmest furs, their strongest dogs, their best meats; but I sold the *hooch* with discretion, and only those were favoured that brought flour and molasses and sugar. And such stores poured in that I set Moosu to build a cache to hold them, for there was soon no space in the igloo. Ere three days had passed Tummasook had gone bankrupt. The shaman, who was never more than half drunk after the first night, watched me closely and hung on for the better part of the week. But before ten days were gone, even the woman Ipsukuk exhausted her provisions, and went home weak and tottery.

"But Moosu complained. 'O master,' he said, 'we have laid by great wealth in molasses and sugar and flour, but our shack is yet mean, our clothes thin, and our sleeping furs mangy. There is a call of the belly for meat the stench of which offends not the stars, and for tea such as Tummasook guzzles, and there is a great yearning for the tobacco of Neewak, who is shaman and who plans to destroy us. I have flour until I am sick, and sugar and molasses without stint, yet is the heart of Moosu sore and his bed empty.'

"'Peace!' I answered, 'thou art weak of understanding and a fool. Walk softly and wait, and we will grasp it all. But grasp now, and we grasp little, and in the end it will be nothing. Thou art a child in the way of the white man's wisdom. Hold thy tongue and watch, and I will show you the way my brothers do overseas, and, so doing, gather to themselves the riches of the earth. It is what is called "business," and what dost thou know about business?'

"But the next day he came in breathless. 'O master, a strange thing happeneth in the igloo of Neewak, the shaman; wherefore we are lost, and we have neither worn the warm furs nor tasted the good tobacco, what of your madness for the molasses and flour. Go thou and witness whilst I watch by the brew.'

"So I went to the igloo of Neewak. And behold, he had made his own still, fashioned cunningly after mine. And as he beheld me he could ill conceal his triumph. For he was a man of parts, and his sleep with the gods when in my igloo had not been sound.

"But I was not disturbed, for I knew what I knew, and when I returned to my own igloo, I descanted to Moosu, and said: 'Happily the property right obtains amongst this people, who otherwise have been blessed with but few of the institutions of men. And because of this respect for property shall you and I wax fat, and, further, we shall introduce amongst them new institutions that other peoples have worked out through great travail and suffering.'

"But Moosu understood dimly, till the shaman came forth, with eyes flashing and a threatening note in his voice, and demanded to trade with me. 'For look you,' he cried, 'there be of flour and molasses none in all the village. The like have you gathered with a shrewd hand from my people, who have slept with your gods and who now have nothing save large heads, and weak knees, and a thirst for cold water that they cannot quench. This is not good, and my voice has power among them; so it were well that we trade, you and I, even as you have traded with them, for molasses and flour.'

"And I made answer: 'This be good talk, and wisdom abideth in thy mouth. We will trade. For this much of flour and molasses givest thou me the caddy of "Star" and the two buckets of smoking.'

"And Moosu groaned, and when the trade was made and the shaman departed, he upbraided me: 'Now, because of thy madness are we, indeed, lost! Neewak maketh *hooch* on his own account, and when the time is ripe, he will command the people to drink of no *hooch* but his *hooch*. And in this way are we undone, and our goods worthless, and our igloo mean, and the bed of Moosu cold and empty!'

"And I answered: 'By the body of the wolf, say I, thou art a fool, and thy father before thee, and thy children after thee, down to the last generation. Thy wisdom is worse than no wisdom and thine eyes blinded to business, of which I have spoken and whereof thou knowest nothing. Go, thou son of a thousand fools, and drink of the *hooch* that Neewak brews in his igloo, and thank thy gods that thou hast a white man's wisdom to make soft the bed thou liest in. Go! and when thou hast drunken, return with the taste still on thy lips, that I may know.'

"And two days after, Neewak sent greeting and invitation to his igloo. Moosu went, but I sat alone, with the song of the still in my ears, and the air thick with the shaman's tobacco; for trade was slack that night, and no one dropped in but Angeit, a young hunter that had faith in me. Later, Moosu came back, his speech thick with chuckling and his eyes wrinkling with laughter.

"'Thou art a great man,' he said. 'Thou art a great man, O master, and because of thy greatness thou wilt not condemn Moosu, thy servant, who ofttimes doubts and cannot be made to understand.'

"'And wherefore now?' I demanded. 'Hast thou drunk overmuch? And are they sleeping sound in the igloo of Neewak, the shaman?'

"'Nay, they are angered and sore of body, and Chief Tummasook has thrust his thumbs in the throat of Neewak, and sworn by the bones of his ancestors to look upon his face no more. For behold! I went to the igloo, and the brew simmered and bubbled, and the steam journeyed through the gooseneck even as thy steam, and even as thine it became water where it met the ice, and dropped into the pot at the far end. And Neewak gave us to drink, and lo, it was not like thine, for there was no bite to the tongue nor tingling to the eyeballs, and of a truth it was water. So we drank, and we drank overmuch; yet did we sit with cold hearts and solemn. And Neewak was perplexed and a cloud came on his brow. And he took Tummasook and Ipsukuk alone of all the company and set them apart, and bade them drink and drink and drink. And they drank and drank and drank, and yet sat solemn and cold, till Tummasook arose in wrath and demanded back the furs and the tea he had paid. And Ipsukuk raised her voice, thin and angry. And the company demanded back what they had given, and there was a great commotion.'

"'Does the son of a dog deem me a whale?' demanded Tummasook, shoving back the skin flap and standing erect, his face black and his brows angry. 'Wherefore I am filled, like a fish-bladder, to bursting, till I can scarce walk, what of the weight within me. Lalah! I have drunken as never before, yet are my eyes clear, my knees strong, my hand steady.'

"'The shaman cannot send us to sleep with the gods,' the people complained, stringing in and joining us, 'and only in thy igloo may the thing be done.'

"So I laughed to myself as I passed the *hooch* around and the guests made merry. For in the flour I had traded to Neewak I had mixed much soda that I had got from the woman Ipsukuk. So how could his brew ferment when the soda kept it sweet? Or his *hooch* be *hooch* when it would not sour?

"After that our wealth flowed in without let or hindrance. Furs we had without number, and the fancy-work of the women, all of the chief's tea, and no end of meat. One day Moosu retold for my benefit, and sadly mangled, the story of Joseph in Egypt, but from it I got an idea, and soon I had half the tribe at work building me great meat caches. And of all they hunted I got the lion's share and stored it away. Nor was Moosu idle. He made himself a pack of cards from birch bark, and taught Neewak the way to play seven-up. He also inveigled the father of Tukeliketa into the game. And one day he married the maiden, and the next day he moved into the shaman's house, which was the finest in the village. The fall of Neewak was complete, for he lost all his possessions, his walrus-hide drums, his incantation tools—everything. And in the end he became a hewer of wood and drawer of water at the beck and call of Moosu. And Moosu—he set himself up as shaman, or high priest, and out of his garbled Scripture created new gods and made incantation before strange altars.

"And I was well pleased, for I thought it good that church and state go hand in hand, and I had certain plans of my own concerning the state. Events were shaping as I had foreseen. Good temper and smiling faces had vanished from the village. The people were morose and sullen. There were quarrels and fighting, and things were in an uproar night and day. Moosu's cards were duplicated and the hunters fell to gambling among themselves. Tummasook beat his wife horribly, and his mother's brother objected and smote him with a tusk of walrus till he cried aloud in the night and was shamed before the people. Also, amid such diversions no hunting was done, and famine fell upon the land. The nights were long and dark, and without meat no *hooch* could be bought; so they murmured against the chief. This I had played for, and when they were well and hungry, I summoned the whole village, made a great harangue, posed as patriarch, and fed the famishing. Moosu made harangue likewise, and because of this and the thing I had done I was made chief. Moosu, who had the ear of God and decreed his judgments, anointed me with whale blubber, and right blubberly he did it, not understanding the ceremony. And between us we interpreted to the people the new theory of the divine right of kings. There was *hooch* galore, and meat and feastings, and they took kindly to the new order.

"So you see, O man, I have sat in the high places, and worn the purple, and ruled populations. And I might yet be a king had the tobacco held out, or had Moosu been more fool and less knave. For he cast eyes upon Esanetuk, eldest daughter to Tummasook, and I objected.

"'O brother,' he explained, 'thou hast seen fit to speak of introducing new institutions amongst this people, and I have listened to thy words and gained wisdom thereby. Thou rulest by the God-given right, and by the God-given right I marry.'

"I noted that he 'brothered' me, and was angry and put my foot down. But he fell back upon the people and made incantations for three days, in which all hands joined; and then, speaking with the voice of God, he decreed polygamy by divine fiat. But he was shrewd, for he limited the number of wives by a property qualification, and because of which he, above all men, was favoured by his wealth. Nor could I fail to admire, though it was plain that power had turned his head, and he would not be satisfied till all the power and all the wealth rested in his own hands. So he became swollen with pride, forgot it was I that had placed him there, and made preparations to destroy me.

"But it was interesting, for the beggar was working out in his own way an evolution of primitive society. Now I, by virtue of the *hooch* monopoly, drew a revenue in which I no longer permitted him to share. So he meditated for a while and evolved a system of ecclesiastical taxation. He laid tithes upon the people, harangued about fat firstlings and such things, and twisted whatever twisted texts he had ever heard to serve his purpose. Even this I bore in silence, but when he instituted what may be likened to a graduated income-tax, I rebelled, and blindly, for this was what he worked for. Thereat, he appealed to the people, and they, envious of my great wealth and well taxed themselves, upheld him. 'Why should we pay,' they asked, 'and not you? Does not the voice of God speak through the lips of Moosu, the shaman?' So I yielded. But at the same time I raised the price of *hooch*, and lo, he was not a whit behind me in raising my taxes.

"Then there was open war. I made a play for Neewak and Tummasook, because of the traditionary rights they possessed; but Moosu won out by creating a priesthood and giving them both high office. The problem of authority presented itself to him, and he worked it out as it has often been worked before. There was my mistake. I should have been made shaman, and he chief; but I saw it too late, and in the clash of spiritual and temporal power I was bound to be worsted. A great controversy waged, but it quickly became one-sided. The people remembered that he had anointed me, and it was clear to them that the source of my authority lay, not in me, but in Moosu. Only a few faithful ones clung to me, chief among whom Angeit was; while he headed the popular party and set whispers afloat that I had it in mind to overthrow him and set up my own gods, which were most unrighteous gods. And in this the clever rascal had anticipated me, for it was just what I had intended—forsake my kingship, you see, and fight spiritual with spiritual. So he frightened the people with the iniquities of my peculiar gods—especially the one he named 'Biz-e-Nass'—and nipped the scheme in the bud.

"Now, it happened that Kluktu, youngest daughter to Tummasook, had caught my fancy, and I likewise hers. So I made overtures, but the ex-chief refused bluntly—after I had paid the purchase price—and informed me that she was set aside for Moosu. This was too much, and I was half of a mind to go to his igloo and slay him with my naked hands; but I recollected that the tobacco was near gone, and went home laughing. The next day he made incantation, and distorted the miracle of the loaves and fishes till it became prophecy, and I, reading between the lines, saw that it was aimed at the wealth of meat stored in my caches. The people also read between the lines, and, as he did not urge them to go on the hunt, they remained at home, and few caribou or bear were brought in.

"But I had plans of my own, seeing that not only the tobacco but the flour and molasses were near gone. And further, I felt it my duty to prove the white man's wisdom and bring sore distress to Moosu, who had waxed high-stomached, what of the power I had given him. So that night I went to my meat caches and toiled mightily, and it was noted next day that all the dogs of the village were lazy. No one suspected, and I toiled thus every night, and the dogs grew fat and fatter, and the people lean and leaner. They grumbled and demanded the fulfilment of prophecy, but Moosu restrained them, waiting for their hunger to grow yet greater. Nor did he dream, to the very last, of the trick I had been playing on the empty caches.

"When all was ready, I sent Angeit, and the faithful ones whom I had fed privily, through the village to call assembly. And the tribe gathered on a great space of beaten snow before my door, with the meat caches towering stilt-legged in the rear. Moosu came also, standing on the inner edge of the circle opposite me, confident that I had some scheme afoot, and prepared at the first break to down me. But I arose, giving him salutation before all men.

106

"'O Moosu, thou blessed of God,' I began, 'doubtless thou hast wondered in that I have called this convocation together; and doubtless, because of my many foolishnesses, art thou prepared for rash sayings and rash doings. Not so. It has been said, that those the gods would destroy they first make mad. And I have been indeed mad. I have crossed thy will, and scoffed at thy authority, and done divers evil and wanton things. Wherefore, last night a vision was vouchsafed me, and I have seen the wickedness of my ways. And thou stoodst forth like a shining star, with brows aflame, and I knew in mine own heart thy greatness. I saw all things clearly. I knew that thou didst command the ear of God, and that when you spoke he listened. And I remembered that whatever of the good deeds that I had done, I had done through the grace of God, and the grace of Moosu.

"'Yes, my children,' I cried, turning to the people, 'whatever right I have done, and whatever good I have done, have been because of the counsel of Moosu. When I listened to him, affairs prospered; when I closed my ears, and acted according to my folly, things came to folly. By his advice it was that I laid my store of meat, and in time of darkness fed the famishing. By his grace it was that I was made chief. And what have I done with my chiefship? Let me tell you. I have done nothing. My head was turned with power, and I deemed myself greater than Moosu, and, behold I have come to grief. My rule has been unwise, and the gods are angered. Lo, ye are pinched with famine, and the mothers are dry-breasted, and the little babies cry through the long nights. Nor do I, who have hardened my heart against Moosu, know what shall be done, nor in what manner of way grub shall be had.'

"At this there was nodding and laughing, and the people put their heads together, and I knew they whispered of the loaves and fishes. I went on hastily. 'So I was made aware of my foolishness and of Moosu's wisdom; of my own unfitness and of Moosu's fitness. And because of this, being no longer mad, I make acknowledgment and rectify evil. I did cast unrighteous eyes upon Kluktu, and lo, she was sealed to Moosu. Yet is she mine, for did I not pay to Tummasook the goods of purchase? But I am well unworthy of her, and she shall go from the igloo of her father to the igloo of Moosu. Can the moon shine in the sunshine? And further, Tummasook shall keep the goods of purchase, and she be a free gift to Moosu, whom God hath ordained her rightful lord.

"'And further yet, because I have used my wealth unwisely, and to oppress ye, O my children, do I make gifts of the kerosene can to Moosu, and the gooseneck, and the gun-barrel, and the copper kettle. Therefore, I can gather to me no more possessions, and when ye are athirst for *hooch*, he will quench ye and without robbery. For he is a great man, and God speaketh through his lips.

"'And yet further, my heart is softened, and I have repented me of my madness. I, who am a fool and a son of fools; I, who am the slave of the bad god Biz-e-Nass; I, who see thy empty bellies and knew not wherewith to fill them—why shall I be chief, and sit above thee, and rule to thine own destruction? Why should I do this, which is not good? But Moosu, who is shaman, and who is wise above men, is so made that he can rule with a soft hand and justly. And because of the things I have related do I make abdication and give my chiefship to Moosu, who alone knoweth how ye may be fed in this day when there be no meat in the land.'

"At this there was a great clapping of hands, and the people cried, '*Kloshe! Kloshe!*' which means 'good.' I had seen the wonder-worry in Moosu's eyes; for he could not understand, and was fearful of my white man's wisdom. I had met his wishes all along the line, and even anticipated some; and standing there, self-shorn of all my power, he knew the time did not favour to stir the people against me.

"Before they could disperse I made announcement that while the still went to Moosu, whatever *hooch* I possessed went to the people. Moosu tried to protest at this, for never had we permitted more than a handful to be drunk at a time; but they cried, '*Kloshe! Kloshe!*' and made festival before my door. And while they waxed uproarious without, as the liquor went to their heads, I held council within with Angeit and the faithful ones. I set them the tasks they were to do, and put into their mouths the words they were to say. Then I slipped away to a place back in the woods where I had two sleds, well loaded, with teams of dogs that were not overfed. Spring was at hand, you see, and there was a crust to the snow; so it was the best time to take the way south. Moreover, the tobacco was gone. There I waited, for I had nothing to fear. Did they bestir themselves on my trail, their dogs were too fat, and themselves too lean, to overtake me; also, I deemed their bestirring would be of an order for which I had made due preparation.

"First came a faithful one, running, and after him another. 'O master,' the first cried, breathless, 'there be great confusion in the village, and no man knoweth his own mind, and they be of many minds. Everybody hath drunken overmuch, and some be stringing bows, and some be quarrelling one with another. Never was there such a trouble.'

"And the second one: 'And I did as thou biddest, O master, whispering shrewd words in thirsty ears, and raising memories of the things that were of old time. The woman Ipsukuk waileth her poverty and the wealth that no longer is hers. And Tummasook thinketh himself once again chief, and the people are hungry and rage up and down.'

"And a third one: 'And Neewak hath overthrown the altars of Moosu, and maketh incantation before the time-honoured and ancient gods. And all the people remember the wealth that ran down their throats, and which they possess no more. And first, Esanetuk, who be *sick tumtum*, fought with Kluktu, and there was much noise. And next, being daughters of the one mother, did they fight with Tukeliketa. And after that did they three fall upon Moosu, like wind-squalls, from every hand, till he ran forth from the igloo, and the people mocked him. For a man who cannot command his womankind is a fool.'

"Then came Angeit: 'Great trouble hath befallen Moosu, O master, for I have whispered to advantage, till the people came to Moosu, saying they were hungry and demanding the fulfilment of prophecy. And there was a loud shout of "Itlwillie! Itlwillie!" (Meat.) So he cried peace to his womenfolk, who were overwrought with anger and with *hooch*, and led the tribe even to thy meat caches. And he bade the men open them and be fed. And lo, the caches were empty. There was no meat. They stood without sound, the people being frightened, and in the silence I lifted my voice. "O Moosu,

109

where is the meat? That there was meat we know. Did we not hunt it and drag it in from the hunt? And it were a lie to say one man hath eaten it; yet have we seen nor hide nor hair. Where is the meat, O Moosu? Thou hast the ear of God. Where is the meat?"

"'And the people cried, "Thou hast the ear of God. Where is the meat?" And they put their heads together and were afraid. Then I went among them, speaking fearsomely of the unknown things, of the dead that come and go like shadows and do evil deeds, till they cried aloud in terror and gathered all together, like little children afraid of the dark. Neewak made harangue, laying this evil that had come upon them at the door of Moosu. When he had done, there was a furious commotion, and they took spears in their hands, and tusks of walrus, and clubs, and stones from the beach. But Moosu ran away home, and because he had not drunken of *hooch* they could not catch him, and fell one over another and made haste slowly. Even now they do howl without his igloo, and his woman-folk within, and what of the noise, he cannot make himself heard.'

"'O Angeit, thou hast done well,' I commanded. 'Go now, taking this empty sled and the lean dogs, and ride fast to the igloo of Moosu; and before the people, who are drunken, are aware, throw him quick upon the sled and bring him to me.'

"I waited and gave good advice to the faithful ones till Angeit returned. Moosu was on the sled, and I saw by the fingermarks on his face that his womankind had done well by him. But he tumbled off and fell in the snow at my feet, crying: 'O master, thou wilt forgive Moosu, thy servant, for the wrong things he has done! Thou art a great man! Surely wilt thou forgive!'

"'Call me "brother," Moosu—call me "brother,"' I chided, lifting him to his feet with the toe of my moccasin. 'Wilt thou evermore obey?'

"'Yea, master,' he whimpered, 'evermore.'

"'Then dispose thy body, so, across the sled,' I shifted the dogwhip to my right hand. 'And direct thy face downwards, toward the snow. And make haste, for we journey south this day.' And when he was well fixed I laid the lash upon him, reciting, at every stroke, the wrongs he had done me. 'This for thy disobedience in general—whack! And this for thy disobedience in particular—whack! whack! And this for Esanetuk! And this for thy soul's welfare! And this for the grace of thy authority! And this for Kluktu! And this for thy rights God-given! And this for thy fat firstlings! And this and this for thy income-tax and thy loaves and fishes! And this for all thy disobedience! And this, finally, that thou mayest henceforth walk softly and with understanding! Now cease thy sniffling and get up! Gird on thy snowshoes and go to the fore and break trail for the dogs. *Chook! Mush-on! Git!*'"

Thomas Stevens smiled quietly to himself as he lighted his fifth cigar and sent curling smoke-rings ceilingward.

"But how about the people of Tattarat?" I asked. "Kind of rough, wasn't it, to leave them flat with famine?"

And he answered, laughing, between two smoke-rings, "Were there not the fat dogs?"

THE FAITH OF MEN

"Tell you what we'll do; we'll shake for it."

"That suits me," said the second man, turning, as he spoke, to the Indian that was mending snowshoes in a corner of the cabin. "Here, you Billebedam, take a run down to Oleson's cabin like a good fellow, and tell him we want to borrow his dice box."

This sudden request in the midst of a council on wages of men, wood, and grub surprised Billebedam. Besides, it was early in the day, and he had never known white men of the calibre of Pentfield and Hutchinson to dice and play till the day's work was done. But his face was impassive as a Yukon Indian's should be, as he pulled on his mittens and went out the door.

Though eight o'clock, it was still dark outside, and the cabin was lighted by a tallow candle thrust into an empty whisky bottle. It stood on the pine-board table in the middle of a disarray of dirty tin dishes. Tallow from innumerable candles had dripped down the long neck of the bottle and hardened into a miniature glacier. The small room, which composed the entire cabin, was as badly littered as the table; while at one end, against the wall, were two bunks, one above the other, with the blankets turned down just as the two men had crawled out in the morning.

Lawrence Pentfield and Corry Hutchinson were millionaires, though they did not look it. There seemed nothing unusual about them, while they would have passed muster as fair specimens of lumbermen in any Michigan camp. But outside, in the darkness, where holes yawned in the ground, were many men engaged in windlassing muck and gravel and gold from the bottoms of the holes where other men received fifteen dollars per day for scraping it from off the bedrock. Each day thousands of dollars' worth of gold were scraped from bedrock and windlassed to the surface, and it all belonged to Pentfield and Hutchinson, who took their rank among the richest kings of Bonanza.

Pentfield broke the silence that followed on Billebedam's departure by heaping the dirty plates higher on the table and drumming a tattoo on the cleared space with his knuckles. Hutchinson snuffed the smoky candle and reflectively rubbed the soot from the wick between thumb and forefinger.

"By Jove, I wish we could both go out!" he abruptly exclaimed. "That would settle it all."

Pentfield looked at him darkly.

"If it weren't for your cursed obstinacy, it'd be settled anyway. All you have to do is get up and go. I'll look after things, and next year I can go out."

"Why should I go? I've no one waiting for me—"

"Your people," Pentfield broke in roughly.

"Like you have," Hutchinson went on. "A girl, I mean, and you know it."

Pentfield shrugged his shoulders gloomily. "She can wait, I guess."

"But she's been waiting two years now."

"And another won't age her beyond recognition."

"That'd be three years. Think of it, old man, three years in this end of the earth, this falling-off place for the damned!" Hutchinson threw up his arm in an almost articulate groan.

He was several years younger than his partner, not more than twenty-six, and there was a certain wistfulness in his face that comes into the faces of men when they yearn vainly for the things they have been long denied. This same wistfulness was in Pentfield's face, and the groan of it was articulate in the heave of his shoulders.

"I dreamed last night I was in Zinkand's," he said. "The music playing, glasses clinking, voices humming, women laughing, and I was ordering eggs—yes, sir, eggs, fried and boiled and poached and scrambled, and in all sorts of ways, and downing them as fast as they arrived."

"I'd have ordered salads and green things," Hutchinson criticized hungrily, "with a big, rare, Porterhouse, and young onions and radishes,—the kind your teeth sink into with a crunch."

"I'd have followed the eggs with them, I guess, if I hadn't awakened," Pentfield replied.

He picked up a trail-scarred banjo from the floor and began to strum a few wandering notes. Hutchinson winced and breathed heavily.

"Quit it!" he burst out with sudden fury, as the other struck into a gaily lifting swing. "It drives me mad. I can't stand it"

Pentfield tossed the banjo into a bunk and quoted:-

"Hear me babble what the weakest won't confess—

I am Memory and Torment—I am Town!

I am all that ever went with evening dress!"

The other man winced where he sat and dropped his head forward on the table. Pentfield resumed the monotonous drumming with his knuckles. A loud snap from the door attracted his attention. The frost was creeping up the inside in a white sheet, and he began to hum:-

"The flocks are folded, boughs are bare,

The salmon takes the sea;

And oh, my fair, would I somewhere

Might house my heart with thee."

Silence fell and was not again broken till Billebedam arrived and threw the dice box on the table.

"Um much cold," he said. "Oleson um speak to me, um say um Yukon freeze last night."

"Hear that, old man!" Pentfield cried, slapping Hutchinson on the shoulder. "Whoever wins can be hitting the trail for God's country this time tomorrow morning!"

He picked up the box, briskly rattling the dice.

"What'll it be?"

"Straight poker dice," Hutchinson answered. "Go on and roll them out."

Pentfield swept the dishes from the table with a crash and rolled out the five dice. Both looked tragedy. The shake was without a pair and five-spot high.

"A stiff!" Pentfield groaned.

After much deliberating Pentfield picked up all the five dice and put them in the box.

"I'd shake to the five if I were you," Hutchinson suggested.

"No, you wouldn't, not when you see this," Pentfield replied, shaking out the dice.

Again they were without a pair, running this time in unbroken sequence from two to six.

"A second stiff!" he groaned. "No use your shaking, Corry. You can't lose."

The other man gathered up the dice without a word, rattled them, rolled them out on the table with a flourish, and saw that he had likewise shaken a six-high stiff.

"Tied you, anyway, but I'll have to do better than that," he said, gathering in four of them and shaking to the six. "And here's what beats you!"

But they rolled out deuce, tray, four, and five—a stiff still and no better nor worse than Pentfield's throw.

Hutchinson sighed.

"Couldn't happen once in a million times," said.

"Nor in a million lives," Pentfield added, catching up the dice and quickly throwing them out. Three fives appeared, and, after much delay, he was rewarded by a fourth five on the second shake. Hutchinson seemed to have lost his last hope.

But three sixes turned up on his first shake. A great doubt rose in the other's eyes, and hope returned into his. He had one more shake. Another six and he would go over the ice to salt water and the States.

He rattled the dice in the box, made as though to cast them, hesitated, and continued rattle them.

"Go on! Go on! Don't take all night about it!" Pentfield cried sharply, bending his nails on the table, so tight was the clutch with which he strove to control himself.

The dice rolled forth, an upturned six meeting their eyes. Both men sat staring at it. There was a long silence. Hutchinson shot a covert glance at his partner, who, still more covertly, caught it, and pursed up his lips in an attempt to advertise his unconcern.

Hutchinson laughed as he got up on his feet. It was a nervous, apprehensive laugh. It was a case where it was more awkward to win than lose. He walked over to his partner, who whirled upon him fiercely:-

"Now you just shut up, Corry! I know all you're going to say—that you'd rather stay in and let me go, and all that; so don't say it. You've your own people in Detroit to see, and that's enough. Besides, you can do for me the very thing I expected to do if I went out."

"And that is—?"

Pentfield read the full question in his partner's eyes, and answered:-

116

"Yes, that very thing. You can bring her in to me. The only difference will be a Dawson wedding instead of a San Franciscan one."

"But, man alike!" Corry Hutchinson objected "how under the sun can I bring her in? We're not exactly brother and sister, seeing that I have not even met her, and it wouldn't be just the proper thing, you know, for us to travel together. Of course, it would be all right—you and I know that; but think of the looks of it, man!"

Pentfield swore under his breath, consigning the looks of it to a less frigid region than Alaska.

"Now, if you'll just listen and not get astride that high horse of yours so blamed quick," his partner went on, "you'll see that the only fair thing under the circumstances is for me to let you go out this year. Next year is only a year away, and then I can take my fling."

Pentfield shook his head, though visibly swayed by the temptation.

"It won't do, Corry, old man. I appreciate your kindness and all that, but it won't do. I'd be ashamed every time I thought of you slaving away in here in my place."

A thought seemed suddenly to strike him. Burrowing into his bunk and disrupting it in his eagerness, he secured a writing-pad and pencil, and sitting down at the table, began to write with swiftness and certitude.

"Here," he said, thrusting the scrawled letter into his partner's hand. "You just deliver that and everything'll be all right."

Hutchinson ran his eye over it and laid it down.

"How do you know the brother will be willing to make that beastly trip in here?" he demanded.

"Oh, he'll do it for me—and for his sister," Pentfield replied. "You see, he's tenderfoot, and I wouldn't trust her with him alone. But with you along it will be an easy trip and a safe one. As soon as you get out, you'll go to her and prepare her. Then you can take your run east to your own people, and

117

in the spring she and her brother'll be ready to start with you. You'll like her, I know, right from the jump; and from that, you'll know her as soon as you lay eyes on her."

So saying he opened the back of his watch and exposed a girl's photograph pasted on the inside of the case. Corry Hutchinson gazed at it with admiration welling up in his eyes.

"Mabel is her name," Pentfield went on. "And it's just as well you should know how to find the house. Soon as you strike 'Frisco, take a cab, and just say, 'Holmes's place, Myrdon Avenue'—I doubt if the Myrdon Avenue is necessary. The cabby'll know where Judge Holmes lives.

"And say," Pentfield continued, after a pause, "it won't be a bad idea for you to get me a few little things which a—er—"

"A married man should have in his business," Hutchinson blurted out with a grin.

Pentfield grinned back.

"Sure, napkins and tablecloths and sheets and pillowslips, and such things. And you might get a good set of china. You know it'll come hard for her to settle down to this sort of thing. You can freight them in by steamer around by Bering Sea. And, I say, what's the matter with a piano?"

Hutchinson seconded the idea heartily. His reluctance had vanished, and he was warming up to his mission.

"By Jove! Lawrence," he said at the conclusion of the council, as they both rose to their feet, "I'll bring back that girl of yours in style. I'll do the cooking and take care of the dogs, and all that brother'll have to do will be to see to her comfort and do for her whatever I've forgotten. And I'll forget damn little, I can tell you."

The next day Lawrence Pentfield shook hands with him for the last time and watched him, running with his dogs, disappear up the frozen Yukon on his way to salt water and the world. Pentfield went back to his Bonanza mine, which was many times more dreary than before, and faced resolutely

118

into the long winter. There was work to be done, men to superintend, and operations to direct in burrowing after the erratic pay streak; but his heart was not in the work. Nor was his heart in any work till the tiered logs of a new cabin began to rise on the hill behind the mine. It was a grand cabin, warmly built and divided into three comfortable rooms. Each log was hand-hewed and squared—an expensive whim when the axemen received a daily wage of fifteen dollars; but to him nothing could be too costly for the home in which Mabel Holmes was to live.

So he went about with the building of the cabin, singing, "And oh, my fair, would I somewhere might house my heart with thee!" Also, he had a calendar pinned on the wall above the table, and his first act each morning was to check off the day and to count the days that were left ere his partner would come booming down the Yukon ice in the spring. Another whim of his was to permit no one to sleep in the new cabin on the hill. It must be as fresh for her occupancy as the square-hewed wood was fresh; and when it stood complete, he put a padlock on the door. No one entered save himself, and he was wont to spend long hours there, and to come forth with his face strangely radiant and in his eyes a glad, warm light.

In December he received a letter from Corry Hutchinson. He had just seen Mabel Holmes. She was all she ought to be, to be Lawrence Pentfield's wife, he wrote. He was enthusiastic, and his letter sent the blood tingling through Pentfield's veins. Other letters followed, one on the heels of another, and sometimes two or three together when the mail lumped up. And they were all in the same tenor. Corry had just come from Myrdon Avenue; Corry was just going to Myrdon Avenue; or Corry was at Myrdon Avenue. And he lingered on and on in San Francisco, nor even mentioned his trip to Detroit.

Lawrence Pentfield began to think that his partner was a great deal in the company of Mabel Holmes for a fellow who was going east to see his people. He even caught himself worrying about it at times, though he would have worried more had he not known Mabel and Corry so well. Mabel's letters, on the other hand, had a great deal to say about Corry. Also, a thread of timidity that was near to disinclination ran through them concerning the trip in over the ice and the Dawson marriage. Pentfield wrote back heartily, laughing at her fears, which he took to be the mere physical ones of danger and hardship rather than those bred of maidenly reserve.

But the long winter and tedious wait, following upon the two previous long winters, were telling upon him. The superintendence of the men and the pursuit of the pay streak could not break the irk of the daily round, and the end of January found him making occasional trips to Dawson, where he could forget his identity for a space at the gambling tables. Because he could afford to lose, he won, and "Pentfield's luck" became a stock phrase among the faro players.

His luck ran with him till the second week in February. How much farther it might have run is conjectural; for, after one big game, he never played again.

It was in the Opera House that it occurred, and for an hour it had seemed that he could not place his money on a card without making the card a winner. In the lull at the end of a deal, while the game-keeper was shuffling the deck, Nick Inwood the owner of the game, remarked, apropos of nothing:-

"I say, Pentfield, I see that partner of yours has been cutting up monkey-shines on the outside."

"Trust Corry to have a good time," Pentfield had answered; "especially when he has earned it."

"Every man to his taste," Nick Inwood laughed; "but I should scarcely call getting married a good time."

"Corry married!" Pentfield cried, incredulous and yet surprised out of himself for the moment.

"Sure," Inwood said. "I saw it in the 'Frisco paper that came in over the ice this morning."

"Well, and who's the girl?" Pentfield demanded, somewhat with the air of patient fortitude with which one takes the bait of a catch and is aware at the time of the large laugh bound to follow at his expense.

Nick Inwood pulled the newspaper from his pocket and began looking it over, saying:-

"I haven't a remarkable memory for names, but it seems to me it's something like Mabel—Mabel—oh yes, here it—'Mabel Holmes, daughter of Judge Holmes,'—whoever he is."

Lawrence Pentfield never turned a hair, though he wondered how any man in the North could know her name. He glanced coolly from face to face to note any vagrant signs of the game that was being played upon him, but beyond a healthy curiosity the faces betrayed nothing. Then he turned to the gambler and said in cold, even tones:-

"Inwood, I've got an even five hundred here that says the print of what you have just said is not in that paper."

The gambler looked at him in quizzical surprise. "Go 'way, child. I don't want your money."

"I thought so," Pentfield sneered, returning to the game and laying a couple of bets.

Nick Inwood's face flushed, and, as though doubting his senses, he ran careful eyes over the print of a quarter of a column. Then be turned on Lawrence Pentfield.

"Look here, Pentfield," he said, in a quiet, nervous manner; "I can't allow that, you know."

"Allow what?" Pentfield demanded brutally.

"You implied that I lied."

"Nothing of the sort," came the reply. "I merely implied that you were trying to be clumsily witty."

"Make your bets, gentlemen," the dealer protested.

"But I tell you it's true," Nick Inwood insisted.

"And I have told you I've five hundred that says it's not in that paper," Pentfield answered, at the same time throwing a heavy sack of dust on the table.

"I am sorry to take your money," was the retort, as Inwood thrust the newspaper into Pentfield's hand.

Pentfield saw, though he could not quite bring himself to believe. Glancing through the headline, "Young Lochinvar came out of the North," and skimming the article until the names of Mabel Holmes and Corry Hutchinson, coupled together, leaped squarely before his eyes, he turned to the top of the page. It was a San Francisco paper.

"The money's yours, Inwood," he remarked, with a short laugh. "There's no telling what that partner of mine will do when he gets started."

Then he returned to the article and read it word for word, very slowly and very carefully. He could no longer doubt. Beyond dispute, Corry Hutchinson had married Mabel Holmes. "One of the Bonanza kings," it described him, "a partner with Lawrence Pentfield (whom San Francisco society has not yet forgotten), and interested with that gentleman in other rich, Klondike properties." Further, and at the end, he read, "It is whispered that Mr. and Mrs. Hutchinson will, after a brief trip east to Detroit, make their real honeymoon journey into the fascinating Klondike country."

"I'll be back again; keep my place for me," Pentfield said, rising to his feet and taking his sack, which meantime had hit the blower and came back lighter by five hundred dollars.

He went down the street and bought a Seattle paper. It contained the same facts, though somewhat condensed. Corry and Mabel were indubitably married. Pentfield returned to the Opera House and resumed his seat in the game. He asked to have the limit removed.

"Trying to get action," Nick Inwood laughed, as he nodded assent to the dealer. "I was going down to the A. C. store, but now I guess I'll stay and watch you do your worst."

This Lawrence Pentfield did at the end of two hours' plunging, when the dealer bit the end off a fresh cigar and struck a match as he announced that the bank was broken. Pentfield cashed in for forty thousand, shook hands with Nick Inwood, and stated that it was the last time he would ever play at his game or at anybody's else's.

No one knew nor guessed that he had been hit, much less hit hard. There was no apparent change in his manner. For a week he went about his work much as he had always done, when he read an account of the marriage in a Portland paper. Then he called in a friend to take charge of his mine and departed up the Yukon behind his dogs. He held to the Salt Water trail till White River was reached, into which he turned. Five days later he came upon a hunting camp of the White River Indians. In the evening there was a feast, and he sat in honour beside the chief; and next morning he headed his dogs back toward the Yukon. But he no longer travelled alone. A young squaw fed his dogs for him that night and helped to pitch camp. She had been mauled by a bear in her childhood and suffered from a slight limp. Her name was Lashka, and she was diffident at first with the strange white man that had come out of the Unknown, married her with scarcely a look or word, and now was carrying her back with him into the Unknown.

But Lashka's was better fortune than falls to most Indian girls that mate with white men in the Northland. No sooner was Dawson reached than the barbaric marriage that had joined them was re-solemnized, in the white man's fashion, before a priest. From Dawson, which to her was all a marvel and a dream, she was taken directly to the Bonanza claim and installed in the square-hewed cabin on the hill.

The nine days' wonder that followed arose not so much out of the fact of the squaw whom Lawrence Pentfield had taken to bed and board as out of the ceremony that had legalized the tie. The properly sanctioned marriage was the one thing that passed the community's comprehension. But no one bothered Pentfield about it. So long as a man's vagaries did no special hurt to the community, the community let the man alone, nor was Pentfield barred from the cabins of men who possessed white wives. The marriage ceremony removed him from the status of squaw-man and placed him beyond moral reproach, though there were men that challenged his taste where women were concerned.

No more letters arrived from the outside. Six sledloads of mails had been lost at the Big Salmon. Besides, Pentfield knew that Corry and his bride must by that time have started in over the trail. They were even then on their honeymoon trip—the honeymoon trip he had dreamed of for himself through two dreary years. His lip curled with bitterness at the thought; but beyond being kinder to Lashka he gave no sign.

March had passed and April was nearing its end, when, one spring morning, Lashka asked permission to go down the creek several miles to Siwash Pete's cabin. Pete's wife, a Stewart River woman, had sent up word that something was wrong with her baby, and Lashka, who was pre-eminently a mother-woman and who held herself to be truly wise in the matter of infantile troubles, missed no opportunity of nursing the children of other women as yet more fortunate than she.

Pentfield harnessed his dogs, and with Lashka behind took the trail down the creek bed of Bonanza. Spring was in the air. The sharpness had gone out of the bite of the frost and though snow still covered the land, the murmur and trickling of water told that the iron grip of winter was relaxing. The bottom was dropping out of the trail, and here and there a new trail had been broken around open holes. At such a place, where there was not room for two sleds to pass, Pentfield heard the jingle of approaching bells and stopped his dogs.

A team of tired-looking dogs appeared around the narrow bend, followed by a heavily-loaded sled. At the gee-pole was a man who steered in a manner familiar to Pentfield, and behind the sled walked two women. His glance returned to the man at the gee-pole. It was Corry. Pentfield got on his feet and waited. He was glad that Lashka was with him. The meeting could not have come about better had it been planned, he thought. And as he waited he wondered what they would say, what they would be able to say. As for himself there was no need to say anything. The explaining was all on their side, and he was ready to listen to them.

As they drew in abreast, Corry recognized him and halted the dogs. With a "Hello, old man," he held out his hand.

Pentfield shook it, but without warmth or speech. By this time the two women had come up, and he noticed that the second one was Dora Holmes. He doffed his fur cap, the flaps of which were flying, shook hands with her, and turned toward Mabel. She swayed forward, splendid and radiant, but faltered before his outstretched hand. He had intended to say, "How do you do, Mrs. Hutchinson?"—but somehow, the Mrs. Hutchinson had choked him, and all he had managed to articulate was the "How do you do?"

There was all the constraint and awkwardness in the situation he could have wished. Mabel betrayed the agitation appropriate to her position, while Dora, evidently brought along as some sort of peacemaker, was saying:-

"Why, what is the matter, Lawrence?"

Before he could answer, Corry plucked him by the sleeve and drew him aside.

"See here, old man, what's this mean?" Corry demanded in a low tone, indicating Lashka with his eyes.

"I can hardly see, Corry, where you can have any concern in the matter," Pentfield answered mockingly.

But Corry drove straight to the point.

"What is that squaw doing on your sled? A nasty job you've given me to explain all this away. I only hope it can be explained away. Who is she? Whose squaw is she?"

Then Lawrence Pentfield delivered his stroke, and he delivered it with a certain calm elation of spirit that seemed somewhat to compensate for the wrong that had been done him.

"She is my squaw," he said; "Mrs. Pentfield, if you please."

Corry Hutchinson gasped, and Pentfield left him and returned to the two women. Mabel, with a worried expression on her face, seemed holding

125

herself aloof. He turned to Dora and asked, quite genially, as though all the world was sunshine:- "How did you stand the trip, anyway? Have any trouble to sleep warm?"

"And, how did Mrs. Hutchinson stand it?" he asked next, his eyes on Mabel.

"Oh, you dear ninny!" Dora cried, throwing her arms around him and hugging him. "Then you saw it, too! I thought something was the matter, you were acting so strangely."

"I—I hardly understand," he stammered.

"It was corrected in next day's paper," Dora chattered on. "We did not dream you would see it. All the other papers had it correctly, and of course that one miserable paper was the very one you saw!"

"Wait a moment! What do you mean?" Pentfield demanded, a sudden fear at his heart, for he felt himself on the verge of a great gulf.

But Dora swept volubly on.

"Why, when it became known that Mabel and I were going to Klondike, *Every Other Week* said that when we were gone, it would be lovely on Myrdon Avenue, meaning, of course, lonely."

"Then—"

"I am Mrs. Hutchinson," Dora answered. "And you thought it was Mabel all the time—"

"Precisely the way of it," Pentfield replied slowly. "But I can see now. The reporter got the names mixed. The Seattle and Portland paper copied."

He stood silently for a minute. Mabel's face was turned toward him again, and he could see the glow of expectancy in it. Corry was deeply interested in the ragged toe of one of his moccasins, while Dora was stealing sidelong glances at the immobile face of Lashka sitting on the sled. Lawrence Pentfield stared straight out before him into a dreary future, through the grey vistas of which he saw himself riding on a sled behind running dogs with lame Lashka by his side.

Then he spoke, quite simply, looking Mabel in the eyes.

"I am very sorry. I did not dream it. I thought you had married Corry. That is Mrs. Pentfield sitting on the sled over there."

Mabel Holmes turned weakly toward her sister, as though all the fatigue of her great journey had suddenly descended on her. Dora caught her around the waist. Corry Hutchinson was still occupied with his moccasins. Pentfield glanced quickly from face to face, then turned to his sled.

"Can't stop here all day, with Pete's baby waiting," he said to Lashka.

The long whip-lash hissed out, the dogs sprang against the breast bands, and the sled lurched and jerked ahead.

"Oh, I say, Corry," Pentfield called back, "you'd better occupy the old cabin. It's not been used for some time. I've built a new one on the hill."

TOO MUCH GOLD

This being a story—and a truer one than it may appear—of a mining country, it is quite to be expected that it will be a hard-luck story. But that depends on the point of view. Hard luck is a mild way of terming it so far as Kink Mitchell and Hootchinoo Bill are concerned; and that they have a decided opinion on the subject is a matter of common knowledge in the Yukon country.

It was in the fall of 1896 that the two partners came down to the east bank of the Yukon, and drew a Peterborough canoe from a moss-covered cache. They were not particularly pleasant-looking objects. A summer's prospecting, filled to repletion with hardship and rather empty of grub, had left their clothes in tatters and themselves worn and cadaverous. A nimbus of mosquitoes buzzed about each man's head. Their faces were coated with blue clay. Each carried a lump of this damp clay, and, whenever it dried and fell from their faces, more was daubed on in its place. There was a querulous plaint in their voices, an irritability of movement and gesture, that told of broken sleep and a losing struggle with the little winged pests.

"Them skeeters'll be the death of me yet," Kink Mitchell whimpered, as the canoe felt the current on her nose, and leaped out from the bank.

"Cheer up, cheer up. We're about done," Hootchinoo Bill answered, with an attempted heartiness in his funereal tones that was ghastly. "We'll be in Forty Mile in forty minutes, and then—cursed little devil!"

One hand left his paddle and landed on the back of his neck with a sharp slap. He put a fresh daub of clay on the injured part, swearing sulphurously the while. Kink Mitchell was not in the least amused. He merely improved the opportunity by putting a thicker coating of clay on his own neck.

They crossed the Yukon to its west bank, shot down-stream with easy stroke, and at the end of forty minutes swung in close to the left around the tail of an island. Forty Mile spread itself suddenly before them. Both men straightened their backs and gazed at the sight. They gazed long and carefully, drifting with the current, in their faces an expression of mingled surprise and consternation slowly gathering. Not a thread of smoke was rising from the hundreds of log-cabins. There was no sound of axes biting sharply into wood, of hammering and sawing. Neither dogs nor men loitered before the big store. No steamboats lay at the bank, no canoes, nor scows, nor poling-boats. The river was as bare of craft as the town was of life.

"Kind of looks like Gabriel's tooted his little horn, and you an' me has turned up missing," remarked Hootchinoo Bill.

His remark was casual, as though there was nothing unusual about the occurrence. Kink Mitchell's reply was just as casual as though he, too, were unaware of any strange perturbation of spirit.

"Looks as they was all Baptists, then, and took the boats to go by water," was his contribution.

"My ol' dad was a Baptist," Hootchinoo Bill supplemented. "An' he always did hold it was forty thousand miles nearer that way."

This was the end of their levity. They ran the canoe in and climbed the high earth bank. A feeling of awe descended upon them as they walked the deserted streets. The sunlight streamed placidly over the town. A gentle wind tapped the halyards against the flagpole before the closed doors of the Caledonia Dance Hall. Mosquitoes buzzed, robins sang, and moose birds tripped hungrily among the cabins; but there was no human life nor sign of human life.

"I'm just dyin' for a drink," Hootchinoo Bill said and unconsciously his voice sank to a hoarse whisper.

His partner nodded his head, loth to hear his own voice break the stillness. They trudged on in uneasy silence till surprised by an open door. Above this door, and stretching the width of the building, a rude sign announced the same as the "Monte Carlo." But beside the door, hat over eyes, chair tilted back, a man sat sunning himself. He was an old man. Beard and hair were long and white and patriarchal.

"If it ain't ol' Jim Cummings, turned up like us, too late for Resurrection!" said Kink Mitchell.

"Most like he didn't hear Gabriel tootin'," was Hootchinoo Bill's suggestion.

"Hello, Jim! Wake up!" he shouted.

The old man unlimbered lamely, blinking his eyes and murmuring automatically: "What'll ye have, gents? What'll ye have?"

They followed him inside and ranged up against the long bar where of yore a half-dozen nimble bar-keepers found little time to loaf. The great room, ordinarily aroar with life, was still and gloomy as a tomb. There was no rattling of chips, no whirring of ivory balls. Roulette and faro tables were like gravestones under their canvas covers. No women's voices drifted merrily from the dance-room behind. Ol' Jim Cummings wiped a glass with palsied hands, and Kink Mitchell scrawled his initials on the dust-covered bar.

"Where's the girls?" Hootchinoo Bill shouted, with affected geniality.

"Gone," was the ancient bar-keeper's reply, in a voice thin and aged as himself, and as unsteady as his hand.

"Where's Bidwell and Barlow?"

"Gone."

"And Sweetwater Charley?"

"Gone."

"And his sister?"

"Gone too."

"Your daughter Sally, then, and her little kid?"

"Gone, all gone." The old man shook his head sadly, rummaging in an absent way among the dusty bottles.

"Great Sardanapolis! Where?" Kink Mitchell exploded, unable longer to restrain himself. "You don't say you've had the plague?"

"Why, ain't you heerd?" The old man chuckled quietly. "They-all's gone to Dawson."

"What-like is that?" Bill demanded. "A creek? or a bar? or a place?"

"Ain't never heered of Dawson, eh?" The old man chuckled exasperatingly. "Why, Dawson's a town, a city, bigger'n Forty Mile. Yes, sir, bigger'n Forty Mile."

"I've ben in this land seven year," Bill announced emphatically, "an' I make free to say I never heard tell of the burg before. Hold on! Let's have some more of that whisky. Your information's flabbergasted me, that it has. Now just whereabouts is this Dawson-place you was a-mentionin'?"

"On the big flat jest below the mouth of Klondike," ol' Jim answered. "But where has you-all ben this summer?"

"Never you mind where we-all's ben," was Kink Mitchell's testy reply. "We-all's ben where the skeeters is that thick you've got to throw a stick into the air so as to see the sun and tell the time of day. Ain't I right, Bill?"

"Right you are," said Bill. "But speakin' of this Dawson-place how like did it happen to be, Jim?"

"Ounce to the pan on a creek called Bonanza, an' they ain't got to bedrock yet."

"Who struck it?"

"Carmack."

At mention of the discoverer's name the partners stared at each other disgustedly. Then they winked with great solemnity.

"Siwash George," sniffed Hootchinoo Bill.

"That squaw-man," sneered Kink Mitchell.

"I wouldn't put on my moccasins to stampede after anything he'd ever find," said Bill.

"Same here," announced his partner. "A cuss that's too plumb lazy to fish his own salmon. That's why he took up with the Indians. S'pose that black brother-in-law of his,—lemme see, Skookum Jim, eh?—s'pose he's in on it?"

The old bar-keeper nodded. "Sure, an' what's more, all Forty Mile, exceptin' me an' a few cripples."

"And drunks," added Kink Mitchell.

"No-sir-ee!" the old man shouted emphatically.

"I bet you the drinks Honkins ain't in on it!" Hootchinoo Bill cried with certitude.

Ol' Jim's face lighted up. "I takes you, Bill, an' you loses."

"However did that ol' soak budge out of Forty Mile?" Mitchell demanded.

"The ties him down an' throws him in the bottom of a polin'-boat," ol' Jim explained. "Come right in here, they did, an' takes him out of that there chair there in the corner, an' three more drunks they finds under the pianny. I tell you-alls the whole camp hits up the Yukon for Dawson jes' like Sam Scratch was after them,—wimmen, children, babes in arms, the whole shebang. Bidwell comes to me an' sez, sez he, 'Jim, I wants you to keep tab on the Monte Carlo. I'm goin'.'

"'Where's Barlow?' sez I. 'Gone,' sez he, 'an' I'm a-followin' with a load of whisky.' An' with that, never waitin' for me to decline, he makes a run for his boat an' away he goes, polin' up river like mad. So here I be, an' these is the first drinks I've passed out in three days."

The partners looked at each other.

"Gosh darn my buttoms!" said Hootchinoo Bill. "Seems likes you and me, Kink, is the kind of folks always caught out with forks when it rains soup."

"Wouldn't it take the saleratus out your dough, now?" said Kink Mitchell. "A stampede of tin-horns, drunks, an' loafers."

"An' squaw-men," added Bill. "Not a genooine miner in the whole caboodle."

"Genooine miners like you an' me, Kink," he went on academically, "is all out an' sweatin' hard over Birch Creek way. Not a genooine miner in this whole crazy Dawson outfit, and I say right here, not a step do I budge for any Carmack strike. I've got to see the colour of the dust first."

"Same here," Mitchell agreed. "Let's have another drink."

Having wet this resolution, they beached the canoe, transferred its contents to their cabin, and cooked dinner. But as the afternoon wore along they grew restive. They were men used to the silence of the great wilderness, but this gravelike silence of a town worried them. They caught themselves listening for familiar sounds—"waitin' for something to make a noise which ain't goin' to make a noise," as Bill put it. They strolled through the deserted streets to the Monte Carlo for more drinks, and wandered along the river bank to the steamer landing, where only water gurgled as the eddy filled and emptied, and an occasional salmon leapt flashing into the sun.

They sat down in the shade in front of the store and talked with the consumptive storekeeper, whose liability to hemorrhage accounted for his presence. Bill and Kink told him how they intended loafing in their cabin and resting up after the hard summer's work. They told him, with a certain insistence, that was half appeal for belief, half challenge for contradiction, how much they were going to enjoy their idleness. But the storekeeper was uninterested. He switched the conversation back to the strike on Klondike, and they could not keep him away from it. He could think of nothing else, talk of nothing else, till Hootchinoo Bill rose up in anger and disgust.

"Gosh darn Dawson, say I!" he cried.

"Same here," said Kink Mitchell, with a brightening face. "One'd think something was doin' up there, 'stead of bein' a mere stampede of greenhorns an' tinhorns."

But a boat came into view from down-stream. It was long and slim. It hugged the bank closely, and its three occupants, standing upright, propelled it against the stiff current by means of long poles.

"Circle City outfit," said the storekeeper. "I was lookin' for 'em along by afternoon. Forty Mile had the start of them by a hundred and seventy miles. But gee! they ain't losin' any time!"

"We'll just sit here quiet-like and watch 'em string by," Bill said complacently.

As he spoke, another boat appeared in sight, followed after a brief interval by two others. By this time the first boat was abreast of the men on the bank. Its occupants did not cease poling while greetings were exchanged, and, though its progress was slow, a half-hour saw it out of sight up river.

Still they came from below, boat after boat, in endless procession. The uneasiness of Bill and Kink increased. They stole speculative, tentative glances at each other, and when their eyes met looked away in embarrassment. Finally, however, their eyes met and neither looked away.

Kink opened his mouth to speak, but words failed him and his mouth remained open while he continued to gaze at his partner.

"Just what I was thinken', Kink," said Bill.

They grinned sheepishly at each other, and by tacit consent started to walk away. Their pace quickened, and by the time they arrived at their cabin they were on the run.

"Can't lose no time with all that multitude a-rushin' by," Kink spluttered, as he jabbed the sour-dough can into the beanpot with one hand and with the other gathered in the frying-pan and coffee-pot.

"Should say not," gasped Bill, his head and shoulders buried in a clothes-sack wherein were stored winter socks and underwear. "I say, Kink, don't forget the saleratus on the corner shelf back of the stove."

Half-an-hour later they were launching the canoe and loading up, while the storekeeper made jocular remarks about poor, weak mortals and the contagiousness of "stampedin' fever." But when Bill and Kink thrust their long poles to bottom and started the canoe against the current, he called after them:-

"Well, so-long and good luck! And don't forget to blaze a stake or two for me!"

They nodded their heads vigorously and felt sorry for the poor wretch who remained perforce behind.

* * * * *

Kink and Bill were sweating hard. According to the revised Northland Scripture, the stampede is to the swift, the blazing of stakes to the strong, and the Crown in royalties, gathers to itself the fulness thereof. Kink and Bill were both swift and strong. They took the soggy trail at a long, swinging gait that broke the hearts of a couple of tender-feet who tried to keep up with them. Behind, strung out between them and Dawson (where the boats were discarded and land travel began), was the vanguard of the Circle City outfit. In the race from Forty Mile the partners had passed every boat, winning from the leading boat by a length in the Dawson eddy, and leaving its occupants sadly behind the moment their feet struck the trail.

"Huh! couldn't see us for smoke," Hootchinoo Bill chuckled, flirting the stinging sweat from his brow and glancing swiftly back along the way they had come.

Three men emerged from where the trail broke through the trees. Two followed close at their heels, and then a man and a woman shot into view.

"Come on, you Kink! Hit her up! Hit her up!"

Bill quickened his pace. Mitchell glanced back in more leisurely fashion.

"I declare if they ain't lopin'!"

"And here's one that's loped himself out," said Bill, pointing to the side of the trail.

A man was lying on his back panting in the culminating stages of violent exhaustion. His face was ghastly, his eyes bloodshot and glazed, for all the world like a dying man.

135

"*Chechaquo!*" Kink Mitchell grunted, and it was the grunt of the old "sour dough" for the green-horn, for the man who outfitted with "self-risin'" flour and used baking-powder in his biscuits.

The partners, true to the old-timer custom, had intended to stake downstream from the strike, but when they saw claim 81 BELOW blazed on a tree,—which meant fully eight miles below Discovery,—they changed their minds. The eight miles were covered in less than two hours. It was a killing pace, over so rough trail, and they passed scores of exhausted men that had fallen by the wayside.

At Discovery little was to be learned of the upper creek. Cormack's Indian brother-in-law, Skookum Jim, had a hazy notion that the creek was staked as high as the 30's; but when Kink and Bill looked at the corner-stakes of 79 ABOVE, they threw their stampeding packs off their backs and sat down to smoke. All their efforts had been vain. Bonanza was staked from mouth to source,—"out of sight and across the next divide." Bill complained that night as they fried their bacon and boiled their coffee over Cormack's fire at Discovery.

"Try that pup," Carmack suggested next morning.

"That pup" was a broad creek that flowed into Bonanza at 7 ABOVE. The partners received his advice with the magnificent contempt of the sour dough for a squaw-man, and, instead, spent the day on Adam's Creek, another and more likely-looking tributary of Bonanza. But it was the old story over again—staked to the sky-line.

For threes days Carmack repeated his advice, and for three days they received it contemptuously. But on the fourth day, there being nowhere else to go, they went up "that pup." They knew that it was practically unstaked, but they had no intention of staking. The trip was made more for the purpose of giving vent to their ill-humour than for anything else. They had become quite cynical, sceptical. They jeered and scoffed at everything, and insulted every *chechaquo* they met along the way.

At No. 23 the stakes ceased. The remainder of the creek was open for location.

"Moose pasture," sneered Kink Mitchell.

But Bill gravely paced off five hundred feet up the creek and blazed the corner-stakes. He had picked up the bottom of a candle-box, and on the smooth side he wrote the notice for his centre-stake:-

THIS MOOSE PASTURE IS RESERVED FOR THE

SWEDES AND *CHECHAQUOS*.

—BILL RADER.

Kink read it over with approval, saying:-

"As them's my sentiments, I reckon I might as well subscribe."

So the name of Charles Mitchell was added to the notice; and many an old sour dough's face relaxed that day at sight of the handiwork of a kindred spirit.

"How's the pup?" Carmack inquired when they strolled back into camp.

"To hell with pups!" was Hootchinoo Bill's reply. "Me and Kink's goin' a-lookin' for Too Much Gold when we get rested up."

Too Much Gold was the fabled creek of which all sour doughs dreamed, whereof it was said the gold was so thick that, in order to wash it, gravel must first be shovelled into the sluice-boxes. But the several days' rest, preliminary to the quest for Too Much Gold, brought a slight change in their plan, inasmuch as it brought one Ans Handerson, a Swede.

Ans Handerson had been working for wages all summer at Miller Creek over on the Sixty Mile, and, the summer done, had strayed up Bonanza like many another waif helplessly adrift on the gold tides that swept willy-nilly across the land. He was tall and lanky. His arms were long, like prehistoric man's, and his hands were like soup-plates, twisted and gnarled, and big-knuckled from toil. He was slow of utterance and movement, and his eyes, pale blue as his hair was pale yellow, seemed filled with an immortal dreaming, the stuff of which no man knew, and himself least of all. Perhaps this appearance of immortal dreaming was due to a supreme and vacuous innocence. At any rate, this was the valuation men of ordinary clay put upon him, and there was nothing extraordinary about the composition of Hootchinoo Bill and Kink Mitchell.

The partners had spent a day of visiting and gossip, and in the evening met in the temporary quarters of the Monte Carlo—a large tent were stampeders rested their weary bones and bad whisky sold at a dollar a drink. Since the only money in circulation was dust, and since the house took the "down-weight" on the scales, a drink cost something more than a dollar. Bill and Kink were not drinking, principally for the reason that their one and common sack was not strong enough to stand many excursions to the scales.

"Say, Bill, I've got a *chechaquo* on the string for a sack of flour," Mitchell announced jubilantly.

Bill looked interested and pleased. Grub as scarce, and they were not over-plentifully supplied for the quest after Too Much Gold.

"Flour's worth a dollar a pound," he answered. "How like do you calculate to get your finger on it?"

"Trade 'm a half-interest in that claim of ourn," Kink answered.

"What claim?" Bill was surprised. Then he remembered the reservation he had staked off for the Swedes, and said, "Oh!"

"I wouldn't be so clost about it, though," he added. "Give 'm the whole thing while you're about it, in a right free-handed way."

Bill shook his head. "If I did, he'd get clean scairt and prance off. I'm lettin' on as how the ground is believed to be valuable, an' that we're lettin' go half just because we're monstrous short on grub. After the dicker we can make him a present of the whole shebang."

"If somebody ain't disregarded our notice," Bill objected, though he was plainly pleased at the prospect of exchanging the claim for a sack of flour.

138

"She ain't jumped," Kink assured him. "It's No. 24, and it stands. The *chechaquos* took it serious, and they begun stakin' where you left off. Staked clean over the divide, too. I was gassin' with one of them which has just got in with cramps in his legs."

It was then, and for the first time, that they heard the slow and groping utterance of Ans Handerson.

"Ay like the looks," he was saying to the bar-keeper. "Ay tank Ay gat a claim."

The partners winked at each other, and a few minutes later a surprised and grateful Swede was drinking bad whisky with two hard-hearted strangers. But he was as hard-headed as they were hard-hearted. The sack made frequent journeys to the scales, followed solicitously each time by Kink Mitchell's eyes, and still Ans Handerson did not loosen up. In his pale blue eyes, as in summer seas, immortal dreams swam up and burned, but the swimming and the burning were due to the tales of gold and prospect pans he heard, rather than to the whisky he slid so easily down his throat.

The partners were in despair, though they appeared boisterous and jovial of speech and action.

"Don't mind me, my friend," Hootchinoo Bill hiccoughed, his hand upon Ans Handerson's shoulder. "Have another drink. We're just celebratin' Kink's birthday here. This is my pardner, Kink, Kink Mitchell. An' what might your name be?"

This learned, his hand descended resoundingly on Kink's back, and Kink simulated clumsy self-consciousness in that he was for the time being the centre of the rejoicing, while Ans Handerson looked pleased and asked them to have a drink with him. It was the first and last time he treated, until the play changed and his canny soul was roused to unwonted prodigality. But he paid for the liquor from a fairly healthy-looking sack. "Not less 'n eight hundred in it," calculated the lynx-eyed Kink; and on the strength of it he took the first opportunity of a privy conversation with Bidwell, proprietor of the bad whisky and the tent.

"Here's my sack, Bidwell," Kink said, with the intimacy and surety of one old-timer to another. "Just weigh fifty dollars into it for a day or so more or less, and we'll be yours truly, Bill an' me."

Thereafter the journeys of the sack to the scales were more frequent, and the celebration of Kink's natal day waxed hilarious. He even essayed to sing the old-timer's classic, "The Juice of the Forbidden Fruit," but broke down and drowned his embarrassment in another round of drinks. Even Bidwell honoured him with a round or two on the house; and he and Bill were decently drunk by the time Ans Handerson's eyelids began to droop and his tongue gave promise of loosening.

Bill grew affectionate, then confidential. He told his troubles and hard luck to the bar-keeper and the world in general, and to Ans Handerson in particular. He required no histrionic powers to act the part. The bad whisky attended to that. He worked himself into a great sorrow for himself and Bill, and his tears were sincere when he told how he and his partner were thinking of selling a half-interest in good ground just because they were short of grub. Even Kink listened and believed.

Ans Handerson's eyes were shining unholily as he asked, "How much you tank you take?"

Bill and Kink did not hear him, and he was compelled to repeat his query. They appeared reluctant. He grew keener. And he swayed back and forward, holding on to the bar and listened with all his ears while they conferred together on one side, and wrangled as to whether they should or not, and disagreed in stage whispers over the price they should set.

"Two hundred and—hic!—fifty," Bill finally announced, "but we reckon as we won't sell."

"Which is monstrous wise if I might chip in my little say," seconded Bidwell.

"Yes, indeedy," added Kink. "We ain't in no charity business a-disgorgin' free an' generous to Swedes an' white men."

140

"Ay tank we haf another drink," hiccoughed Ans Handerson, craftily changing the subject against a more propitious time.

And thereafter, to bring about that propitious time, his own sack began to see-saw between his hip pocket and the scales. Bill and Kink were coy, but they finally yielded to his blandishments. Whereupon he grew shy and drew Bidwell to one side. He staggered exceedingly, and held on to Bidwell for support as he asked—

"They ban all right, them men, you tank so?"

"Sure," Bidwell answered heartily. "Known 'em for years. Old sour doughs. When they sell a claim, they sell a claim. They ain't no air-dealers."

"Ay tank Ay buy," Ans Handerson announced, tottering back to the two men.

But by now he was dreaming deeply, and he proclaimed he would have the whole claim or nothing. This was the cause of great pain to Hootchinoo Bill. He orated grandly against the "hawgishness" of *chechaquos* and Swedes, albeit he dozed between periods, his voice dying away to a gurgle, and his head sinking forward on his breast. But whenever roused by a nudge from Kink or Bidwell, he never failed to explode another volley of abuse and insult.

Ans Handerson was calm under it all. Each insult added to the value of the claim. Such unamiable reluctance to sell advertised but one thing to him, and he was aware of a great relief when Hootchinoo Bill sank snoring to the floor, and he was free to turn his attention to his less intractable partner.

Kink Mitchell was persuadable, though a poor mathematician. He wept dolefully, but was willing to sell a half-interest for two hundred and fifty dollars or the whole claim for seven hundred and fifty. Ans Handerson and Bidwell laboured to clear away his erroneous ideas concerning fractions, but their labour was vain. He spilled tears and regrets all over the bar and on their shoulders, which tears, however, did not wash away his opinion, that if one half was worth two hundred and fifty, two halves were worth three times as much.

In the end,—and even Bidwell retained no more than hazy recollections of how the night terminated,—a bill of sale was drawn up, wherein Bill Rader and Charles Mitchell yielded up all right and title to the claim known as 24 ELDORADO, the same being the name the creek had received from some optimistic *chechaquo.*

When Kink had signed, it took the united efforts of the three to arouse Bill. Pen in hand, he swayed long over the document; and, each time he rocked back and forth, in Ans Handerson's eyes flashed and faded a wondrous golden vision. When the precious signature was at last appended and the dust paid over, he breathed a great sigh, and sank to sleep under a table, where he dreamed immortally until morning.

But the day was chill and grey. He felt bad. His first act, unconscious and automatic, was to feel for his sack. Its lightness startled him. Then, slowly, memories of the night thronged into his brain. Rough voices disturbed him. He opened his eyes and peered out from under the table. A couple of early risers, or, rather, men who had been out on trail all night, were vociferating their opinions concerning the utter and loathsome worthlessness of Eldorado Creek. He grew frightened, felt in his pocket, and found the deed to 24 ELDORADO.

Ten minutes later Hootchinoo Bill and Kink Mitchell were roused from their blankets by a wild-eyed Swede that strove to force upon them an ink-scrawled and very blotty piece of paper.

"Ay tank Ay take my money back," he gibbered. "Ay tank Ay take my money back."

Tears were in his eyes and throat. They ran down his cheeks as he knelt before them and pleaded and implored. But Bill and Kink did not laugh. They might have been harder hearted.

"First time I ever hear a man squeal over a minin' deal," Bill said. "An' I make free to say 'tis too onusual for me to savvy."

"Same here," Kink Mitchell remarked. "Minin' deals is like horse-tradin'."

They were honest in their wonderment. They could not conceive of themselves raising a wail over a business transaction, so they could not understand it in another man.

"The poor, ornery *chechaquo*," murmured Hootchinoo Bill, as they watched the sorrowing Swede disappear up the trail.

"But this ain't Too Much Gold," Kink Mitchell said cheerfully.

And ere the day was out they purchased flour and bacon at exorbitant prices with Ans Handerson's dust and crossed over the divide in the direction of the creeks that lie between Klondike and Indian River.

Three months later they came back over the divide in the midst of a snow-storm and dropped down the trail to 24 ELDORADO. It merely chanced that the trail led them that way. They were not looking for the claim. Nor could they see much through the driving white till they set foot upon the claim itself. And then the air lightened, and they beheld a dump, capped by a windlass that a man was turning. They saw him draw a bucket of gravel from the hole and tilt it on the edge of the dump. Likewise they saw another, man, strangely familiar, filling a pan with the fresh gravel. His hands were large; his hair wets pale yellow. But before they reached him, he turned with the pan and fled toward a cabin. He wore no hat, and the snow falling down his neck accounted for his haste. Bill and Kink ran after him, and came upon him in the cabin, kneeling by the stove and washing the pan of gravel in a tub of water.

He was too deeply engaged to notice more than that somebody had entered the cabin. They stood at his shoulder and looked on. He imparted to the pan a deft circular motion, pausing once or twice to rake out the larger particles of gravel with his fingers. The water was muddy, and, with the pan buried in it, they could see nothing of its contents. Suddenly he lifted the pan clear and sent the water out of it with a flirt. A mass of yellow, like butter in a churn, showed across the bottom.

Hootchinoo Bill swallowed. Never in his life had he dreamed of so rich a test-pan.

"Kind of thick, my friend," he said huskily. "How much might you reckon that-all to be?"

Ans Handerson did not look up as he replied, "Ay tank fafty ounces."

"You must be scrumptious rich, then, eh?"

Still Ans Handerson kept his head down, absorbed in putting in the fine touches which wash out the last particles of dross, though he answered, "Ay tank Ay ban wort' five hundred t'ousand dollar."

"Gosh!" said Hootchinoo Bill, and he said it reverently.

"Yes, Bill, gosh!" said Kink Mitchell; and they went out softly and closed the door.

THE ONE THOUSAND DOZEN

David Rasmunsen was a hustler, and, like many a greater man, a man of the one idea. Wherefore, when the clarion call of the North rang on his ear, he conceived an adventure in eggs and bent all his energy to its achievement. He figured briefly and to the point, and the adventure became iridescent-hued, splendid. That eggs would sell at Dawson for five dollars a dozen was a safe working premise. Whence it was incontrovertible that one thousand dozen would bring, in the Golden Metropolis, five thousand dollars.

On the other hand, expense was to be considered, and he considered it well, for he was a careful man, keenly practical, with a hard head and a heart that imagination never warmed. At fifteen cents a dozen, the initial cost of his thousand dozen would be one hundred and fifty dollars, a mere bagatelle in face of the enormous profit. And suppose, just suppose, to be wildly extravagant for once, that transportation for himself and eggs should run up eight hundred and fifty more; he would still have four thousand clear cash and clean when the last egg was disposed of and the last dust had rippled into his sack.

"You see, *Alma*,"—he figured it over with his wife, the cosy dining-room submerged in a sea of maps, government surveys, guide-books, and Alaskan itineraries,—"you see, expenses don't really begin till you make Dyea—fifty dollars'll cover it with a first-class passage thrown in. Now from Dyea to Lake Linderman, Indian packers take your goods over for twelve cents a pound, twelve dollars a hundred, or one hundred and twenty dollars a thousand. Say I have fifteen hundred pounds, it'll cost one hundred and eighty dollars—call it two hundred and be safe. I am creditably informed by a Klondiker just come out that I can buy a boat for three hundred. But the same man says I'm sure to get a couple of passengers for one hundred and fifty each, which will give me the boat for nothing, and, further, they can help me manage it. And . . . that's all; I put my eggs ashore from the boat at Dawson. Now let me see how much is that?"

"Fifty dollars from San Francisco to Dyea, two hundred from Dyea to Linderman, passengers pay for the boat—two hundred and fifty all told," she summed up swiftly.

"And a hundred for my clothes and personal outfit," he went on happily; "that leaves a margin of five hundred for emergencies. And what possible emergencies can arise?"

Alma shrugged her shoulders and elevated her brows. If that vast Northland was capable of swallowing up a man and a thousand dozen eggs, surely there was room and to spare for whatever else he might happen to possess. So she thought, but she said nothing. She knew David Rasmunsen too well to say anything.

"Doubling the time because of chance delays, I should make the trip in two months. Think of it, *Alma*! Four thousand in two months! Beats the paltry hundred a month I'm getting now. Why, we'll build further out where we'll have more space, gas in every room, and a view, and the rent of the cottage'll pay taxes, insurance, and water, and leave something over. And then there's always the chance of my striking it and coming out a millionaire. Now tell me, *Alma*, don't you think I'm very moderate?"

And *Alma* could hardly think otherwise. Besides, had not her own cousin,—though a remote and distant one to be sure, the black sheep, the harum-scarum, the ne'er-do-well,—had not he come down out of that weird North country with a hundred thousand in yellow dust, to say nothing of a half-ownership in the hole from which it came?

David Rasmunsen's grocer was surprised when he found him weighing eggs in the scales at the end of the counter, and Rasmunsen himself was more surprised when he found that a dozen eggs weighed a pound and a half—fifteen hundred pounds for his thousand dozen! There would be no weight left for his clothes, blankets, and cooking utensils, to say nothing of the grub he must necessarily consume by the way. His calculations were all thrown out, and he was just proceeding to recast them when he hit upon the idea of weighing small eggs. "For whether they be large or small, a dozen eggs is a dozen eggs," he observed sagely to himself; and a dozen small ones he found to weigh but a pound and a quarter. Thereat the city of San Francisco was overrun by anxious-eyed emissaries, and commission houses and dairy associations were startled by a sudden demand for eggs running not more than twenty ounces to the dozen.

Rasmunsen mortgaged the little cottage for a thousand dollars, arranged for his wife to make a prolonged stay among her own people, threw up his job, and started North. To keep within his schedule he compromised on a second-class passage, which, because of the rush, was worse than steerage; and in the late summer, a pale and wabbly man, he disembarked with his eggs on the Dyea beach. But it did not take him long to recover his land legs and appetite. His first interview with the Chilkoot packers straightened him up and stiffened his backbone. Forty cents a pound they demanded for the twenty-eight-mile portage, and while he caught his breath and swallowed, the price went up to forty-three. Fifteen husky Indians put the straps on his packs at forty-five, but took them off at an offer of forty-seven from a Skaguay Croesus in dirty shirt and ragged overalls who had lost his horses on the White Pass trail and was now making a last desperate drive at the country by way of Chilkoot.

But Rasmunsen was clean grit, and at fifty cents found takers, who, two days later, set his eggs down intact at Linderman. But fifty cents a pound is a thousand dollars a ton, and his fifteen hundred pounds had exhausted his emergency fund and left him stranded at the Tantalus point where each day he saw the fresh-whipsawed boats departing for Dawson. Further, a great anxiety brooded over the camp where the boats were built. Men worked frantically, early and late, at the height of their endurance, caulking, nailing, and pitching in a frenzy of haste for which adequate explanation was not far to seek. Each day the snow-line crept farther down the bleak, rock-shouldered peaks, and gale followed gale, with sleet and slush and snow, and in the eddies and quiet places young ice formed and thickened through the fleeting hours. And each morn, toil-stiffened men turned wan faces across the lake to see if the freeze-up had come. For the freeze-up heralded the death of their hope—the hope that they would be floating down the swift river ere navigation closed on the chain of lakes.

To harrow Rasmunsen's soul further, he discovered three competitors in the egg business. It was true that one, a little German, had gone broke and was himself forlornly back-tripping the last pack of the portage; but the other two had boats nearly completed, and were daily supplicating the god of merchants and traders to stay the iron hand of winter for just another day. But the iron hand closed down over the land. Men were being frozen in the blizzard which swept Chilkoot, and Rasmunsen frosted his toes ere he was aware. He found a chance to go passenger with his freight in a boat just shoving off through the rubble, but two hundred hard cash, was required, and he had no money.

"Ay tank you yust wait one leedle w'ile," said the Swedish boat-builder, who had struck his Klondike right there and was wise enough to know it— "one leedle w'ile und I make you a tam fine skiff boat, sure Pete."

With this unpledged word to go on, Rasmunsen hit the back trail to Crater Lake, where he fell in with two press correspondents whose tangled baggage was strewn from Stone House, over across the Pass, and as far as Happy Camp.

"Yes," he said with consequence. "I've a thousand dozen eggs at Linderman, and my boat's just about got the last seam caulked. Consider myself in luck to get it. Boats are at a premium, you know, and none to be had."

Whereupon and almost with bodily violence the correspondents clamoured to go with him, fluttered greenbacks before his eyes, and spilled yellow twenties from hand to hand. He could not hear of it, but they over-persuaded him, and he reluctantly consented to take them at three hundred apiece. Also they pressed upon him the passage money in advance. And while they wrote to their respective journals concerning the Good Samaritan with the thousand dozen eggs, the Good Samaritan was hurrying back to the Swede at Linderman.

"Here, you! Gimme that boat!" was his salutation, his hand jingling the correspondents' gold pieces and his eyes hungrily bent upon the finished craft.

148

The Swede regarded him stolidly and shook his head.

"How much is the other fellow paying? Three hundred? Well, here's four. Take it."

He tried to press it upon him, but the man backed away.

"Ay tank not. Ay say him get der skiff boat. You yust wait—"

"Here's six hundred. Last call. Take it or leave it. Tell 'm it's a mistake."

The Swede wavered. "Ay tank yes," he finally said, and the last Rasmunsen saw of him his vocabulary was going to wreck in a vain effort to explain the mistake to the other fellows.

The German slipped and broke his ankle on the steep hogback above Deep Lake, sold out his stock for a dollar a dozen, and with the proceeds hired Indian packers to carry him back to Dyea. But on the morning Rasmunsen shoved off with his correspondents, his two rivals followed suit.

"How many you got?" one of them, a lean little New Englander, called out.

"One thousand dozen," Rasmunsen answered proudly.

"Huh! I'll go you even stakes I beat you in with my eight hundred."

The correspondents offered to lend him the money; but Rasmunsen declined, and the Yankee closed with the remaining rival, a brawny son of the sea and sailor of ships and things, who promised to show them all a wrinkle or two when it came to cracking on. And crack on he did, with a large tarpaulin square-sail which pressed the bow half under at every jump. He was the first to run out of Linderman, but, disdaining the portage, piled his loaded boat on the rocks in the boiling rapids. Rasmunsen and the Yankee, who likewise had two passengers, portaged across on their backs and then lined their empty boats down through the bad water to Bennett.

Bennett was a twenty-five-mile lake, narrow and deep, a funnel between the mountains through which storms ever romped. Rasmunsen camped on the sand-pit at its head, where were many men and boats bound north in the teeth of the Arctic winter. He awoke in the morning to find a piping gale from the south, which caught the chill from the whited peaks and glacial valleys and blew as cold as north wind ever blew. But it was fair, and he also found the Yankee staggering past the first bold headland with all sail set. Boat after boat was getting under way, and the correspondents fell to with enthusiasm.

"We'll catch him before Cariboo Crossing," they assured Rasmunsen, as they ran up the sail and the *Alma* took the first icy spray over her bow.

Now Rasmunsen all his life had been prone to cowardice on water, but he clung to the kicking steering-oar with set face and determined jaw. His thousand dozen were there in the boat before his eyes, safely secured beneath the correspondents' baggage, and somehow, before his eyes were the little cottage and the mortgage for a thousand dollars.

It was bitter cold. Now and again he hauled in the steering-sweep and put out a fresh one while his passengers chopped the ice from the blade. Wherever the spray struck, it turned instantly to frost, and the dipping boom of the spritsail was quickly fringed with icicles. The *Alma* strained and hammered through the big seas till the seams and butts began to spread, but in lieu of bailing the correspondents chopped ice and flung it overboard. There was no let-up. The mad race with winter was on, and the boats tore along in a desperate string.

"W-w-we can't stop to save our souls!" one of the correspondents chattered, from cold, not fright.

"That's right! Keep her down the middle, old man!" the other encouraged.

Rasmunsen replied with an idiotic grin. The iron-bound shores were in a lather of foam, and even down the middle the only hope was to keep running away from the big seas. To lower sail was to be overtaken and swamped. Time and again they passed boats pounding among the rocks, and once they saw one on the edge of the breakers about to strike. A little craft behind them, with two men, jibed over and turned bottom up.

"W-w-watch out, old man," cried he of the chattering teeth.

Rasmunsen grinned and tightened his aching grip on the sweep. Scores of times had the send of the sea caught the big square stern of the *Alma* and thrown her off from dead before it till the after leach of the spritsail fluttered hollowly, and each time, and only with all his strength, had he forced her back. His grin by then had become fixed, and it disturbed the correspondents to look at him.

They roared down past an isolated rock a hundred yards from shore. From its wave-drenched top a man shrieked wildly, for the instant cutting the storm with his voice. But the next instant the *Alma* was by, and the rock growing a black speck in the troubled froth.

"That settles the Yankee!   Where's the sailor?" shouted one of his passengers.

Rasmunsen shot a glance over his shoulder at a black square-sail.   He had seen it leap up out of the grey to windward, and for an hour, off and on, had been watching it grow.   The sailor had evidently repaired damages and was making up for lost time.

"Look at him come!"

Both passengers stopped chopping ice to watch.   Twenty miles of Bennett were behind them—room and to spare for the sea to toss up its mountains toward the sky.   Sinking and soaring like a storm-god, the sailor drove by them.   The huge sail seemed to grip the boat from the crests of the waves, to tear it bodily out of the water, and fling it crashing and smothering down into the yawning troughs.

"The sea'll never catch him!"

"But he'll r-r-run her nose under!"

Even as they spoke, the black tarpaulin swooped from sight behind a big comber.   The next wave rolled over the spot, and the next, but the boat did not reappear.   The *Alma* rushed by the place.   A little riffraff of oats and boxes was seen.   An arm thrust up and a shaggy head broke surface a score of yards away.

For a time there was silence. As the end of the lake came in sight, the waves began to leap aboard with such steady recurrence that the correspondents no longer chopped ice but flung the water out with buckets. Even this would not do, and, after a shouted conference with Rasmunsen, they attacked the baggage. Flour, bacon, beans, blankets, cooking-stove, ropes, odds and ends, everything they could get hands on, flew overboard. The boat acknowledged it at once, taking less water and rising more buoyantly.

"That'll do!" Rasmunsen called sternly, as they applied themselves to the top layer of eggs.

"The h-hell it will!" answered the shivering one, savagely. With the exception of their notes, films, and cameras, they had sacrificed their outfit. He bent over, laid hold of an egg-box, and began to worry it out from under the lashing.

"Drop it! Drop it, I say!"

Rasmunsen had managed to draw his revolver, and with the crook of his arm over the sweep head, was taking aim. The correspondent stood up on the thwart, balancing back and forth, his face twisted with menace and speechless anger.

"My God!"

So cried his brother correspondent, hurling himself, face downward, into the bottom of the boat. The *Alma*, under the divided attention of Rasmunsen, had been caught by a great mass of water and whirled around. The after leach hollowed, the sail emptied and jibed, and the boom, sweeping with terrific force across the boat, carried the angry correspondent overboard with a broken back. Mast and sail had gone over the side as well. A drenching sea followed, as the boat lost headway, and Rasmunsen sprang to the bailing bucket.

Several boats hurtled past them in the next half-hour,—small boats, boats of their own size, boats afraid, unable to do aught but run madly on. Then a ten-ton barge, at imminent risk of destruction, lowered sail to windward and lumbered down upon them.

"Keep off! Keep off!" Rasmunsen screamed.

But his low gunwale ground against the heavy craft, and the remaining correspondent clambered aboard. Rasmunsen was over the eggs like a cat and in the bow of the *Alma*, striving with numb fingers to bend the hauling-lines together.

"Come on!" a red-whiskered man yelled at him.

"I've a thousand dozen eggs here," he shouted back. "Gimme a tow! I'll pay you!"

"Come on!" they howled in chorus.

A big whitecap broke just beyond, washing over the barge and leaving the *Alma* half swamped. The men cast off, cursing him as they ran up their sail. Rasmunsen cursed back and fell to bailing. The mast and sail, like a sea anchor, still fast by the halyards, held the boat head on to wind and sea and gave him a chance to fight the water out.

Three hours later, numbed, exhausted, blathering like a lunatic, but still bailing, he went ashore on an ice-strewn beach near Cariboo Crossing. Two men, a government courier and a half-breed voyageur, dragged him out of the surf, saved his cargo, and beached the *Alma*. They were paddling out of the country in a Peterborough, and gave him shelter for the night in their storm-bound camp. Next morning they departed, but he elected to stay by his eggs. And thereafter the name and fame of the man with the thousand dozen eggs began to spread through the land. Gold-seekers who made in before the freeze-up carried the news of his coming. Grizzled old-timers of Forty Mile and Circle City, sour doughs with leathern jaws and bean-calloused stomachs, called up dream memories of chickens and green things at mention of his name. Dyea and Skaguay took an interest in his being, and questioned his progress from every man who came over the passes, while Dawson—golden, omeletless Dawson—fretted and worried, and way-laid every chance arrival for word of him.

But of this Rasmunsen knew nothing. The day after the wreck he patched up the *Alma* and pulled out. A cruel east wind blew in his teeth from

153

Tagish, but he got the oars over the side and bucked manfully into it, though half the time he was drifting backward and chopping ice from the blades. According to the custom of the country, he was driven ashore at Windy Arm; three times on Tagish saw him swamped and beached; and Lake Marsh held him at the freeze-up. The *Alma* was crushed in the jamming of the floes, but the eggs were intact. These he back-tripped two miles across the ice to the shore, where he built a cache, which stood for years after and was pointed out by men who knew.

Half a thousand frozen miles stretched between him and Dawson, and the waterway was closed. But Rasmunsen, with a peculiar tense look in his face, struck back up the lakes on foot. What he suffered on that lone trip, with nought but a single blanket, an axe, and a handful of beans, is not given to ordinary mortals to know. Only the Arctic adventurer may understand. Suffice that he was caught in a blizzard on Chilkoot and left two of his toes with the surgeon at Sheep Camp. Yet he stood on his feet and washed dishes in the scullery of the *Pawona* to the Puget Sound, and from there passed coal on a P. S. boat to San Francisco.

It was a haggard, unkempt man who limped across the shining office floor to raise a second mortgage from the bank people. His hollow cheeks betrayed themselves through the scraggy beard, and his eyes seemed to have retired into deep caverns where they burned with cold fires. His hands were grained from exposure and hard work, and the nails were rimmed with tight-packed dirt and coal-dust. He spoke vaguely of eggs and ice-packs, winds and tides; but when they declined to let him have more than a second thousand, his talk became incoherent, concerning itself chiefly with the price of dogs and dog-food, and such things as snowshoes and moccasins and winter trails. They let him have fifteen hundred, which was more than the cottage warranted, and breathed easier when he scrawled his signature and passed out the door.

Two weeks later he went over Chilkoot with three dog sleds of five dogs each. One team he drove, the two Indians with him driving the others. At Lake Marsh they broke out the cache and loaded up. But there was no trail. He was the first in over the ice, and to him fell the task of packing the snow and hammering away through the rough river jams. Behind him he often observed a camp-fire smoke trickling thinly up through the quiet air, and he wondered why the people did not overtake him. For he was a stranger to the land and did not understand. Nor could he understand his Indians when they tried to explain. This they conceived to be a hardship, but when they balked and refused to break camp of mornings, he drove them to their work at pistol point.

When he slipped through an ice bridge near the White Horse and froze his foot, tender yet and oversensitive from the previous freezing, the Indians looked for him to lie up. But he sacrificed a blanket, and, with his foot incased in an enormous moccasin, big as a water-bucket, continued to take his regular turn with the front sled. Here was the cruellest work, and they respected him, though on the side they rapped their foreheads with their knuckles and significantly shook their heads. One night they tried to run away, but the zip-zip of his bullets in the snow brought them back, snarling but convinced. Whereupon, being only savage Chilkat men, they put their heads together to kill him; but he slept like a cat, and, waking or sleeping, the chance never came. Often they tried to tell him the import of the smoke wreath in the rear, but he could not comprehend and grew suspicious of them. And when they sulked or shirked, he was quick to let drive at them between the eyes, and quick to cool their heated souls with sight of his ready revolver.

And so it went—with mutinous men, wild dogs, and a trail that broke the heart. He fought the men to stay with him, fought the dogs to keep them away from the eggs, fought the ice, the cold, and the pain of his foot, which would not heal. As fast as the young tissue renewed, it was bitten and scared by the frost, so that a running sore developed, into which he could almost shove his fist. In the mornings, when he first put his weight upon it, his head went dizzy, and he was near to fainting from the pain; but later on in the day it usually grew numb, to recommence when he crawled into his blankets and tried to sleep. Yet he, who had been a clerk and sat at a desk all his days, toiled till the Indians were exhausted, and even out-worked the dogs. How hard he worked, how much he suffered, he did not know.

Being a man of the one idea, now that the idea had come, it mastered him. In the foreground of his consciousness was Dawson, in the background his thousand dozen eggs, and midway between the two his ego fluttered, striving always to draw them together to a glittering golden point. This golden point was the five thousand dollars, the consummation of the idea and the point of departure for whatever new idea might present itself. For the rest, he was a mere automaton. He was unaware of other things, seeing them as through a glass darkly, and giving them no thought. The work of his hands he did with machine-like wisdom; likewise the work of his head. So the look on his face grew very tense, till even the Indians were afraid of it, and marvelled at the strange white man who had made them slaves and forced them to toil with such foolishness.

Then came a snap on Lake Le Barge, when the cold of outer space smote the tip of the planet, and the force ranged sixty and odd degrees below zero. Here, labouring with open mouth that he might breathe more freely, he chilled his lungs, and for the rest of the trip he was troubled with a dry, hacking cough, especially irritable in smoke of camp or under stress of undue exertion. On the Thirty Mile river he found much open water, spanned by precarious ice bridges and fringed with narrow rim ice, tricky and uncertain. The rim ice was impossible to reckon on, and he dared it without reckoning, falling back on his revolver when his drivers demurred. But on the ice bridges, covered with snow though they were, precautions could be taken. These they crossed on their snowshoes, with long poles, held crosswise in their hands, to which to cling in case of accident. Once over, the dogs were called to follow. And on such a bridge, where the absence of the centre ice was masked by the snow, one of the Indians met his end. He went through as quickly and neatly as a knife through thin cream, and the current swept him from view down under the stream ice.

That night his mate fled away through the pale moonlight, Rasmunsen futilely puncturing the silence with his revolver—a thing that he handled with more celerity than cleverness. Thirty-six hours later the Indian made a police camp on the Big Salmon.

"Um—um—um funny mans—what you call?—top um head all loose," the interpreter explained to the puzzled captain. "Eh? Yep, clazy, much clazy mans. Eggs, eggs, all a time eggs—savvy? Come bime-by."

It was several days before Rasmunsen arrived, the three sleds lashed together, and all the dogs in a single team. It was awkward, and where the going was bad he was compelled to back-trip it sled by sled, though he managed most of the time, through herculean efforts, to bring all along on the one haul. He did not seem moved when the captain of police told him his man was hitting the high places for Dawson, and was by that time, probably, half-way between Selkirk and Stewart. Nor did he appear interested when informed that the police had broken the trail as far as Pelly; for he had attained to a fatalistic acceptance of all natural dispensations, good or ill. But when they told him that Dawson was in the bitter clutch of famine, he smiled, threw the harness on his dogs, and pulled out.

But it was at his next halt that the mystery of the smoke was explained. With the word at Big Salmon that the trail was broken to Pelly, there was no longer any need for the smoke wreath to linger in his wake; and Rasmunsen, crouching over lonely fire, saw a motley string of sleds go by. First came the courier and the half-breed who had hauled him out from Bennett; then mail-carriers for Circle City, two sleds of them, and a mixed following of ingoing Klondikers. Dogs and men were fresh and fat, while Rasmunsen and his brutes were jaded and worn down to the skin and bone. They of the smoke wreath had travelled one day in three, resting and reserving their strength for the dash to come when broken trail was met with; while each day he had plunged and floundered forward, breaking the spirit of his dogs and robbing them of their mettle.

As for himself, he was unbreakable. They thanked him kindly for his efforts in their behalf, those fat, fresh men,—thanked him kindly, with broad grins and ribald laughter; and now, when he understood, he made no answer. Nor did he cherish silent bitterness. It was immaterial. The idea—the fact behind the idea—was not changed. Here he was and his thousand dozen; there was Dawson; the problem was unaltered.

At the Little Salmon, being short of dog food, the dogs got into his grub, and from there to Selkirk he lived on beans—coarse, brown beans, big beans, grossly nutritive, which griped his stomach and doubled him up at two-hour intervals. But the Factor at Selkirk had a notice on the door of the Post to the effect that no steamer had been up the Yukon for two years, and in consequence grub was beyond price. He offered to swap flour, however, at the rate of a cupful of each egg, but Rasmunsen shook his head and hit the trail. Below the Post he managed to buy frozen horse hide for the dogs, the horses having been slain by the Chilkat cattle men, and the scraps and offal preserved by the Indians. He tackled the hide himself, but the hair worked into the bean sores of his mouth, and was beyond endurance.

Here at Selkirk he met the forerunners of the hungry exodus of Dawson, and from there on they crept over the trail, a dismal throng. "No grub!" was the song they sang. "No grub, and had to go." "Everybody holding candles for a rise in the spring." "Flour dollar 'n a half a pound, and no sellers."

"Eggs?" one of them answered. "Dollar apiece, but there ain't none."

Rasmunsen made a rapid calculation. "Twelve thousand dollars," he said aloud.

"Hey?" the man asked.

"Nothing," he answered, and *mushed* the dogs along.

When he arrived at Stewart River, seventy from Dawson, five of his dogs were gone, and the remainder were falling in the traces. He, also, was in the traces, hauling with what little strength was left in him. Even then he was barely crawling along ten miles a day. His cheek-bones and nose, frost-bitten again and again, were turned bloody-black and hideous. The thumb, which was separated from the fingers by the gee-pole, had likewise been nipped and gave him great pain. The monstrous moccasin still incased his foot, and strange pains were beginning to rack the leg. At Sixty Mile, the last beans, which he had been rationing for some time, were finished; yet he steadfastly refused to touch the eggs. He could not reconcile his mind to the legitimacy of it, and staggered and fell along the way to Indian River. Here a fresh-killed moose and an open-handed old-timer gave him and his dogs new strength, and at Ainslie's he felt repaid for it all when a stampede, ripe from Dawson in five hours, was sure he could get a dollar and a quarter for every egg he possessed.

He came up the steep bank by the Dawson barracks with fluttering heart and shaking knees. The dogs were so weak that he was forced to rest them, and, waiting, he leaned limply against the gee-pole. A man, an eminently decorous-looking man, came sauntering by in a great bearskin coat. He glanced at Rasmunsen curiously, then stopped and ran a speculative eye over the dogs and the three lashed sleds.

"What you got?" he asked.

"Eggs," Rasmunsen answered huskily, hardly able to pitch his voice above a whisper.

"Eggs! Whoopee! Whoopee!" He sprang up into the air, gyrated madly, and finished with half-a-dozen war steps. "You don't say—all of 'em?"

"All of 'em."

"Say, you must be the Egg Man." He walked around and viewed Rasmunsen from the other side. "Come, now, ain't you the Egg Man?"

Rasmunsen didn't know, but supposed he was, and the man sobered down a bit.

"What d'ye expect to get for 'em?" he asked cautiously.

Rasmunsen became audacious. "Dollar 'n a half," he said.

"Done!" the man came back promptly. "Gimme a dozen."

"I—I mean a dollar 'n a half apiece," Rasmunsen hesitatingly explained.

"Sure. I heard you. Make it two dozen. Here's the dust."

The man pulled out a healthy gold sack the size of a small sausage and knocked it negligently against the gee-pole. Rasmunsen felt a strange trembling in the pit of his stomach, a tickling of the nostrils, and an almost overwhelming desire to sit down and cry. But a curious, wide-eyed crowd was beginning to collect, and man after man was calling out for eggs. He was without scales, but the man with the bearskin coat fetched a pair and obligingly weighed in the dust while Rasmunsen passed out the goods. Soon there was a pushing and shoving and shouldering, and a great clamour. Everybody wanted to buy and to be served first. And as the excitement grew, Rasmunsen cooled down. This would never do. There must be something behind the fact of their buying so eagerly. It would be wiser if he rested first and sized up the market. Perhaps eggs were worth two dollars apiece. Anyway, whenever he wished to sell, he was sure of a dollar and a half. "Stop!" he cried, when a couple of hundred had been sold. "No more now. I'm played out. I've got to get a cabin, and then you can come and see me."

A groan went up at this, but the man with the bearskin coat approved. Twenty-four of the frozen eggs went rattling in his capacious pockets, and he didn't care whether the rest of the town ate or not. Besides, he could see Rasmunsen was on his last legs.

"There's a cabin right around the second corner from the Monte Carlo," he told him—"the one with the sody-bottle window. It ain't mine, but I've got charge of it. Rents for ten a day and cheap for the money. You move right in, and I'll see you later. Don't forget the sody-bottle window."

"Tra-la-loo!" he called back a moment later. "I'm goin' up the hill to eat eggs and dream of home."

On his way to the cabin, Rasmunsen recollected he was hungry and bought a small supply of provisions at the N. A. T. & T. store—also a beefsteak at the butcher shop and dried salmon for the dogs. He found the cabin without difficulty, and left the dogs in the harness while he started the fire and got the coffee under way.

"A dollar 'n a half apiece—one thousand dozen—eighteen thousand dollars!" he kept muttering it to himself, over and over, as he went about his work.

As he flopped the steak into the frying-pan the door opened. He turned. It was the man with the bearskin coat. He seemed to come in with determination, as though bound on some explicit errand, but as he looked at Rasmunsen an expression of perplexity came into his face.

"I say—now I say—" he began, then halted.

Rasmunsen wondered if he wanted the rent.

"I say, damn it, you know, them eggs is bad."

Rasmunsen staggered. He felt as though some one had struck him an astounding blow between the eyes. The walls of the cabin reeled and tilted up. He put out his hand to steady himself and rested it on the stove. The sharp pain and the smell of the burning flesh brought him back to himself.

"I see," he said slowly, fumbling in his pocket for the sack. "You want your money back."

"It ain't the money," the man said, "but hain't you got any eggs—good?"

Rasmunsen shook his head. "You'd better take the money."

But the man refused and backed away. "I'll come back," he said, "when you've taken stock, and get what's comin'."

Rasmunsen rolled the chopping-block into the cabin and carried in the eggs. He went about it quite calmly. He took up the hand-axe, and, one by one, chopped the eggs in half. These halves he examined carefully and let fall to the floor. At first he sampled from the different cases, then deliberately emptied one case at a time. The heap on the floor grew larger. The coffee boiled over and the smoke of the burning beefsteak filled the cabin. He chopped steadfastly and monotonously till the last case was finished.

Somebody knocked at the door, knocked again, and let himself in.

"What a mess!" he remarked, as he paused and surveyed the scene.

The severed eggs were beginning to thaw in the heat of the stove, and a miserable odour was growing stronger.

161

"Must a-happened on the steamer," he suggested.

Rasmunsen looked at him long and blankly.

"I'm Murray, Big Jim Murray, everybody knows me," the man volunteered. "I'm just hearin' your eggs is rotten, and I'm offerin' you two hundred for the batch. They ain't good as salmon, but still they're fair scoffin's for dogs."

Rasmunsen seemed turned to stone. He did not move. "You go to hell," he said passionlessly.

"Now just consider. I pride myself it's a decent price for a mess like that, and it's better 'n nothin'. Two hundred. What you say?"

"You go to hell," Rasmunsen repeated softly, "and get out of here."

Murray gaped with a great awe, then went out carefully, backward, with his eyes fixed an the other's face.

Rasmunsen followed him out and turned the dogs loose. He threw them all the salmon he had bought, and coiled a sled-lashing up in his hand. Then he re-entered the cabin and drew the latch in after him. The smoke from the cindered steak made his eyes smart. He stood on the bunk, passed the lashing over the ridge-pole, and measured the swing-off with his eye. It did not seem to satisfy, for he put the stool on the bunk and climbed upon the stool. He drove a noose in the end of the lashing and slipped his head through. The other end he made fast. Then he kicked the stool out from under.

THE MARRIAGE OF LIT-LIT

When John Fox came into a country where whisky freezes solid and may be used as a paper-weight for a large part of the year, he came without the ideals and illusions that usually hamper the progress of more delicately nurtured adventurers. Born and reared on the frontier fringe of the United States, he took with him into Canada a primitive cast of mind, an elemental simplicity and grip on things, as it were, that insured him immediate success in his new career. From a mere servant of the Hudson Bay Company, driving a paddle with the voyageurs and carrying goods on his back across the portages, he swiftly rose to a Factorship and took charge of a trading post at Fort Angelus.

Here, because of his elemental simplicity, he took to himself a native wife, and, by reason of the connubial bliss that followed, he escaped the unrest and vain longings that curse the days of more fastidious men, spoil their work, and conquer them in the end. He lived contentedly, was at single purposes with the business he was set there to do, and achieved a brilliant record in the service of the Company. About this time his wife died, was claimed by her people, and buried with savage circumstance in a tin trunk in the top of a tree.

Two sons she had borne him, and when the Company promoted him, he journeyed with them still deeper into the vastness of the North-West Territory to a place called Sin Rock, where he took charge of a new post in a more important fur field. Here he spent several lonely and depressing months, eminently disgusted with the unprepossessing appearance of the Indian maidens, and greatly worried by his growing sons who stood in need of a mother's care. Then his eyes chanced upon Lit-lit.

"Lit-lit—well, she is Lit-lit," was the fashion in which he despairingly described her to his chief clerk, Alexander McLean.

McLean was too fresh from his Scottish upbringing—"not dry behind the ears yet," John Fox put it—to take to the marriage customs of the country. Nevertheless he was not averse to the Factor's imperilling his own immortal soul, and, especially, feeling an ominous attraction himself for Lit-lit, he was sombrely content to clinch his own soul's safety by seeing her married to the Factor.

Nor is it to be wondered that McLean's austere Scotch soul stood in danger of being thawed in the sunshine of Lit-lit's eyes. She was pretty, and slender, and willowy; without the massive face and temperamental stolidity of the average squaw. "Lit-lit," so called from her fashion, even as a child, of being fluttery, of darting about from place to place like a butterfly, of being inconsequent and merry, and of laughing as lightly as she darted and danced about.

Lit-lit was the daughter of Snettishane, a prominent chief in the tribe, by a half-breed mother, and to him the Factor fared casually one summer day to open negotiations of marriage. He sat with the chief in the smoke of a mosquito smudge before his lodge, and together they talked about everything under the sun, or, at least, everything that in the Northland is under the sun, with the sole exception of marriage. John Fox had come particularly to talk of marriage; Snettishane knew it, and John Fox knew he knew it, wherefore the subject was religiously avoided. This is alleged to be Indian subtlety. In reality it is transparent simplicity.

The hours slipped by, and Fox and Snettishane smoked interminable pipes, looking each other in the eyes with a guilelessness superbly histrionic. In the mid-afternoon McLean and his brother clerk, McTavish, strolled past, innocently uninterested, on their way to the river. When they strolled back again an hour later, Fox and Snettishane had attained to a ceremonious discussion of the condition and quality of the gunpowder and bacon which the Company was offering in trade. Meanwhile Lit-lit, divining the Factor's errand, had crept in under the rear wall of the lodge, and through the front flap was peeping out at the two logomachists by the mosquito smudge. She was flushed and happy-eyed, proud that no less a man than the Factor (who stood next to God in the Northland hierarchy) had singled her out, femininely curious to see at close range what manner of man he was. Sunglare on the ice, camp smoke, and weather beat had burned his face to a copper-brown, so that her father was as fair as he, while she was fairer. She was remotely glad of this, and more immediately glad that he was large and strong, though his great black beard half frightened her, it was so strange.

Being very young, she was unversed in the ways of men. Seventeen times she had seen the sun travel south and lose itself beyond the sky-line, and seventeen times she had seen it travel back again and ride the sky day and night till there was no night at all. And through these years she had been cherished jealously by Snettishane, who stood between her and all suitors, listening disdainfully to the young hunters as they bid for her hand, and turning them away as though she were beyond price. Snettishane was mercenary. Lit-lit was to him an investment. She represented so much capital, from which he expected to receive, not a certain definite interest, but an incalculable interest.

And having thus been reared in a manner as near to that of the nunnery as tribal conditions would permit, it was with a great and maidenly anxiety that she peeped out at the man who had surely come for her, at the husband who was to teach her all that was yet unlearned of life, at the masterful being whose word was to be her law, and who was to mete and bound her actions and comportment for the rest of her days.

But, peeping through the front flap of the lodge, flushed and thrilling at the strange destiny reaching out for her, she grew disappointed as the day wore along, and the Factor and her father still talked pompously of matters concerning other things and not pertaining to marriage things at all. As the sun sank lower and lower toward the north and midnight approached, the Factor began making unmistakable preparations for departure. As he turned to stride away Lit-lit's heart sank; but it rose again as he halted, half turning on one heel.

"Oh, by the way, Snettishane," he said, "I want a squaw to wash for me and mend my clothes."

Snettishane grunted and suggested Wanidani, who was an old woman and toothless.

"No, no," interposed the Factor. "What I want is a wife. I've been kind of thinking about it, and the thought just struck me that you might know of some one that would suit."

Snettishane looked interested, whereupon the Factor retraced his steps, casually and carelessly to linger and discuss this new and incidental topic.

"Kattou?" suggested Snettishane.

"She has but one eye," objected the Factor.

"Laska?"

"Her knees be wide apart when she stands upright. Kips, your biggest dog, can leap between her knees when she stands upright."

"Senatee?" went on the imperturbable Snettishane.

But John Fox feigned anger, crying: "What foolishness is this? Am I old, that thou shouldst mate me with old women? Am I toothless? lame of leg? blind of eye? Or am I poor that no bright-eyed maiden may look with favour upon me? Behold! I am the Factor, both rich and great, a power in the land, whose speech makes men tremble and is obeyed!"

Snettishane was inwardly pleased, though his sphinx-like visage never relaxed. He was drawing the Factor, and making him break ground. Being a creature so elemental as to have room for but one idea at a time, Snettishane could pursue that one idea a greater distance than could John Fox. For John Fox, elemental as he was, was still complex enough to entertain several glimmering ideas at a time, which debarred him from pursuing the one as single-heartedly or as far as did the chief.

Snettishane calmly continued calling the roster of eligible maidens, which, name by name, as fast as uttered, were stamped ineligible by John Fox, with specified objections appended. Again he gave it up and started to return to the Fort. Snettishane watched him go, making no effort to stop him, but seeing him, in the end, stop himself.

"Come to think of it," the Factor remarked, "we both of us forgot Lit-lit. Now I wonder if she'll suit me?"

166

Snettishane met the suggestion with a mirthless face, behind the mask of which his soul grinned wide. It was a distinct victory. Had the Factor gone but one step farther, perforce Snettishane would himself have mentioned the name of Lit-lit, but—the Factor had not gone that one step farther.

The chief was non-committal concerning Lit-lit's suitability, till he drove the white man into taking the next step in order of procedure.

"Well," the Factor meditated aloud, "the only way to find out is to make a try of it." He raised his voice. "So I will give for Lit-lit ten blankets and three pounds of tobacco which is good tobacco."

Snettishane replied with a gesture which seemed to say that all the blankets and tobacco in all the world could not compensate him for the loss of Lit-lit and her manifold virtues. When pressed by the Factor to set a price, he coolly placed it at five hundred blankets, ten guns, fifty pounds of tobacco, twenty scarlet cloths, ten bottles of rum, a music-box, and lastly the good-will and best offices of the Factor, with a place by his fire.

The Factor apparently suffered a stroke of apoplexy, which stroke was successful in reducing the blankets to two hundred and in cutting out the place by the fire—an unheard-of condition in the marriages of white men with the daughters of the soil. In the end, after three hours more of chaffering, they came to an agreement. For Lit-lit Snettishane was to receive one hundred blankets, five pounds of tobacco, three guns, and a bottle of rum, goodwill and best offices included, which according to John Fox, was ten blankets and a gun more than she was worth. And as he went home through the wee sma' hours, the three-o'clock sun blazing in the due north-east, he was unpleasantly aware that Snettishane had bested him over the bargain.

Snettishane, tired and victorious, sought his bed, and discovered Lit-lit before she could escape from the lodge.

He grunted knowingly: "Thou hast seen. Thou has heard. Wherefore it be plain to thee thy father's very great wisdom and understanding. I have made for thee a great match. Heed my words and walk in the way of my words, go when I say go, come when I bid thee come, and we shall grow fat with the wealth of this big white man who is a fool according to his bigness."

167

The next day no trading was done at the store. The Factor opened whisky before breakfast, to the delight of McLean and McTavish, gave his dogs double rations, and wore his best moccasins. Outside the Fort preparations were under way for a *potlatch*. *Potlatch* means "a giving," and John Fox's intention was to signalize his marriage with Lit-lit by a *potlatch* as generous as she was good-looking. In the afternoon the whole tribe gathered to the feast. Men, women, children, and dogs gorged to repletion, nor was there one person, even among the chance visitors and stray hunters from other tribes, who failed to receive some token of the bridegroom's largess.

Lit-lit, tearfully shy and frightened, was bedecked by her bearded husband with a new calico dress, splendidly beaded moccasins, a gorgeous silk handkerchief over her raven hair, a purple scarf about her throat, brass ear-rings and finger-rings, and a whole pint of pinchbeck jewellery, including a Waterbury watch. Snettishane could scarce contain himself at the spectacle, but watching his chance drew her aside from the feast.

"Not this night, nor the next night," he began ponderously, "but in the nights to come, when I shall call like a raven by the river bank, it is for thee to rise up from thy big husband, who is a fool, and come to me.

"Nay, nay," he went on hastily, at sight of the dismay in her face at turning her back upon her wonderful new life. "For no sooner shall this happen than thy big husband, who is a fool, will come wailing to my lodge. Then it is for thee to wail likewise, claiming that this thing is not well, and that the other thing thou dost not like, and that to be the wife of the Factor is more than thou didst bargain for, only wilt thou be content with more blankets, and more tobacco, and more wealth of various sorts for thy poor old father, Snettishane. Remember well, when I call in the night, like a raven, from the river bank."

Lit-lit nodded; for to disobey her father was a peril she knew well; and, furthermore, it was a little thing he asked, a short separation from the Factor, who would know only greater gladness at having her back. She returned to the feast, and, midnight being well at hand, the Factor sought her out and led her away to the Fort amid joking and outcry, in which the squaws were especially conspicuous.

Lit-lit quickly found that married life with the head-man of a fort was even better than she had dreamed. No longer did she have to fetch wood and water and wait hand and foot upon cantankerous menfolk. For the first time in her life she could lie abed till breakfast was on the table. And what a bed!—clean and soft, and comfortable as no bed she had ever known. And such food! Flour, cooked into biscuits, hot-cakes and bread, three times a day and every day, and all one wanted! Such prodigality was hardly believable.

To add to her contentment, the Factor was cunningly kind. He had buried one wife, and he knew how to drive with a slack rein that went firm only on occasion, and then went very firm. "Lit-lit is boss of this place," he announced significantly at the table the morning after the wedding. "What she says goes. Understand?" And McLean and McTavish understood. Also, they knew that the Factor had a heavy hand.

But Lit-lit did not take advantage. Taking a leaf from the book of her husband, she at once assumed charge of his own growing sons, giving them added comforts and a measure of freedom like to that which he gave her. The two sons were loud in the praise of their new mother; McLean and McTavish lifted their voices; and the Factor bragged of the joys of matrimony till the story of her good behaviour and her husband's satisfaction became the property of all the dwellers in the Sin Rock district.

Whereupon Snettishane, with visions of his incalculable interest keeping him awake of nights, thought it time to bestir himself. On the tenth night of her wedded life Lit-lit was awakened by the croaking of a raven, and she knew that Snettishane was waiting for her by the river bank. In her great happiness she had forgotten her pact, and now it came back to her with behind it all the childish terror of her father. For a time she lay in fear and trembling, loath to go, afraid to stay. But in the end the Factor won the silent victory, and his kindness plus his great muscles and square jaw, nerved her to disregard Snettishane's call.

But in the morning she arose very much afraid, and went about her duties in momentary fear of her father's coming. As the day wore along, however, she began to recover her spirits. John Fox, soundly berating McLean and

The Abysmal Brute & The Faith of Men

McTavish for some petty dereliction of duty, helped her to pluck up courage. She tried not to let him go out of her sight, and when she followed him into the huge cache and saw him twirling and tossing great bales around as though they were feather pillows, she felt strengthened in her disobedience to her father. Also (it was her first visit to the warehouse, and Sin Rock was the chief distributing point to several chains of lesser posts), she was astounded at the endlessness of the wealth there stored away.

This sight and the picture in her mind's eye of the bare lodge of Snettishane, put all doubts at rest. Yet she capped her conviction by a brief word with one of her step-sons. "White daddy good?" was what she asked, and the boy answered that his father was the best man he had ever known. That night the raven croaked again. On the night following the croaking was more persistent. It awoke the Factor, who tossed restlessly for a while. Then he said aloud, "Damn that raven," and Lit-lit laughed quietly under the blankets.

In the morning, bright and early, Snettishane put in an ominous appearance and was set to breakfast in the kitchen with Wanidani. He refused "squaw food," and a little later bearded his son-in-law in the store where the trading was done. Having learned, he said, that his daughter was such a jewel, he had come for more blankets, more tobacco, and more guns—especially more guns. He had certainly been cheated in her price, he held, and he had come for justice. But the Factor had neither blankets nor justice to spare. Whereupon he was informed that Snettishane had seen the missionary at Three Forks, who had notified him that such marriages were not made in heaven, and that it was his father's duty to demand his daughter back.

"I am good Christian man now," Snettishane concluded. "I want my Lit-lit to go to heaven."

The Factor's reply was short and to the point; for he directed his father-in-law to go to the heavenly antipodes, and by the scruff of the neck and the slack of the blanket propelled him on that trail as far as the door.

But Snettishane sneaked around and in by the kitchen, cornering Lit-lit in the great living-room of the Fort.

170

"Mayhap thou didst sleep over-sound last night when I called by the river bank," he began, glowering darkly.

"Nay, I was awake and heard." Her heart was beating as though it would choke her, but she went on steadily, "And the night before I was awake and heard, and yet again the night before."

And thereat, out of her great happiness and out of the fear that it might be taken from her, she launched into an original and glowing address upon the status and rights of woman—the first new-woman lecture delivered north of Fifty-three.

But it fell on unheeding ears. Snettishane was still in the dark ages. As she paused for breath, he said threateningly, "To-night I shall call again like the raven."

At this moment the Factor entered the room and again helped Snettishane on his way to the heavenly antipodes.

That night the raven croaked more persistently than ever. Lit-lit, who was a light sleeper, heard and smiled. John Fox tossed restlessly. Then he awoke and tossed about with greater restlessness. He grumbled and snorted, swore under his breath and over his breath, and finally flung out of bed. He groped his way to the great living-room, and from the rack took down a loaded shot-gun—loaded with bird-shot, left therein by the careless McTavish.

The Factor crept carefully out of the Fort and down to the river. The croaking had ceased, but he stretched out in the long grass and waited. The air seemed a chilly balm, and the earth, after the heat of the day, now and again breathed soothingly against him. The Factor, gathered into the rhythm of it all, dozed off, with his head upon his arm, and slept.

Fifty yards away, head resting on knees, and with his back to John Fox, Snettishane likewise slept, gently conquered by the quietude of the night. An hour slipped by and then he awoke, and, without lifting his head, set the night vibrating with the hoarse gutturals of the raven call.

The Factor roused, not with the abrupt start of civilized man, but with the swift and comprehensive glide from sleep to waking of the savage. In the night-light he made out a dark object in the midst of the grass and brought his gun to bear upon it. A second croak began to rise, and he pulled the trigger. The crickets ceased from their sing-song chant, the wildfowl from their squabbling, and the raven croak broke midmost and died away in gasping silence.

John Fox ran to the spot and reached for the thing he had killed, but his fingers closed on a coarse mop of hair and he turned Snettishane's face upward to the starlight. He knew how a shotgun scattered at fifty yards, and he knew that he had peppered Snettishane across the shoulders and in the small of the back. And Snettishane knew that he knew, but neither referred to it.

"What dost thou here?" the Factor demanded. "It were time old bones should be in bed."

But Snettishane was stately in spite of the bird-shot burning under his skin.

"Old bones will not sleep," he said solemnly. "I weep for my daughter, for my daughter Lit-lit, who liveth and who yet is dead, and who goeth without doubt to the white man's hell."

"Weep henceforth on the far bank, beyond ear-shot of the Fort," said John Fox, turning on his heel, "for the noise of thy weeping is exceeding great and will not let one sleep of nights."

"My heart is sore," Snettishane answered, "and my days and nights be black with sorrow."

"As the raven is black," said John Fox.

"As the raven is black," Snettishane said.

Never again was the voice of the raven heard by the river bank. Lit-lit grows matronly day by day and is very happy. Also, there are sisters to the sons of John Fox's first wife who lies buried in a tree. Old Snettishane is no longer a visitor at the Fort, and spends long hours raising a thin, aged voice against the filial ingratitude of children in general and of his daughter Lit-lit in particular. His declining years are embittered by the knowledge that he was cheated, and even John Fox has withdrawn the assertion that the price for Lit-lit was too much by ten blankets and a gun.

BÂTARD

Bâtard was a devil. This was recognized throughout the Northland. "Hell's Spawn" he was called by many men, but his master, Black Leclère, chose for him the shameful name "Bâtard." Now Black Leclère was also a devil, and the twain were well matched. There is a saying that when two devils come together, hell is to pay. This is to be expected, and this certainly was to be expected when Bâtard and Black Leclère came together. The first time they met, Bâtard was a part-grown puppy, lean and hungry, with bitter eyes; and they met with snap and snarl, and wicked looks, for Leclère's upper lip had a wolfish way of lifting and showing the white, cruel teeth. And it lifted then, and his eyes glinted viciously, as he reached for Bâtard and dragged him out from the squirming litter. It was certain that they divined each other, for on the instant Bâtard had buried his puppy fangs in Leclère's hand, and Leclère, thumb and finger, was coolly choking his young life out of him.

"*Sacredam*," the Frenchman said softly, flirting the quick blood from his bitten hand and gazing down on the little puppy choking and gasping in the snow.

Leclère turned to John Hamlin, storekeeper of the Sixty Mile Post. "Dat fo' w'at Ah lak heem. 'Ow moch, eh, you, *M'sieu*? 'Ow moch? Ah buy heem, now; Ah buy heem queek."

And because he hated him with an exceeding bitter hate, Leclère bought Bâtard and gave him his shameful name. And for five years the twain adventured across the Northland, from St. Michael's and the Yukon delta to the head-reaches of the Pelly and even so far as the Peace River, Athabasca, and the Great Slave. And they acquired a reputation for uncompromising wickedness, the like of which never before attached itself to man and dog.

Bâtard did not know his father—hence his name—but, as John Hamlin knew, his father was a great grey timber wolf. But the mother of Bâtard, as he dimly remembered her, was snarling, bickering, obscene, husky, full-fronted and heavy-chested, with a malign eye, a cat-like grip on life, and a genius for trickery and evil. There was neither faith nor trust in her. Her treachery alone could be relied upon, and her wild-wood amours attested her general depravity. Much of evil and much of strength were there in these, Bâtard's progenitors, and, bone and flesh of their bone and flesh, he had inherited it all. And then came Black Leclère, to lay his heavy hand on the bit of pulsating puppy life, to press and prod and mould till it became a big bristling beast, acute in knavery, overspilling with hate, sinister, malignant, diabolical. With a proper master Bâtard might have made an ordinary, fairly efficient sled-dog. He never got the chance: Leclère but confirmed him in his congenital iniquity.

The history of Bâtard and Leclère is a history of war—of five cruel, relentless years, of which their first meeting is fit summary. To begin with, it was Leclère's fault, for he hated with understanding and intelligence, while the long-legged, ungainly puppy hated only blindly, instinctively, without reason or method. At first there were no refinements of cruelty (these were to come later), but simple beatings and crude brutalities. In one of these Bâtard had an ear injured. He never regained control of the riven muscles, and ever after the ear drooped limply down to keep keen the memory of his tormentor. And he never forgot.

His puppyhood was a period of foolish rebellion. He was always worsted, but he fought back because it was his nature to fight back. And he was unconquerable. Yelping shrilly from the pain of lash and club, he none the less contrived always to throw in the defiant snarl, the bitter vindictive menace of his soul which fetched without fail more blows and beatings. But his was his mother's tenacious grip on life. Nothing could kill him. He flourished under misfortune, grew fat with famine, and out of his terrible struggle for life developed a preternatural intelligence. His were the stealth and cunning of the husky, his mother, and the fierceness and valour of the wolf, his father.

Possibly it was because of his father that he never wailed. His puppy yelps passed with his lanky legs, so that he became grim and taciturn, quick to strike, slow to warn. He answered curse with snarl, and blow with

175

snap, grinning the while his implacable hatred; but never again, under the extremest agony, did Leclère bring from him the cry of fear nor of pain. This unconquerableness but fanned Leclère's wrath and stirred him to greater deviltries.

Did Leclère give Bâtard half a fish and to his mates whole ones, Bâtard went forth to rob other dogs of their fish. Also he robbed caches and expressed himself in a thousand rogueries, till he became a terror to all dogs and masters of dogs. Did Leclère beat Bâtard and fondle Babette—Babette who was not half the worker he was—why, Bâtard threw her down in the snow and broke her hind leg in his heavy jaws, so that Leclère was forced to shoot her. Likewise, in bloody battles, Bâtard mastered all his team-mates, set them the law of trail and forage, and made them live to the law he set.

In five years he heard but one kind word, received but one soft stroke of a hand, and then he did not know what manner of things they were. He leaped like the untamed thing he was, and his jaws were together in a flash. It was the missionary at Sunrise, a newcomer in the country, who spoke the kind word and gave the soft stroke of the hand. And for six months after, he wrote no letters home to the States, and the surgeon at McQuestion travelled two hundred miles on the ice to save him from blood-poisoning.

Men and dogs looked askance at Bâtard when he drifted into their camps and posts. The men greeted him with feet threateningly lifted for the kick, the dogs with bristling manes and bared fangs. Once a man did kick Bâtard, and Bâtard, with quick wolf snap, closed his jaws like a steel trap on the man's calf and crunched down to the bone. Whereat the man was determined to have his life, only Black Leclère, with ominous eyes and naked hunting-knife, stepped in between. The killing of Bâtard—ah, *sacredam*, *that* was a pleasure Leclère reserved for himself. Some day it would happen, or else—bah! who was to know? Anyway, the problem would be solved.

For they had become problems to each other. The very breath each drew was a challenge and a menace to the other. Their hate bound them together as love could never bind. Leclère was bent on the coming of the day when Bâtard should wilt in spirit and cringe and whimper at his feet. And

176

Bâtard—Leclère knew what was in Bâtard's mind, and more than once had read it in Bâtard's eyes. And so clearly had he read, that when Bâtard was at his back, he made it a point to glance often over his shoulder.

Men marvelled when Leclère refused large money for the dog. "Some day you'll kill him and be out his price," said John Hamlin once, when Bâtard lay panting in the snow where Leclère had kicked him, and no one knew whether his ribs were broken, and no one dared look to see.

"Dat," said Leclère, dryly, "dat is my biz'ness, *M'sieu'*."

And the men marvelled that Bâtard did not run away. They did not understand. But Leclère understood. He was a man who lived much in the open, beyond the sound of human tongue, and he had learned the voices of wind and storm, the sigh of night, the whisper of dawn, the clash of day. In a dim way he could hear the green things growing, the running of the sap, the bursting of the bud. And he knew the subtle speech of the things that moved, of the rabbit in the snare, the moody raven beating the air with hollow wing, the baldface shuffling under the moon, the wolf like a grey shadow gliding betwixt the twilight and the dark. And to him Bâtard spoke clear and direct. Full well he understood why Bâtard did not run away, and he looked more often over his shoulder.

When in anger, Bâtard was not nice to look upon, and more than once had he leapt for Leclère's throat, to be stretched quivering and senseless in the snow, by the butt of the ever ready dogwhip. And so Bâtard learned to bide his time. When he reached his full strength and prime of youth, he thought the time had come. He was broad-chested, powerfully muscled, of far more than ordinary size, and his neck from head to shoulders was a mass of bristling hair—to all appearances a full-blooded wolf. Leclère was lying asleep in his furs when Bâtard deemed the time to be ripe. He crept upon him stealthily, head low to earth and lone ear laid back, with a feline softness of tread. Bâtard breathed gently, very gently, and not till he was close at hand did he raise his head. He paused for a moment and looked at the bronzed bull throat, naked and knotty, and swelling to a deep steady pulse. The slaver dripped down his fangs and slid off his tongue at the sight, and in that moment he remembered his drooping ear, his uncounted blows and prodigious wrongs, and without a sound sprang on the sleeping man.

Leclère awoke to the pang of the fangs in his throat, and, perfect animal that he was, he awoke clear-headed and with full comprehension. He closed on Bâtard's windpipe with both his hands, and rolled out of his furs to get his weight uppermost. But the thousands of Bâtard's ancestors had clung at the throats of unnumbered moose and caribou and dragged them down, and the wisdom of those ancestors was his. When Leclère's weight came on top of him, he drove his hind legs upwards and in, and clawed down chest and abdomen, ripping and tearing through skin and muscle. And when he felt the man's body wince above him and lift, he worried and shook at the man's throat. His team-mates closed around in a snarling circle, and Bâtard, with failing breath and fading sense, knew that their jaws were hungry for him. But that did not matter—it was the man, the man above him, and he ripped and clawed, and shook and worried, to the last ounce of his strength. But Leclère choked him with both his hands, till Bâtard's chest heaved and writhed for the air denied, and his eyes glazed and set, and his jaws slowly loosened, and his tongue protruded black and swollen.

"Eh? *Bon*, you devil!" Leclère gurgled mouth and throat clogged with his own blood, as he shoved the dizzy dog from him.

And then Leclère cursed the other dogs off as they fell upon Bâtard. They drew back into a wider circle, squatting alertly on their haunches and licking their chops, the hair on every neck bristling and erect.

Bâtard recovered quickly, and at sound of Leclère's voice, tottered to his feet and swayed weakly back and forth.

"A-h-ah! You beeg devil!" Leclère spluttered. "Ah fix you; Ah fix you plentee, by *Gar*!"

Bâtard, the air biting into his exhausted lungs like wine, flashed full into the man's face, his jaws missing and coming together with a metallic clip. They rolled over and over on the snow, Leclère striking madly with his fists. Then they separated, face to face, and circled back and forth before each other. Leclère could have drawn his knife. His rifle was at his feet. But the beast in him was up and raging. He would do the thing with his hands—and his teeth. Bâtard sprang in, but Leclère knocked him over with a blow of the fist, fell upon him, and buried his teeth to the bone in the dog's shoulder.

It was a primordial setting and a primordial scene, such as might have been in the savage youth of the world. An open space in a dark forest, a ring of grinning wolf-dogs, and in the centre two beasts, locked in combat, snapping and snarling raging madly about panting, sobbing, cursing, straining, wild with passion, in a fury of murder, ripping and tearing and clawing in elemental brutishness.

But Leclère caught Bâtard behind the ear with a blow from his fist, knocking him over, and, for the instant, stunning him. Then Leclère leaped upon him with his feet, and sprang up and down, striving to grind him into the earth. Both Bâtard's hind legs were broken ere Leclère ceased that he might catch breath.

"A-a-ah! A-a-ah!" he screamed, incapable of speech, shaking his fist, through sheer impotence of throat and larynx.

But Bâtard was indomitable. He lay there in a helpless welter, his lip feebly lifting and writhing to the snarl he had not the strength to utter. Leclère kicked him, and the tired jaws closed on the ankle, but could not break the skin.

Then Leclère picked up the whip and proceeded almost to cut him to pieces, at each stroke of the lash crying: "Dis taim Ah break you! Eh? By *Gar*! Ah break you!"

In the end, exhausted, fainting from loss of blood, he crumpled up and fell by his victim, and when the wolf-dogs closed in to take their vengeance, with his last consciousness dragged his body on top of Bâtard to shield him from their fangs.

This occurred not far from Sunrise, and the missionary, opening the door to Leclère a few hours later, was surprised to note the absence of Bâtard from the team. Nor did his surprise lessen when Leclère threw back the robes from the sled, gathered Bâtard into his arms and staggered across the threshold. It happened that the surgeon of McQuestion, who was something of a gadabout, was up on a gossip, and between them they proceeded to repair Leclère,

"*Merci, non,*" said he. "Do you fix firs' de dog. To die? *Non.* Eet is not good. Becos' heem Ah mus' yet break. Dat fo' w'at he mus' not die."

The surgeon called it a marvel, the missionary a miracle, that Leclère pulled through at all; and so weakened was he, that in the spring the fever got him, and he went on his back again. Bâtard had been in even worse plight, but his grip on life prevailed, and the bones of his hind legs knit, and his organs righted themselves, during the several weeks he lay strapped to the floor. And by the time Leclère, finally convalescent, sallow and shaky, took the sun by the cabin door, Bâtard had reasserted his supremacy among his kind, and brought not only his own team-mates but the missionary's dogs into subjection.

He moved never a muscle, nor twitched a hair, when, for the first time, Leclère tottered out on the missionary's arm, and sank down slowly and with infinite caution on the three-legged stool.

"*Bon!*" he said. "*Bon!* De good sun!" And he stretched out his wasted hands and washed them in the warmth.

Then his gaze fell on the dog, and the old light blazed back in his eyes. He touched the missionary lightly on the arm. "*Mon père,* dat is one beeg devil, dat Bâtard. You will bring me one pistol, so, dat Ah drink de sun in peace."

And thenceforth for many days he sat in the sun before the cabin door. He never dozed, and the pistol lay always across his knees. Bâtard had a way, the first thing each day, of looking for the weapon in its wonted place. At sight of it he would lift his lip faintly in token that he understood, and Leclère would lift his own lip in an answering grin. One day the missionary took note of the trick.

"Bless me!" he said. "I really believe the brute comprehends."

Leclère laughed softly. "Look you, *mon père*. Dat w'at Ah now spik, to dat does he lissen."

As if in confirmation, Bâtard just perceptibly wriggled his lone ear up to catch the sound.

"Ah say 'keel'."

Bâtard growled deep down in his throat, the hair bristled along his neck, and every muscle went tense and expectant.

"Ah lift de gun, so, like dat." And suiting action to word, he sighted the pistol at Bâtard. Bâtard, with a single leap, sideways, landed around the corner of the cabin out of sight.

"Bless me!" he repeated at intervals. Leclère grinned proudly.

"But why does he not run away?"

The Frenchman's shoulders went up in the racial shrug that means all things from total ignorance to infinite understanding.

"Then why do you not kill him?"

Again the shoulders went up.

"*Mon père*," he said after a pause, "de taim is not yet. He is one beeg devil. Some taim Ah break heem, so an' so, all to leetle bits. Hey? some taim. *Bon!*"

A day came when Leclère gathered his dogs together and floated down in a bateau to Forty Mile, and on to the Porcupine, where he took a commission from the P. C. Company, and went exploring for the better part of a year. After that he poled up the Koyokuk to deserted Arctic City, and later came drifting back, from camp to camp, along the Yukon. And during the long months Bâtard was well lessoned. He learned many tortures, and, notably, the torture of hunger, the torture of thirst, the torture of fire, and, worst of all, the torture of music.

Like the rest of his kind, he did not enjoy music. It gave him exquisite anguish, racking him nerve by nerve, and ripping apart every fibre of his being. It made him howl, long and wolf-life, as when the wolves bay the stars on frosty nights. He could not help howling. It was his one weakness in the contest with Leclère, and it was his shame. Leclère, on the other hand, passionately loved music—as passionately as he loved strong drink. And when his soul clamoured for expression, it usually uttered itself in one or the other of the two ways, and more usually in both ways. And when he had drunk, his brain a-lilt with unsung song and the devil in him aroused and rampant, his soul found its supreme utterance in torturing Bâtard.

"Now we will haf a leetle museek," he would say. "Eh? W'at you t'ink, Bâtard?"

It was only an old and battered harmonica, tenderly treasured and patiently repaired; but it was the best that money could buy, and out of its silver reeds he drew weird vagrant airs that men had never heard before. Then Bâtard, dumb of throat, with teeth tight clenched, would back away, inch by inch, to the farthest cabin corner. And Leclère, playing, playing, a stout club tucked under his arm, followed the animal up, inch by inch, step by step, till there was no further retreat.

At first Bâtard would crowd himself into the smallest possible space, grovelling close to the floor; but as the music came nearer and nearer, he was forced to uprear, his back jammed into the logs, his fore legs fanning the air as though to beat off the rippling waves of sound. He still kept his teeth together, but severe muscular contractions attacked his body, strange twitchings and jerkings, till he was all a-quiver and writhing in silent torment. As he lost control, his jaws spasmodically wrenched apart, and deep throaty vibrations issued forth, too low in the register of sound for human ear to catch. And then, nostrils distended, eyes dilated, hair bristling in helpless rage, arose the long wolf howl. It came with a slurring rush upwards, swelling to a great heart-breaking burst of sound, and dying away in sadly cadenced woe—then the next rush upward, octave upon octave; the bursting heart; and the infinite sorrow and misery, fainting, fading, falling, and dying slowly away.

It was fit for hell. And Leclère, with fiendish ken, seemed to divine each particular nerve and heartstring, and with long wails and tremblings and sobbing minors to make it yield up its last shred of grief. It was frightful, and for twenty-four hours after, Bâtard was nervous and unstrung, starting at common sounds, tripping over his own shadow, but, withal, vicious and masterful with his team-mates. Nor did he show signs of a breaking spirit. Rather did he grow more grim and taciturn, biding his time with an inscrutable patience that began to puzzle and weigh upon Leclère. The dog would lie in the firelight, motionless, for hours, gazing straight before him at Leclère, and hating him with his bitter eyes.

Often the man felt that he had bucked against the very essence of life— the unconquerable essence that swept the hawk down out of the sky like a feathered thunderbolt, that drove the great grey goose across the zones, that hurled the spawning salmon through two thousand miles of boiling Yukon flood. At such times he felt impelled to—express his own unconquerable essence; and with strong drink, wild music, and Bâtard, he indulged in vast orgies, wherein he pitted his puny strength in the face of things, and challenged all that was, and had been, and was yet to be.

"Dere is somet'ing dere," he affirmed, when the rhythmed vagaries of his mind touched the secret chords of Bâtard's being and brought forth the long lugubrious howl. "Ah pool eet out wid bot' my han's, so, an' so. Ha! ha! Eet is fonee! Eet is ver' fonee! De priest chant, de womans pray, de mans swear, de leetle bird go *peep-peep*, Bâtard, heem go *yow-yow*—an' eet is all de ver' same t'ing. Ha! ha!"

Father Gautier, a worthy priest, one reproved him with instances of concrete perdition. He never reproved him again.

"Eet may be so, *mon père*," he made answer. "An' Ah t'ink Ah go troo hell a-snappin', lak de hemlock troo de fire. Eh, *mon père?*"

But all bad things come to an end as well as good, and so with Black Leclère. On the summer low water, in a poling boat, he left McDougall for Sunrise. He left McDougall in company with Timothy Brown, and arrived at Sunrise by himself. Further, it was known that they had quarrelled just previous to pulling out; for the *Lizzie*, a wheezy ten-ton stern-wheeler, twenty-four hours behind, beat Leclère in by three days. And when he did get in, it was with a clean-drilled bullet-hole through his shoulder muscle, and a tale of ambush and murder.

A strike had been made at Sunrise, and things had changed considerably. With the infusion of several hundred gold-seekers, a deal of whisky, and half-a-dozen equipped gamblers, the missionary had seen the page of his years of labour with the Indians wiped clean. When the squaws became preoccupied with cooking beans and keeping the fire going for the wifeless miners, and the bucks with swapping their warm furs for black bottles and broken time-pieces, he took to his bed, said "Bless me" several times, and departed to his final accounting in a rough-hewn, oblong box. Whereupon the gamblers moved their roulette and faro tables into the mission house, and the click of chips and clink of glasses went up from dawn till dark and to dawn again.

Now Timothy Brown was well beloved among these adventurers of the North. The one thing against him was his quick temper and ready fist—a little thing, for which his kind heart and forgiving hand more than atoned. On the other hand, there was nothing to atone for Black Leclère. He was "black," as more than one remembered deed bore witness, while he was as well hated as the other was beloved. So the men of Sunrise put an antiseptic dressing on his shoulder and haled him before Judge Lynch.

It was a simple affair. He had quarrelled with Timothy Brown at McDougall. With Timothy Brown he had left McDougall. Without Timothy Brown he had arrived at Sunrise. Considered in the light of his evilness, the unanimous conclusion was that he had killed Timothy Brown. On the other hand, Leclère acknowledged their facts, but challenged their conclusion, and gave his own explanation. Twenty miles out of Sunrise he and Timothy Brown were poling the boat along the rocky shore. From that shore two rifle-shots rang out. Timothy Brown pitched out of the boat and went down bubbling red, and that was the last of Timothy Brown. He, Leclère, pitched into the bottom of the boat with a stinging shoulder. He lay very quiet, peeping at the shore. After a time two Indians stuck up their heads and came out to the water's edge, carrying between them a birch-bark canoe. As they launched

184

it, Leclère let fly. He potted one, who went over the side after the manner of Timothy Brown. The other dropped into the bottom of the canoe, and then canoe and poling boat went down the stream in a drifting battle. After that they hung up on a split current, and the canoe passed on one side of an island, the poling boat on the other. That was the last of the canoe, and he came on into Sunrise. Yes, from the way the Indian in the canoe jumped, he was sure he had potted him. That was all. This explanation was not deemed adequate. They gave him ten hours' grace while the *Lizzie* steamed down to investigate. Ten hours later she came wheezing back to Sunrise. There had been nothing to investigate. No evidence had been found to back up his statements. They told him to make his will, for he possessed a fifty-thousand dollar Sunrise claim, and they were a law-abiding as well as a law-giving breed.

Leclère shrugged his shoulders. "Bot one t'ing," he said; "a leetle, w'at you call, favour—a leetle favour, dat is eet. I gif my feefty t'ousan' dollair to de church. I gif my husky dog, Bâtard, to de devil. De leetle favour? Firs' you hang heem, an' den you hang me. Eet is good, eh?"

Good it was, they agreed, that Hell's Spawn should break trail for his master across the last divide, and the court was adjourned down to the river bank, where a big spruce tree stood by itself. Slackwater Charley put a hangman's knot in the end of a hauling-line, and the noose was slipped over Leclère's head and pulled tight around his neck. His hands were tied behind his back, and he was assisted to the top of a cracker box. Then the running end of the line was passed over an over-hanging branch, drawn taut, and made fast. To kick the box out from under would leave him dancing on the air.

"Now for the dog," said Webster Shaw, sometime mining engineer. "You'll have to rope him, Slackwater."

Leclère grinned. Slackwater took a chew of tobacco, rove a running noose, and proceeded leisurely to coil a few turns in his hand. He paused once or twice to brush particularly offensive mosquitoes from off his face. Everybody was brushing mosquitoes, except Leclère, about whose head a small cloud was visible. Even Bâtard, lying full-stretched on the ground with his fore paws rubbed the pests away from eyes and mouth.

But while Slackwater waited for Bâtard to lift his head, a faint call came from the quiet air, and a man was seen waving his arms and running across the flat from Sunrise. It was the storekeeper.

"C-call 'er off, boys," he panted, as he came in among them.

"Little Sandy and Bernadotte's jes' got in," he explained with returning breath. "Landed down below an' come up by the short cut. Got the Beaver with 'm. Picked 'm up in his canoe, stuck in a back channel, with a couple of bullet-holes in 'm. Other buck was Klok Kutz, the one that knocked spots out of his squaw and dusted."

"Eh? W'at Ah say? Eh?" Leclère cried exultantly. "Dat de one fo' sure! Ah know. Ah spik true."

"The thing to do is to teach these damned Siwashes a little manners," spoke Webster Shaw. "They're getting fat and sassy, and we'll have to bring them down a peg. Round in all the bucks and string up the Beaver for an object lesson. That's the programme. Come on and let's see what he's got to say for himself."

"Heh, *M'sieu*!" Leclère called, as the crowd began to melt away through the twilight in the direction of Sunrise. "Ah lak ver' moch to see de fon."

"Oh, we'll turn you loose when we come back," Webster Shaw shouted over his shoulder. "In the meantime meditate on your sins and the ways of Providence. It will do you good, so be grateful."

As is the way with men who are accustomed to great hazards, whose nerves are healthy and trained in patience, so it was with Leclère who settled himself to the long wait—which is to say that he reconciled his mind to it. There was no settling of the body, for the taut rope forced him to stand rigidly erect. The least relaxation of the leg muscles pressed the rough-fibred noose into his neck, while the upright position caused him much pain in his wounded shoulder. He projected his under lip and expelled his breath upwards along his face to blow the mosquitoes away from his eyes. But the situation had its compensation. To be snatched from the maw of death was well worth a little bodily suffering, only it was unfortunate that he should miss the hanging of the Beaver.

And so he mused, till his eyes chanced to fall upon Bâtard, head between fore paws and stretched on the ground asleep. And their Leclère ceased to muse. He studied the animal closely, striving to sense if the sleep were real or feigned. Bâtard's sides were heaving regularly, but Leclère felt that the breath came and went a shade too quickly; also he felt that there was a vigilance or alertness to every hair that belied unshackling sleep. He would have given his Sunrise claim to be assured that the dog was not awake, and once, when one of his joints cracked, he looked quickly and guiltily at Bâtard to see if he roused. He did not rouse then but a few minutes later he got up slowly and lazily, stretched, and looked carefully about him.

"*Sacredam*," said Leclère under his breath.

Assured that no one was in sight or hearing, Bâtard sat down, curled his upper lip almost into a smile, looked up at Leclère, and licked his chops.

"Ah see my feenish," the man said, and laughed sardonically aloud.

Bâtard came nearer, the useless ear wabbling, the good ear cocked forward with devilish comprehension. He thrust his head on one side quizzically, and advanced with mincing, playful steps. He rubbed his body gently against the box till it shook and shook again. Leclère teetered carefully to maintain his equilibrium.

"Bâtard," he said calmly, "look out. Ah keel you."

Bâtard snarled at the word and shook the box with greater force. Then he upreared, and with his fore paws threw his weight against it higher up. Leclère kicked out with one foot, but the rope bit into his neck and checked so abruptly as nearly to overbalance him.

"Hi, ya! *Chook*! *Mush-on*!" he screamed.

Bâtard retreated, for twenty feet or so, with a fiendish levity in his bearing that Leclère could not mistake. He remembered the dog often breaking the scum of ice on the water hole by lifting up and throwing his weight upon it; and remembering, he understood what he now had in mind. Bâtard faced about and paused. He showed his white teeth in a grin, which

Leclère answered; and then hurled his body through the air, in full charge, straight for the box.

Fifteen minutes later, Slackwater Charley and Webster Shaw returning, caught a glimpse of a ghostly pendulum swinging back and forth in the dim light. As they hurriedly drew in closer, they made out the man's inert body, and a live thing that clung to it, and shook and worried, and gave to it the swaying motion.

"Hi, ya! *Chook*! you Spawn of Hell!" yelled Webster Shaw.

But Bâtard glared at him, and snarled threateningly, without loosing his jaws.

Slackwater Charley got out his revolver, but his hand was shaking, as with a chill, and he fumbled.

"Here you take it," he said, passing the weapon over.

Webster Shaw laughed shortly, drew a sight between the gleaming eyes, and pressed the trigger. Bâtard's body twitched with the shock, threshed the ground spasmodically for a moment, and went suddenly limp. But his teeth still held fast locked.

THE STORY OF JEES UCK

There have been renunciations and renunciations. But, in its essence, renunciation is ever the same. And the paradox of it is, that men and women forego the dearest thing in the world for something dearer. It was never otherwise. Thus it was when Abel brought of the firstlings of his flock and of the fat thereof. The firstlings and the fat thereof were to him the dearest things in the world; yet he gave them over that he might be on good terms with God. So it was with Abraham when he prepared to offer up his son Isaac on a stone. Isaac was very dear to him; but God, in incomprehensible ways, was yet dearer. It may be that Abraham feared the Lord. But whether that be true or not it has since been determined by a few billion people that he loved the Lord and desired to serve him.

And since it has been determined that love is service, and since to renounce is to serve, then Jees Uck, who was merely a woman of a swart-skinned breed, loved with a great love. She was unversed in history, having learned to read only the signs of weather and of game; so she had never heard of Abel nor of Abraham; nor, having escaped the good sisters at Holy Cross, had she been told the story of Ruth, the Moabitess, who renounced her very God for the sake of a stranger woman from a strange land. Jees Uck had learned only one way of renouncing, and that was with a club as the dynamic factor, in much the same manner as a dog is made to renounce a stolen marrow-bone. Yet, when the time came, she proved herself capable of rising to the height of the fair-faced royal races and of renouncing in right regal fashion.

So this is the story of Jees Uck, which is also the story of Neil Bonner, and Kitty Bonner, and a couple of Neil Bonner's progeny. Jees Uck was of a swart-skinned breed, it is true, but she was not an Indian; nor was she an Eskimo; nor even an Innuit. Going backward into mouth tradition, there appears the figure of one Skolkz, a Toyaat Indian of the Yukon, who journeyed down in his youth to the Great Delta where dwell the Innuits, and where he foregathered with a woman remembered as Olillie. Now the woman Olillie had been bred from an Eskimo mother by an Innuit man. And from Skolkz and Olillie came Halie, who was one-half Toyaat Indian, one-quarter Innuit, and one-quarter Eskimo. And Halie was the grandmother of Jees Uck.

Now Halie, in whom three stocks had been bastardized, who cherished no prejudice against further admixture, mated with a Russian fur trader called Shpack, also known in his time as the Big Fat. Shpack is herein classed Russian for lack of a more adequate term; for Shpack's father, a Slavonic convict from the Lower Provinces, had escaped from the quicksilver mines into Northern Siberia, where he knew Zimba, who was a woman of the Deer People and who became the mother of Shpack, who became the grandfather of Jees Uck.

Now had not Shpack been captured in his boyhood by the Sea People, who fringe the rim of the Arctic Sea with their misery, he would not have become the grandfather of Jees Uck and there would be no story at all. But he *was* captured by the Sea People, from whom he escaped to Kamchatka, and thence, on a Norwegian whale-ship, to the Baltic. Not long after that he turned up in St. Petersburg, and the years were not many till he went drifting east over the same weary road his father had measured with blood and groans a half-century before. But Shpack was a free man, in the employ of the great Russian Fur Company. And in that employ he fared farther and farther east, until he crossed Bering Sea into Russian America; and at Pastolik, which is hard by the Great Delta of the Yukon, became the husband of Halie, who was the grandmother of Jees Uck. Out of this union came the woman-child, Tukesan.

Shpack, under the orders of the Company, made a canoe voyage of a few hundred miles up the Yukon to the post of Nulato. With him he took Halie and the babe Tukesan. This was in 1850, and in 1850 it was that the river Indians fell upon Nulato and wiped it from the face of the earth. And that was the end of Shpack and Halie. On that terrible night Tukesan disappeared. To this day the Toyaats aver they had no hand in the trouble; but, be that as it may, the fact remains that the babe Tukesan grew up among them.

190

Tukesan was married successively to two Toyaat brothers, to both of whom she was barren. Because of this, other women shook their heads, and no third Toyaat man could be found to dare matrimony with the childless widow. But at this time, many hundred miles above, at Fort Yukon, was a man, Spike O'Brien. Fort Yukon was a Hudson Bay Company post, and Spike O'Brien one of the Company's servants. He was a good servant, but he achieved an opinion that the service was bad, and in the course of time vindicated that opinion by deserting. It was a year's journey, by the chain of posts, back to York Factory on Hudson's Bay. Further, being Company posts, he knew he could not evade the Company's clutches. Nothing retained but to go down the Yukon. It was true no white man had ever gone down the Yukon, and no white man knew whether the Yukon emptied into the Arctic Ocean or Bering Sea; but Spike O'Brien was a Celt, and the promise of danger was a lure he had ever followed.

A few weeks later, somewhat battered, rather famished, and about dead with river-fever, he drove the nose of his canoe into the earth bank by the village of the Toyaats and promptly fainted away. While getting his strength back, in the weeks that followed, he looked upon Tukesan and found her good. Like the father of Shpack, who lived to a ripe old age among the Siberian Deer People, Spike O'Brien might have left his aged bones with the Toyaats. But romance gripped his heart-strings and would not let him stay. As he had journeyed from York Factory to Fort Yukon, so, first among men, might he journey from Fort Yukon to the sea and win the honour of being the first man to make the North-West Passage by land. So he departed down the river, won the honour, and was unannaled and unsung. In after years he ran a sailors' boarding-house in San Francisco, where he became esteemed a most remarkable liar by virtue of the gospel truths he told. But a child was born to Tukesan, who had been childless. And this child was Jees Uck. Her lineage has been traced at length to show that she was neither Indian, nor Eskimo, nor Innuit, nor much of anything else; also to show what waifs of the generations we are, all of us, and the strange meanderings of the seed from which we spring.

191

What with the vagrant blood in her and the heritage compounded of many races, Jees Uck developed a wonderful young beauty. Bizarre, perhaps, it was, and Oriental enough to puzzle any passing ethnologist. A lithe and slender grace characterized her. Beyond a quickened lilt to the imagination, the contribution of the Celt was in no wise apparent. It might possibly have put the warm blood under her skin, which made her face less swart and her body fairer; but that, in turn, might have come from Shpack, the Big Fat, who inherited the colour of his Slavonic father. And, finally, she had great, blazing black eyes—the half-caste eye, round, full-orbed, and sensuous, which marks the collision of the dark races with the light. Also, the white blood in her, combined with her knowledge that it was in her, made her, in a way, ambitious. Otherwise by upbringing and in outlook on life, she was wholly and utterly a Toyaat Indian.

One winter, when she was a young woman, Neil Bonner came into her life. But he came into her life, as he had come into the country, somewhat reluctantly. In fact, it was very much against his will, coming into the country. Between a father who clipped coupons and cultivated roses, and a mother who loved the social round, Neil Bonner had gone rather wild. He was not vicious, but a man with meat in his belly and without work in the world has to expend his energy somehow, and Neil Bonner was such a man. And he expended his energy in such a fashion and to such extent that when the inevitable climax came, his father, Neil Bonner, senior, crawled out of his roses in a panic and looked on his son with a wondering eye. Then he hied himself away to a crony of kindred pursuits, with whom he was wont to confer over coupons and roses, and between the two the destiny of young Neil Bonner was made manifest. He must go away, on probation, to live down his harmless follies in order that he might live up to their own excellent standard.

This determined upon, and young Neil a little repentant and a great deal ashamed, the rest was easy. The cronies were heavy stockholders in the P. C. Company. The P. C. Company owned fleets of river-steamers and ocean-going craft, and, in addition to farming the sea, exploited a hundred thousand square miles or so of the land that, on the maps of geographers, usually occupies the white spaces. So the P. C. Company sent young Neil Bonner north, where the white spaces are, to do its work and to learn to be good like his father. "Five years of simplicity, close to the soil and far from temptation, will make a man of him," said old Neil Bonner, and forthwith crawled back among his roses. Young Neil set his jaw, pitched his chin at the proper angle, and went to work. As an underling he did his work well and gained the commendation of his superiors. Not that he delighted in the work, but that it was the one thing that prevented him from going mad.

The first year he wished he was dead. The second year he cursed God. The third year he was divided between the two emotions, and in the confusion quarrelled with a man in authority. He had the best of the quarrel, though the man in authority had the last word,—a word that sent Neil Bonner into an exile that made his old billet appear as paradise. But he went without a whimper, for the North had succeeded in making him into a man.

Here and there, on the white spaces on the map, little circlets like the letter "o" are to be found, and, appended to these circlets, on one side or the other, are names such as "Fort Hamilton," "Yanana Station," "Twenty Mile," thus leading one to imagine that the white spaces are plentifully besprinkled with towns and villages. But it is a vain imagining. Twenty Mile, which is very like the rest of the posts, is a log building the size of a corner grocery with rooms to let up-stairs. A long-legged cache on stilts may be found in the back yard; also a couple of outhouses. The back yard is unfenced, and extends to the sky-line and an unascertainable bit beyond. There are no other houses in sight, though the Toyaats sometimes pitch a winter camp a mile or two down the Yukon. And this is Twenty Mile, one tentacle of the many-tentacled P. C. Company. Here the agent, with an assistant, barters with the Indians for their furs, and does an erratic trade on a gold-dust basis with the wandering miners. Here, also, the agent and his assistant yearn all winter for the spring, and when the spring comes, camp blasphemously on the roof while the Yukon washes out the establishment. And here, also, in the fourth year of his sojourn in the land, came Neil Bonner to take charge.

He had displaced no agent; for the man that previously ran the post had made away with himself; "because of the rigours of the place," said the assistant, who still remained; though the Toyaats, by their fires, had another version. The assistant was a shrunken-shouldered, hollow-chested man, with a cadaverous face and cavernous cheeks that his sparse black beard could not hide. He coughed much, as though consumption gripped his lungs, while his eyes had that mad, fevered light common to consumptives in the last stage. Pentley was his name—Amos Pentley—and Bonner did not like him, though he felt a pity for the forlorn and hopeless devil. They did not get along together, these two men who, of all men, should have been on good terms in the face of the cold and silence and darkness of the long winter.

In the end, Bonner concluded that Amos was partly demented, and left him alone, doing all the work himself except the cooking. Even then, Amos had nothing but bitter looks and an undisguised hatred for him. This was a great loss to Bonner; for the smiling face of one of his own kind, the cheery word, the sympathy of comradeship shared with misfortune—these things meant much; and the winter was yet young when he began to realize the added reasons, with such an assistant, that the previous agent had found to impel his own hand against his life.

It was very lonely at Twenty Mile. The bleak vastness stretched away on every side to the horizon. The snow, which was really frost, flung its mantle over the land and buried everything in the silence of death. For days it was clear and cold, the thermometer steadily recording forty to fifty degrees below zero. Then a change came over the face of things. What little moisture had oozed into the atmosphere gathered into dull grey, formless clouds; it became quite warm, the thermometer rising to twenty below; and the moisture fell out of the sky in hard frost-granules that hissed like dry sugar or driving sand when kicked underfoot. After that it became clear and cold again, until enough moisture had gathered to blanket the earth from the cold of outer space. That was all. Nothing happened. No storms, no churning waters and threshing forests, nothing but the machine-like precipitation of accumulated moisture. Possibly the most notable thing that occurred through the weary weeks was the gliding of the temperature up to the unprecedented height of fifteen below. To atone for this, outer space smote the earth with its cold till the mercury froze and the spirit thermometer remained more than seventy below for a fortnight, when it burst. There was no telling how much colder it was after that. Another occurrence, monotonous in its regularity, was the lengthening of the nights, till day became a mere blink of light between the darkness.

Neil Bonner was a social animal. The very follies for which he was doing penance had been bred of his excessive sociability. And here, in the fourth year of his exile, he found himself in company—which were to travesty the word—with a morose and speechless creature in whose sombre eyes smouldered a hatred as bitter as it was unwarranted. And Bonner, to whom speech and fellowship were as the breath of life, went about as a ghost might go, tantalized by the gregarious revelries of some former life. In the day his lips were compressed, his face stern; but in the night he clenched his hands, rolled about in his blankets, and cried aloud like a little child. And he would remember a certain man in authority and curse him through the long hours. Also, he cursed God. But God understands. He cannot find it in his heart to blame weak mortals who blaspheme in Alaska.

And here, to the post of Twenty Mile, came Jees Uck, to trade for flour and bacon, and beads, and bright scarlet cloths for her fancy work. And further, and unwittingly, she came to the post of Twenty Mile to make a lonely man more lonely, make him reach out empty arms in his sleep. For Neil Bonner was only a man. When she first came into the store, he looked at her long, as a thirsty man may look at a flowing well. And she, with the heritage bequeathed her by Spike O'Brien, imagined daringly and smiled up into his eyes, not as the swart-skinned peoples should smile at the royal races, but as a woman smiles at a man. The thing was inevitable; only, he did not see it, and fought against her as fiercely and passionately as he was drawn towards her. And she? She was Jees Uck, by upbringing wholly and utterly a Toyaat Indian woman.

She came often to the post to trade. And often she sat by the big wood stove and chatted in broken English with Neil Bonner. And he came to look for her coming; and on the days she did not come he was worried and restless. Sometimes he stopped to think, and then she was met coldly, with a resolve that perplexed and piqued her, and which, she was convinced, was not sincere. But more often he did not dare to think, and then all went well and there were smiles and laughter. And Amos Pentley, gasping like a stranded catfish, his hollow cough a-reek with the grave, looked upon it all and grinned. He, who loved life, could not live, and it rankled his soul that others should be able to live. Wherefore he hated Bonner, who was so very much alive and into whose eyes sprang joy at the sight of Jees Uck. As for Amos, the very thought of the girl was sufficient to send his blood pounding up into a hemorrhage.

Jees Uck, whose mind was simple, who thought elementally and was unused to weighing life in its subtler quantities, read Amos Pentley like a book. She warned Bonner, openly and bluntly, in few words; but the complexities of higher existence confused the situation to him, and he laughed at her evident anxiety. To him, Amos was a poor, miserable devil, tottering desperately into the grave. And Bonner, who had suffered much, found it easy to forgive greatly.

But one morning, during a bitter snap, he got up from the breakfast-table and went into the store. Jees Uck was already there, rosy from the trail, to buy a sack of flour. A few minutes later, he was out in the snow lashing the flour on her sled. As he bent over he noticed a stiffness in his neck and felt a premonition of impending physical misfortune. And as he put the last half-hitch into the lashing and attempted to straighten up, a quick spasm seized him and he sank into the snow. Tense and quivering, head jerked back, limbs extended, back arched and mouth twisted and distorted, he appeared as though being racked limb from limb. Without cry or sound, Jees Uck was in the snow beside him; but he clutched both her wrists spasmodically, and as long as the convulsion endured she was helpless. In a few moments the spasm relaxed and he was left weak and fainting, his forehead beaded with sweat, and his lips flecked with foam.

"Quick!" he muttered, in a strange, hoarse voice. "Quick! Inside!"

He started to crawl on hands and knees, but she raised him up, and, supported by her young arm, he made faster progress. As he entered the store the spasm seized him again, and his body writhed irresistibly away from her

196

and rolled and curled on the floor. Amos Pentley came and looked on with curious eyes.

"Oh, Amos!" she cried in an agony of apprehension and helplessness, "him die, you think?" But Amos shrugged his shoulders and continued to look on.

Bonner's body went slack, the tense muscles easing down and an expression of relief coming into his face. "Quick!" he gritted between his teeth, his mouth twisting with the on-coming of the next spasm and with his effort to control it. "Quick, Jees Uck! The medicine! Never mind! Drag me!"

She knew where the medicine-chest stood, at the rear of the room beyond the stove, and thither, by the legs, she dragged the struggling man. As the spasm passed he began, very faint and very sick, to overhaul the chest. He had seen dogs die exhibiting symptoms similar to his own, and he knew what should be done. He held up a vial of chloral hydrate, but his fingers were too weak and nerveless to draw the cork. This Jees Uck did for him, while he was plunged into another convulsion. As he came out of it he found the open bottle proffered him, and looked into the great black eyes of the woman and read what men have always read in the Mate-woman's eyes. Taking a full dose of the stuff, he sank back until another spasm had passed. Then he raised himself limply on his elbow.

"Listen, Jees Uck!" he said very slowly, as though aware of the necessity for haste and yet afraid to hasten. "Do what I say. Stay by my side, but do not touch me. I must be very quiet, but you must not go away." His jaw began to set and his face to quiver and distort with the fore-running pangs, but he gulped and struggled to master them. "Do not got away. And do not let Amos go away. Understand! Amos must stay right here."

She nodded her head, and he passed off into the first of many convulsions, which gradually diminished in force and frequency. Jees Uck hung over him remembering his injunction and not daring to touch him. Once Amos grew restless and made as though to go into the kitchen; but a quick blaze from her eyes quelled him, and after that, save for his laboured breathing and charnel cough, he was very quiet.

Bonner slept. The blink of light that marked the day disappeared. Amos, followed about by the woman's eyes, lighted the kerosene lamps. Evening came on. Through the north window the heavens were emblazoned with an auroral display, which flamed and flared and died down into blackness. Some time after that, Neil Bonner roused. First he looked to see that Amos was still there, then smiled at Jees Uck and pulled himself up. Every muscle was stiff and sore, and he smiled ruefully, pressing and prodding himself as if to ascertain the extent of the ravage. Then his face went stern and businesslike.

"Jees Uck," he said, "take a candle. Go into the kitchen. There is food on the table—biscuits and beans and bacon; also, coffee in the pot on the stove. Bring it here on the counter. Also, bring tumblers and water and whisky, which you will find on the top shelf of the locker. Do not forget the whisky."

Having swallowed a stiff glass of the whisky, he went carefully through the medicine chest, now and again putting aside, with definite purpose, certain bottles and vials. Then he set to work on the food, attempting a crude analysis. He had not been unused to the laboratory in his college days and was possessed of sufficient imagination to achieve results with his limited materials. The condition of tetanus, which had marked his paroxysms, simplified matters, and he made but one test. The coffee yielded nothing; nor did the beans. To the biscuits he devoted the utmost care. Amos, who knew nothing of chemistry, looked on with steady curiosity. But Jees Uck, who had boundless faith in the white man's wisdom, and especially in Neil Bonner's wisdom, and who not only knew nothing but knew that she knew nothing watched his face rather than his hands.

Step by step he eliminated possibilities, until he came to the final test. He was using a thin medicine vial for a tube, and this he held between him and the light, watching the slow precipitation of a salt through the solution contained in the tube. He said nothing, but he saw what he had expected to see. And Jees Uck, her eyes riveted on his face, saw something too,—something that made her spring like a tigress upon Amos, and with splendid suppleness and strength bend his body back across her knee. Her knife was out of its sheaf and uplifted, glinting in the lamplight. Amos was snarling; but Bonner intervened ere the blade could fall.

"That's a good girl, Jees Uck. But never mind. Let him go!"

She dropped the man obediently, though with protest writ large on her face; and his body thudded to the floor. Bonner nudged him with his moccasined foot.

"Get up, Amos!" he commanded. "You've got to pack an outfit yet tonight and hit the trail."

"You don't mean to say—" Amos blurted savagely.

"I mean to say that you tried to kill me," Neil went on in cold, even tones. "I mean to say that you killed Birdsall, for all the Company believes he killed himself. You used strychnine in my case. God knows with what you fixed him. Now I can't hang you. You're too near dead as it is. But Twenty Mile is too small for the pair of us, and you've got to mush. It's two hundred miles to Holy Cross. You can make it if you're careful not to over-exert. I'll give you grub, a sled, and three dogs. You'll be as safe as if you were in jail, for you can't get out of the country. And I'll give you one chance. You're almost dead. Very well. I shall send no word to the Company until the spring. In the meantime, the thing for you to do is to die. Now *mush!*"

"You go to bed!" Jees Uck insisted, when Amos had churned away into the night towards Holy Cross. "You sick man yet, Neil."

"And you're a good girl, Jees Uck," he answered. "And here's my hand on it. But you must go home."

"You don't like me," she said simply.

He smiled, helped her on with her *parka*, and led her to the door. "Only too well, Jees Uck," he said softly; "only too well."

After that the pall of the Arctic night fell deeper and blacker on the land. Neil Bonner discovered that he had failed to put proper valuation upon even the sullen face of the murderous and death-stricken Amos. It became very lonely at Twenty Mile. "For the love of God, Prentiss, send me a man," he wrote to the agent at Fort Hamilton, three hundred miles up river. Six weeks later the Indian messenger brought back a reply. It was characteristic: "Hell. Both feet frozen. Need him myself—Prentiss."

To make matters worse, most of the Toyaats were in the back country on the flanks of a caribou herd, and Jees Uck was with them. Removing to a distance seemed to bring her closer than ever, and Neil Bonner found himself picturing her, day by day, in camp and on trail. It is not good to be alone. Often he went out of the quiet store, bare-headed and frantic, and shook his fist at the blink of day that came over the southern sky-line. And on still, cold nights he left his bed and stumbled into the frost, where he assaulted the silence at the top of his lungs, as though it were some tangible, sentiment thing that he might arouse; or he shouted at the sleeping dogs till they howled and howled again. One shaggy brute he brought into the post, playing that it was the new man sent by Prentiss. He strove to make it sleep decently under blankets at nights and to sit at table and eat as a man should; but the beast, mere domesticated wolf that it was, rebelled, and sought out dark corners and snarled and bit him in the leg, and was finally beaten and driven forth.

Then the trick of personification seized upon Neil Bonner and mastered him. All the forces of his environment metamorphosed into living, breathing entities and came to live with him. He recreated the primitive pantheon; reared an altar to the sun and burned candle fat and bacon grease thereon; and in the unfenced yard, by the long-legged cache, made a frost devil, which he was wont to make faces at and mock when the mercury oozed down into the bulb. All this in play, of course. He said it to himself that it was in play, and repeated it over and over to make sure, unaware that madness is ever prone to express itself in make-believe and play.

One midwinter day, Father Champreau, a Jesuit missionary, pulled into Twenty Mile. Bonner fell upon him and dragged him into the post, and clung to him and wept, until the priest wept with him from sheer compassion. Then Bonner became madly hilarious and made lavish entertainment, swearing valiantly that his guest should not depart. But Father Champreau was pressing to Salt Water on urgent business for his order, and pulled out next morning, with Bonner's blood threatened on his head.

And the threat was in a fair way toward realization, when the Toyaats returned from their long hunt to the winter camp. They had many furs, and there was much trading and stir at Twenty Mile. Also, Jees Uck came to buy beads and scarlet cloths and things, and Bonner began to find himself again. He fought for a week against her. Then the end came one night when she rose to leave. She had not forgotten her repulse, and the pride that drove Spike O'Brien on to complete the North-West Passage by land was her pride.

"I go now," she said; "good-night, Neil."

But he came up behind her. "Nay, it is not well," he said.

And as she turned her face toward his with a sudden joyful flash, he bent forward, slowly and gravely, as it were a sacred thing, and kissed her on the lips. The Toyaats had never taught her the meaning of a kiss upon the lips, but she understood and was glad.

With the coming of Jees Uck, at once things brightened up. She was regal in her happiness, a source of unending delight. The elemental workings of her mind and her naive little ways made an immense sum of pleasurable surprise to the over-civilized man that had stooped to catch her up. Not alone was she solace to his loneliness, but her primitiveness rejuvenated his jaded mind. It was as though, after long wandering, he had returned to pillow his head in the lap of Mother Earth. In short, in Jees Uck he found the youth of the world—the youth and the strength and the joy.

And to fill the full round of his need, and that they might not see overmuch of each other, there arrived at Twenty Mile one Sandy MacPherson, as companionable a man as ever whistled along the trail or raised a ballad by a camp-fire. A Jesuit priest had run into his camp, a couple of hundred miles up the Yukon, in the nick of time to say a last word over the body of Sandy's partner. And on departing, the priest had said, "My son, you will be lonely now." And Sandy had bowed his head brokenly. "At Twenty Mile," the priest added, "there is a lonely man. You have need of each other, my son."

So it was that Sandy became a welcome third at the post, brother to the man and woman that resided there. He took Bonner moose-hunting and wolf-trapping; and, in return, Bonner resurrected a battered and way-worn volume and made him friends with Shakespeare, till Sandy declaimed iambic pentameters to his sled-dogs whenever they waxed mutinous. And of the long evenings they played cribbage and talked and disagreed about the universe, the while Jees Uck rocked matronly in an easy-chair and darned their moccasins and socks.

Spring came. The sun shot up out of the south. The land exchanged its austere robes for the garb of a smiling wanton. Everywhere light laughed and life invited. The days stretched out their balmy length and the nights passed from blinks of darkness to no darkness at all. The river bared its bosom, and snorting steamboats challenged the wilderness. There were stir and bustle, new faces, and fresh facts. An assistant arrived at Twenty Mile, and Sandy MacPherson wandered off with a bunch of prospectors to invade the Koyokuk country. And there were newspapers and magazines and letters for Neil Bonner. And Jees Uck looked on in worriment, for she knew his kindred talked with him across the world.

Without much shock, it came to him that his father was dead. There was a sweet letter of forgiveness, dictated in his last hours. There were official letters from the Company, graciously ordering him to turn the post over to the assistant and permitting him to depart at his earliest pleasure. A long, legal affair from the lawyers informed him of interminable lists of stocks and bonds, real estate, rents, and chattels that were his by his father's will. And a dainty bit of stationery, sealed and monogramed, implored dear Neil's return to his heart-broken and loving mother.

Neil Bonner did some swift thinking, and when the *Yukon Belle* coughed in to the bank on her way down to Bering Sea, he departed—departed with the ancient lie of quick return young and blithe on his lips.

"I'll come back, dear Jees Uck, before the first snow flies," he promised her, between the last kisses at the gang-plank.

And not only did he promise, but, like the majority of men under the same circumstances, he really meant it. To John Thompson, the new agent, he gave orders for the extension of unlimited credit to his wife, Jees Uck. Also, with his last look from the deck of the *Yukon Belle*, he saw a dozen men at work rearing the logs that were to make the most comfortable house along a thousand miles of river front—the house of Jees Uck, and likewise the house of Neil Bonner—ere the first flurry of snow. For he fully and fondly meant to come back. Jees Uck was dear to him, and, further, a golden future awaited the north. With his father's money he intended to verify that future. An ambitious dream allured him. With his four years of experience, and aided by the friendly coöperation of the P. C. Company, he would return to become the Rhodes of Alaska. And he would return, fast as steam could drive, as soon as he had put into shape the affairs of his father, whom he had never known, and comforted his mother, whom he had forgotten.

There was much ado when Neil Bonner came back from the Arctic. The fires were lighted and the fleshpots slung, and he took of it all and called it good. Not only was he bronzed and creased, but he was a new man under his skin, with a grip on things and a seriousness and control. His old companions were amazed when he declined to hit up the pace in the good old way, while his father's crony rubbed hands gleefully, and became an authority upon the reclamation of wayward and idle youth.

For four years Neil Bonner's mind had lain fallow. Little that was new had been added to it, but it had undergone a process of selection. It had, so to say, been purged of the trivial and superfluous. He had lived quick years, down in the world; and, up in the wilds, time had been given him to organize the confused mass of his experiences. His superficial standards had been flung to the winds and new standards erected on deeper and broader generalizations. Concerning civilization, he had gone away with one set of values, had returned with another set of values. Aided, also, by the earth smells in his nostrils and the earth sights in his eyes, he laid hold of the inner significance of civilization, beholding with clear vision its futilities and powers. It was a simple little philosophy he evolved. Clean living was the way to grace. Duty performed was sanctification. One must live clean and do his duty in order that he might work. Work was salvation. And to work toward life abundant, and more abundant, was to be in line with the scheme of things and the will of God.

Primarily, he was of the city. And his fresh earth grip and virile conception of humanity gave him a finer sense of civilization and endeared civilization to him. Day by day the people of the city clung closer to him and the world loomed more colossal. And, day by day, Alaska grew more remote and less real. And then he met Kitty Sharon—a woman of his own flesh and blood and kind; a woman who put her hand into his hand and drew him to her, till he forgot the day and hour and the time of the year the first snow flies on the Yukon.

Jees Uck moved into her grand log-house and dreamed away three golden summer months. Then came the autumn, post-haste before the down rush of winter. The air grew thin and sharp, the days thin and short. The river ran sluggishly, and skin ice formed in the quiet eddies. All migratory life departed south, and silence fell upon the land. The first snow flurries came, and the last homing steamboat bucked desperately into the running mush ice. Then came the hard ice, solid cakes and sheets, till the Yukon ran level with its banks. And when all this ceased the river stood still and the blinking days lost themselves in the darkness.

John Thompson, the new agent, laughed; but Jees Uck had faith in the mischances of sea and river. Neil Bonner might be frozen in anywhere between Chilkoot Pass and St. Michael's, for the last travellers of the year are always caught by the ice, when they exchange boat for sled and dash on through the long hours behind the flying dogs.

But no flying dogs came up the trail, nor down the trail, to Twenty Mile. And John Thompson told Jees Uck, with a certain gladness ill concealed, that Bonner would never come back again. Also, and brutally, he suggested his own eligibility. Jees Uck laughed in his face and went back to her grand log-house. But when midwinter came, when hope dies down and life is at its lowest ebb, Jees Uck found she had no credit at the store. This was Thompson's doing, and he rubbed his hands, and walked up and down, and came to his door and looked up at Jees Uck's house and waited. And he continued to wait. She sold her dog-team to a party of miners and paid cash for her food. And when Thompson refused to honour even her coin, Toyaat Indians made her purchases, and sledded them up to her house in the dark.

In February the first post came in over the ice, and John Thompson read in the society column of a five-months-old paper of the marriage of Neil

204

Bonner and Kitty Sharon. Jees Uck held the door ajar and him outside while he imparted the information; and, when he had done, laughed pridefully and did not believe. In March, and all alone, she gave birth to a man-child, a brave bit of new life at which she marvelled. And at that hour, a year later, Neil Bonner sat by another bed, marvelling at another bit of new life that had fared into the world.

The snow went off the ground and the ice broke out of the Yukon. The sun journeyed north, and journeyed south again; and, the money from the being spent, Jees Uck went back to her own people. Oche Ish, a shrewd hunter, proposed to kill the meat for her and her babe, and catch the salmon, if she would marry him. And Imego and Hah Yo and Wy Nooch, husky young hunters all, made similar proposals. But she elected to live alone and seek her own meat and fish. She sewed moccasins and parkas and mittens—warm, serviceable things, and pleasing to the eye, withal, what of the ornamental hair-tufts and bead-work. These she sold to the miners, who were drifting faster into the land each year. And not only did she win food that was good and plentiful, but she laid money by, and one day took passage on the *Yukon Belle* down the river.

At St. Michael's she washed dishes in the kitchen of the post. The servants of the Company wondered at the remarkable woman with the remarkable child, though they asked no questions and she vouchsafed nothing. But just before Bering Sea closed in for the year, she bought a passage south on a strayed sealing schooner. That winter she cooked for Captain Markheim's household at Unalaska, and in the spring continued south to Sitka on a whisky sloop. Later on appeared at Metlakahtla, which is near to St. Mary's on the end of the Pan-Handle, where she worked in the cannery through the salmon season. When autumn came and the Siwash fishermen prepared to return to Puget Sound, she embarked with a couple of families in a big cedar canoe; and with them she threaded the hazardous chaos of the Alaskan and Canadian coasts, till the Straits of Juan de Fuca were passed and she led her boy by the hand up the hard pave of Seattle.

There she met Sandy MacPherson, on a windy corner, very much surprised and, when he had heard her story, very wroth—not so wroth as he might have been, had he known of Kitty Sharon; but of her Jees Uck breathed not a word, for she had never believed. Sandy, who read commonplace and sordid desertion into the circumstance, strove to dissuade her from her trip to San Francisco, where Neil Bonner was supposed to live when he was at home. And, having striven, he made her comfortable, bought her tickets and saw her off, the while smiling in her face and muttering "dam-shame" into his beard.

With roar and rumble, through daylight and dark, swaying and lurching between the dawns, soaring into the winter snows and sinking to summer valleys, skirting depths, leaping chasms, piercing mountains, Jees Uck and her boy were hurled south. But she had no fear of the iron stallion; nor was she stunned by this masterful civilization of Neil Bonner's people. It seemed, rather, that she saw with greater clearness the wonder that a man of such godlike race had held her in his arms. The screaming medley of San Francisco, with its restless shipping, belching factories, and thundering traffic, did not confuse her; instead, she comprehended swiftly the pitiful sordidness of Twenty Mile and the skin-lodged Toyaat village. And she looked down at the boy that clutched her hand and wondered that she had borne him by such a man.

She paid the hack-driver five pieces and went up the stone steps of Neil Bonner's front door. A slant-eyed Japanese parleyed with her for a fruitless space, then led her inside and disappeared. She remained in the hall, which to her simply fancy seemed to be the guest-room—the show-place wherein were arrayed all the household treasures with the frank purpose of parade and dazzlement. The walls and ceiling were of oiled and panelled redwood. The floor was more glassy than glare-ice, and she sought standing place on one of the great skins that gave a sense of security to the polished surface. A huge fireplace—an extravagant fireplace, she deemed it—yawned in the farther wall. A flood of light, mellowed by stained glass, fell across the room, and from the far end came the white gleam of a marble figure.

This much she saw, and more, when the slant-eyed servant led the way past another room—of which she caught a fleeting glance—and into a third, both of which dimmed the brave show of the entrance hall. And to her eyes the great house seemed to hold out the promise of endless similar rooms.

There was such length and breadth to them, and the ceilings were so far away! For the first time since her advent into the white man's civilization, a feeling of awe laid hold of her. Neil, her Neil, lived in this house, breathed the air of it, and lay down at night and slept! It was beautiful, all this that she saw, and it pleased her; but she felt, also, the wisdom and mastery behind. It was the concrete expression of power in terms of beauty, and it was the power that she unerringly divined.

And then came a woman, queenly tall, crowned with a glory of hair that was like a golden sun. She seemed to come toward Jees Uck as a ripple of music across still water; her sweeping garment itself a song, her body playing rhythmically beneath. Jees Uck herself was a man compeller. There were Oche Ish and Imego and Hah Yo and Wy Nooch, to say nothing of Neil Bonner and John Thompson and other white men that had looked upon her and felt her power. But she gazed upon the wide blue eyes and rose-white skin of this woman that advanced to meet her, and she measured her with woman's eyes looking through man's eyes; and as a man compeller she felt herself diminish and grow insignificant before this radiant and flashing creature.

"You wish to see my husband?" the woman asked; and Jees Uck gasped at the liquid silver of a voice that had never sounded harsh cries at snarling wolf-dogs, nor moulded itself to a guttural speech, nor toughened in storm and frost and camp smoke.

"No," Jees Uck answered slowly and gropingly, in order that she might do justice to her English. "I come to see Neil Bonner."

"He is my husband," the woman laughed.

Then it was true! John Thompson had not lied that bleak February day, when she laughed pridefully and shut the door in his face. As once she had thrown Amos Pentley across her knee and ripped her knife into the air, so now she felt impelled to spring upon this woman and bear her back and down, and tear the life out of her fair body. But Jees Uck was thinking quickly and gave no sign, and Kitty Bonner little dreamed how intimately she had for an instant been related with sudden death.

Jees Uck nodded her head that she understood, and Kitty Bonner explained that Neil was expected at any moment. Then they sat down on ridiculously comfortable chairs, and Kitty sought to entertain her strange visitor, and Jees Uck strove to help her.

"You knew my husband in the North?" Kitty asked, once.

"Sure. I wash um clothes," Jees Uck had answered, her English abruptly beginning to grow atrocious.

"And this is your boy? I have a little girl."

Kitty caused her daughter to be brought, and while the children, after their manner, struck an acquaintance, the mothers indulged in the talk of mothers and drank tea from cups so fragile that Jees Uck feared lest hers should crumble to pieces beneath her fingers. Never had she seen such cups, so delicate and dainty. In her mind she compared them with the woman who poured the tea, and there uprose in contrast the gourds and pannikins of the Toyaat village and the clumsy mugs of Twenty Mile, to which she likened herself. And in such fashion and such terms the problem presented itself. She was beaten. There was a woman other than herself better fitted to bear and upbring Neil Bonner's children. Just as his people exceeded her people, so did his womankind exceed her. They were the man compellers, as their men were the world compellers. She looked at the rose-white tenderness of Kitty Bonner's skin and remembered the sun-beat on her own face. Likewise she looked from brown hand to white—the one, work-worn and hardened by whip-handle and paddle, the other as guiltless of toil and soft as a newborn babe's. And, for all the obvious softness and apparent weakness, Jees Uck looked into the blue eyes and saw the mastery she had seen in Neil Bonner's eyes and in the eyes of Neil Bonner's people.

"Why, it's Jees Uck!" Neil Bonner said, when he entered. He said it calmly, with even a ring of joyful cordiality, coming over to her and shaking both her hands, but looking into her eyes with a worry in his own that she understood.

"Hello, Neil!" she said. "You look much good."

"Fine, fine, Jees Uck," he answered heartily, though secretly studying Kitty for some sign of what had passed between the two. Yet he knew his wife too well to expect, even though the worst had passed, such a sign.

"Well, I can't say how glad I am to see you," he went on. "What's happened? Did you strike a mine? And when did you get in?"

"Oo-a, I get in to-day," she replied, her voice instinctively seeking its guttural parts. "I no strike it, Neil. You known Cap'n Markheim, Unalaska? I cook, his house, long time. No spend money. Bime-by, plenty. Pretty good, I think, go down and see White Man's Land. Very fine, White Man's Land, very fine," she added. Her English puzzled him, for Sandy and he had sought, constantly, to better her speech, and she had proved an apt pupil. Now it seemed that she had sunk back into her race. Her face was guileless, stolidly guileless, giving no cue. Kitty's untroubled brow likewise baffled him. What had happened? How much had been said? and how much guessed?

While he wrestled with these questions and while Jees Uck wrestled with her problem—never had he looked so wonderful and great—a silence fell.

"To think that you knew my husband in Alaska!" Kitty said softly.

Knew him! Jees Uck could not forbear a glance at the boy she had borne him, and his eyes followed hers mechanically to the window where played the two children. An iron hand seemed to tighten across his forehead. His knees went weak and his heart leaped up and pounded like a fist against his breast. His boy! He had never dreamed it!

Little Kitty Bonner, fairylike in gauzy lawn, with pinkest of cheeks and bluest of dancing eyes, arms outstretched and lips puckered in invitation, was striving to kiss the boy. And the boy, lean and lithe, sunbeaten and browned, skin-clad and in hair-fringed and hair-tufted *muclucs* that showed the wear of the sea and rough work, coolly withstood her advances, his body straight and stiff with the peculiar erectness common to children of savage people. A stranger in a strange land, unabashed and unafraid, he appeared more like an untamed animal, silent and watchful, his black eyes flashing from face to face, quiet so long as quiet endured, but prepared to spring and fight and tear and scratch for life, at the first sign of danger.

The contrast between boy and girl was striking, but not pitiful. There was too much strength in the boy for that, waif that he was of the generations of Shpack, Spike O'Brien, and Bonner. In his features, clean cut as a cameo and almost classic in their severity, there were the power and achievement of his father, and his grandfather, and the one known as the Big Fat, who was captured by the Sea people and escaped to Kamchatka.

Neil Bonner fought his emotion down, swallowed it down, and choked over it, though his face smiled with good-humour and the joy with which one meets a friend.

"Your boy, eh, Jees Uck?" he said. And then turning to Kitty: "Handsome fellow! He'll do something with those two hands of his in this our world."

Kitty nodded concurrence. "What is your name?" she asked.

The young savage flashed his quick eyes upon her and dwelt over her for a space, seeking out, as it were, the motive beneath the question.

"Neil," he answered deliberately when the scrutiny had satisfied him.

"Injun talk," Jees Uck interposed, glibly manufacturing languages on the spur of the moment. "Him Injun talk, *nee-al* all the same 'cracker.' Him baby, him like cracker; him cry for cracker. Him say, '*Nee-al, nee-al,*' all time him say, 'Nee-al.' Then I say that um name. So um name all time *Nee-al.*"

Never did sound more blessed fall upon Neil Bonner's ear than that lie from Jees Uck's lips. It was the cue, and he knew there was reason for Kitty's untroubled brow.

"And his father?" Kitty asked. "He must be a fine man."

"Oo-a, yes," was the reply. "Um father fine man. Sure!"

"Did you know him, Neil?" queried Kitty.

"Know him? Most intimately," Neil answered, and harked back to dreary Twenty Mile and the man alone in the silence with his thoughts.

210

And here might well end the story of Jees Uck but for the crown she put upon her renunciation. When she returned to the North to dwell in her grand log-house, John Thompson found that the P. C. Company could make a shift somehow to carry on its business without his aid. Also, the new agent and the succeeding agents received instructions that the woman Jees Uck should be given whatsoever goods and grub she desired, in whatsoever quantities she ordered, and that no charge should be placed upon the books. Further, the Company paid yearly to the woman Jees Uck a pension of five thousand dollars.

When he had attained suitable age, Father Champreau laid hands upon the boy, and the time was not long when Jees Uck received letters regularly from the Jesuit college in Maryland. Later on these letters came from Italy, and still later from France. And in the end there returned to Alaska one Father Neil, a man mighty for good in the land, who loved his mother and who ultimately went into a wider field and rose to high authority in the order.

Jees Uck was a young woman when she went back into the North, and men still looked upon her and yearned. But she lived straight, and no breath was ever raised save in commendation. She stayed for a while with the good sisters at Holy Cross, where she learned to read and write and became versed in practical medicine and surgery. After that she returned to her grand log-house and gathered about her the young girls of the Toyaat village, to show them the way of their feet in the world. It is neither Protestant nor Catholic, this school in the house built by Neil Bonner for Jees Uck, his wife; but the missionaries of all the sects look upon it with equal favour. The latchstring is always out, and tired prospectors and trail-weary men turn aside from the flowing river or frozen trail to rest there for a space and be warm by her fire. And, down in the States, Kitty Bonner is pleased at the interest her husband takes in Alaskan education and the large sums he devotes to that purpose; and, though she often smiles and chaffs, deep down and secretly she is but the prouder of him.

About Author

John Griffith London (born John Griffith Chaney; January 12, 1876 – November 22, 1916) was an American novelist, journalist, and social activist. A pioneer in the world of commercial magazine fiction, he was one of the first writers to become a worldwide celebrity and earn a large fortune from writing. He was also an innovator in the genre that would later become known as science fiction.

His most famous works include The Call of the Wild and White Fang, both set in the Klondike Gold Rush, as well as the short stories "To Build a Fire", "An Odyssey of the North", and "Love of Life". He also wrote about the South Pacific in stories such as "The Pearls of Parlay", and "The Heathen".

London was part of the radical literary group "The Crowd" in San Francisco and a passionate advocate of unionization, workers' rights, socialism, and eugenics. He wrote several works dealing with these topics, such as his dystopian novel The Iron Heel, his non-fiction exposé The People of the Abyss, The War of the Classes, and Before Adam.

Family

Jack London's mother, Flora Wellman, was the fifth and youngest child of Pennsylvania Canal builder Marshall Wellman and his first wife, Eleanor Garrett Jones. Marshall Wellman was descended from Thomas Wellman, an early Puritan settler in the Massachusetts Bay Colony. Flora left Ohio and moved to the Pacific coast when her father remarried after her mother died. In San Francisco, Flora worked as a music teacher and spiritualist, claiming to channel the spirit of a Sauk chief, Black Hawk.

Biographer Clarice Stasz and others believe London's father was astrologer William Chaney. Flora Wellman was living with Chaney in San Francisco when she became pregnant. Whether Wellman and Chaney were legally married is unknown. Stasz notes that in his memoirs, Chaney refers to London's mother Flora Wellman as having been his "wife"; he also cites an advertisement in which Flora called herself "Florence Wellman Chaney".

According to Flora Wellman's account, as recorded in the San Francisco Chronicle of June 4, 1875, Chaney demanded that she have an abortion. When she refused, he disclaimed responsibility for the child. In desperation, she shot herself. She was not seriously wounded, but she was temporarily deranged. After giving birth, Flora turned the baby over for care to Virginia Prentiss, an African-American woman and former slave. She was a major maternal figure throughout London's life. Late in 1876, Flora Wellman married John London, a partially disabled Civil War veteran, and brought her baby John, later known as Jack, to live with the newly married couple. The family moved around the San Francisco Bay Area before settling in Oakland, where London completed public grade school.

In 1897, when he was 21 and a student at the University of California, Berkeley, London searched for and read the newspaper accounts of his mother's suicide attempt and the name of his biological father. He wrote to William Chaney, then living in Chicago. Chaney responded that he could not be London's father because he was impotent; he casually asserted that London's mother had relations with other men and averred that she had slandered him when she said he insisted on an abortion. Chaney concluded by saying that he was more to be pitied than London. London was devastated by his father's letter; in the months following, he quit school at Berkeley and went to the Klondike during the gold rush boom.

Early life

London was born near Third and Brannan Streets in San Francisco. The house burned down in the fire after the 1906 San Francisco earthquake; the California Historical Society placed a plaque at the site in 1953. Although the family was working class, it was not as impoverished as London's later accounts claimed. London was largely self-educated.

In 1885, London found and read Ouida's long Victorian novel Signa. He credited this as the seed of his literary success. In 1886, he went to the Oakland Public Library and found a sympathetic librarian, Ina Coolbrith, who encouraged his learning. (She later became California's first poet laureate and an important figure in the San Francisco literary community).

In 1889, London began working 12 to 18 hours a day at Hickmott's Cannery. Seeking a way out, he borrowed money from his foster mother Virginia Prentiss, bought the sloop Razzle-Dazzle from an oyster pirate named French Frank, and became an oyster pirate himself. In his memoir, John Barleycorn, he claims also to have stolen French Frank's mistress Mamie. After a few months, his sloop became damaged beyond repair. London hired on as a member of the California Fish Patrol.

In 1893, he signed on to the sealing schooner Sophie Sutherland, bound for the coast of Japan. When he returned, the country was in the grip of the panic of '93 and Oakland was swept by labor unrest. After grueling jobs in a jute mill and a street-railway power plant, London joined Coxey's Army and began his career as a tramp. In 1894, he spent 30 days for vagrancy in the Erie County Penitentiary at Buffalo, New York. In The Road, he wrote:

> Man-handling was merely one of the very minor unprintable horrors of the Erie County Pen. I say 'unprintable'; and in justice I must also say undescribable. They were unthinkable to me until I saw them, and I was no spring chicken in the ways of the world and the awful abysses of human degradation. It would take a deep plummet to reach bottom in the Erie County Pen, and I do but skim lightly and facetiously the surface of things as I there saw them.

— Jack London, The Road

After many experiences as a hobo and a sailor, he returned to Oakland and attended Oakland High School. He contributed a number of articles to the high school's magazine, The Aegis. His first published work was "Typhoon off the Coast of Japan", an account of his sailing experiences.

As a schoolboy, London often studied at Heinold's First and Last Chance Saloon, a port-side bar in Oakland. At 17, he confessed to the bar's owner, John Heinold, his desire to attend university and pursue a career as a writer. Heinold lent London tuition money to attend college.

London desperately wanted to attend the University of California, located in Berkeley. In 1896, after a summer of intense studying to pass certification exams, he was admitted. Financial circumstances forced him to leave in 1897 and he never graduated. No evidence has surfaced that he ever wrote for student publications while studying at Berkeley.

While at Berkeley, London continued to study and spend time at Heinold's saloon, where he was introduced to the sailors and adventurers who would influence his writing. In his autobiographical novel, John Barleycorn, London mentioned the pub's likeness seventeen times. Heinold's was the place where London met Alexander McLean, a captain known for his cruelty at sea. London based his protagonist Wolf Larsen, in the novel The Sea-Wolf, on McLean.

Heinold's First and Last Chance Saloon is now unofficially named Jack London's Rendezvous in his honor.

Gold rush and first success

On July 12, 1897, London (age 21) and his sister's husband Captain Shepard sailed to join the Klondike Gold Rush. This was the setting for some of his first successful stories. London's time in the harsh Klondike, however, was detrimental to his health. Like so many other men who were malnourished in the goldfields, London developed scurvy. His gums became swollen, leading to the loss of his four front teeth. A constant gnawing pain affected his hip and leg muscles, and his face was stricken with marks that always reminded him of the struggles he faced in the Klondike. Father William Judge, "The Saint of Dawson", had a facility in Dawson that provided shelter, food and any available medicine to London and others. His struggles there inspired London's short story, "To Build a Fire" (1902, revised in 1908), which many critics assess as his best.

His landlords in Dawson were mining engineers Marshall Latham Bond and Louis Whitford Bond, educated at Yale and Stanford, respectively. The brothers' father, Judge Hiram Bond, was a wealthy mining investor. The Bonds, especially Hiram, were active Republicans. Marshall Bond's diary mentions friendly sparring with London on political issues as a camp pastime.

London left Oakland with a social conscience and socialist leanings; he returned to become an activist for socialism. He concluded that his only hope of escaping the work "trap" was to get an education and "sell his brains". He saw his writing as a business, his ticket out of poverty, and, he hoped, a means of beating the wealthy at their own game. On returning to California in 1898, London began working to get published, a struggle described in his novel, Martin Eden (serialized in 1908, published in 1909). His first published story since high school was "To the Man On Trail", which has frequently been collected in anthologies. When The Overland Monthly offered him only five dollars for it—and was slow paying—London came close to abandoning his writing career. In his words, "literally and literarily I was saved" when The Black Cat accepted his story "A Thousand Deaths", and paid him $40—the "first money I ever received for a story".

London began his writing career just as new printing technologies enabled lower-cost production of magazines. This resulted in a boom in popular magazines aimed at a wide public audience and a strong market for short fiction. In 1900, he made $2,500 in writing, about $77,000 in today's currency. Among the works he sold to magazines was a short story known as either "Diable" (1902) or "Bâtard" (1904), two editions of the same basic story; London received $141.25 for this story on May 27, 1902. In the text, a cruel French Canadian brutalizes his dog, and the dog retaliates and kills the man. London told some of his critics that man's actions are the main cause of the behavior of their animals, and he would show this in another story, The Call of the Wild.

In early 1903, London sold The Call of the Wild to The Saturday Evening Post for $750, and the book rights to Macmillan for $2,000. Macmillan's promotional campaign propelled it to swift success.

While living at his rented villa on Lake Merritt in Oakland, California, London met poet George Sterling; in time they became best friends. In 1902, Sterling helped London find a home closer to his own in nearby Piedmont. In his letters London addressed Sterling as "Greek", owing to Sterling's aquiline nose and classical profile, and he signed them as "Wolf". London was later to depict Sterling as Russ Brissenden in his autobiographical novel Martin Eden (1910) and as Mark Hall in The Valley of the Moon (1913).

In later life London indulged his wide-ranging interests by accumulating a personal library of 15,000 volumes. He referred to his books as "the tools of my trade".

First marriage (1900–04)

London married Elizabeth "Bessie" Maddern on April 7, 1900, the same day The Son of the Wolf was published. Bess had been part of his circle of friends for a number of years. She was related to stage actresses Minnie Maddern Fiske and Emily Stevens. Stasz says, "Both acknowledged publicly that they were not marrying out of love, but from friendship and a belief that they would produce sturdy children." Kingman says, "they were comfortable together... Jack had made it clear to Bessie that he did not love her, but that he liked her enough to make a successful marriage."

London met Bessie through his friend at Oakland High School, Fred Jacobs; she was Fred's fiancée. Bessie, who tutored at Anderson's University Academy in Alameda California, tutored Jack in preparation for his entrance exams for the University of California at Berkeley in 1896. Jacobs was killed aboard the USAT Scandia in 1897, but Jack and Bessie continued their friendship, which included taking photos and developing the film together. This was the beginning of Jack's passion for photography.

During the marriage, London continued his friendship with Anna Strunsky, co-authoring The Kempton-Wace Letters, an epistolary novel contrasting two philosophies of love. Anna, writing "Dane Kempton's" letters, arguing for a romantic view of marriage, while London, writing "Herbert Wace's" letters, argued for a scientific view, based on Darwinism and eugenics. In the novel, his fictional character contrasted two women he had known.

London's pet name for Bess was "Mother-Girl" and Bess's for London was "Daddy-Boy". Their first child, Joan, was born on January 15, 1901, and their second, Bessie (later called Becky), on October 20, 1902. Both children were born in Piedmont, California. Here London wrote one of his most celebrated works, The Call of the Wild.

While London had pride in his children, the marriage was strained. Kingman says that by 1903 the couple were close to separation as they were "extremely incompatible". "Jack was still so kind and gentle with Bessie that when Cloudsley Johns was a house guest in February 1903 he didn't suspect a breakup of their marriage."

London reportedly complained to friends Joseph Noel and George Sterling:

> [Bessie] is devoted to purity. When I tell her morality is only evidence of low blood pressure, she hates me. She'd sell me and the children out for her damned purity. It's terrible. Every time I come back after being away from home for a night she won't let me be in the same room with her if she can help it.

Stasz writes that these were "code words for fear that was consorting with prostitutes and might bring home venereal disease."

On July 24, 1903, London told Bessie he was leaving and moved out. During 1904, London and Bess negotiated the terms of a divorce, and the decree was granted on November 11, 1904.

War correspondent (1904)

London accepted an assignment of the San Francisco Examiner to cover the Russo-Japanese War in early 1904, arriving in Yokohama on January 25, 1904. He was arrested by Japanese authorities in Shimonoseki, but released through the intervention of American ambassador Lloyd Griscom. After travelling to Korea, he was again arrested by Japanese authorities for straying too close to the border with Manchuria without official permission, and was sent back to Seoul. Released again, London was permitted to travel with the Imperial Japanese Army to the border, and to observe the Battle of the Yalu.

London asked William Randolph Hearst, the owner of the San Francisco Examiner, to be allowed to transfer to the Imperial Russian Army, where he felt that restrictions on his reporting and his movements would be less severe. However, before this could be arranged, he was arrested for a third time in four months, this time for assaulting his Japanese assistants, whom he accused of stealing the fodder for his horse. Released through the personal intervention of President Theodore Roosevelt, London departed the front in June 1904.

Bohemian Club

On August 18, 1904, London went with his close friend, the poet George Sterling, to "Summer High Jinks" at the Bohemian Grove. London was elected to honorary membership in the Bohemian Club and took part in many activities. Other noted members of the Bohemian Club during this time included Ambrose Bierce, Gelett Burgess, Allan Dunn, John Muir, Frank Norris, and Herman George Scheffauer.

Beginning in December 1914, London worked on The Acorn Planter, A California Forest Play, to be performed as one of the annual Grove Plays, but it was never selected. It was described as too difficult to set to music. London published The Acorn Planter in 1916.

Second marriage

After divorcing Maddern, London married Charmian Kittredge in 1905. London had been introduced to Kittredge in 1900 by her aunt Netta Eames, who was an editor at Overland Monthly magazine in San Francisco. The two met prior to his first marriage but became lovers years later after Jack and Bessie London visited Wake Robin, Netta Eames' Sonoma County resort, in 1903. London was injured when he fell from a buggy, and Netta arranged for Charmian to care for him. The two developed a friendship, as Charmian, Netta, her husband Roscoe, and London were politically aligned with socialist causes. At some point the relationship became romantic, and Jack divorced his wife to marry Charmian, who was five years his senior.

Biographer Russ Kingman called Charmian "Jack's soul-mate, always at his side, and a perfect match." Their time together included numerous trips, including a 1907 cruise on the yacht Snark to Hawaii and Australia. Many of London's stories are based on his visits to Hawaii, the last one for 10 months beginning in December 1915.

220

The couple also visited Goldfield, Nevada, in 1907, where they were guests of the Bond brothers, London's Dawson City landlords. The Bond brothers were working in Nevada as mining engineers.

London had contrasted the concepts of the "Mother Girl" and the "Mate Woman" in The Kempton-Wace Letters. His pet name for Bess had been "Mother-Girl;" his pet name for Charmian was "Mate-Woman."Charmian's aunt and foster mother, a disciple of Victoria Woodhull, had raised her without prudishness.Every biographer alludes to Charmian's uninhibited sexuality.

Joseph Noel calls the events from 1903 to 1905 "a domestic drama that would have intrigued the pen of an Ibsen.... London's had comedy relief in it and a sort of easy-going romance." In broad outline, London was restless in his first marriage, sought extramarital sexual affairs, and found, in Charmian Kittredge, not only a sexually active and adventurous partner, but his future life-companion. They attempted to have children; one child died at birth, and another pregnancy ended in a miscarriage.

In 1906, London published in Collier's magazine his eye-witness report of the San Francisco earthquake.

Beauty Ranch (1905–16)

In 1905, London purchased a 1,000 acres (4.0 km2) ranch in Glen Ellen, Sonoma County, California, on the eastern slope of Sonoma Mountain.He wrote: "Next to my wife, the ranch is the dearest thing in the world to me." He desperately wanted the ranch to become a successful business enterprise. Writing, always a commercial enterprise with London, now became even more a means to an end: "I write for no other purpose than to add to the beauty that now belongs to me. I write a book for no other reason than to add three or four hundred acres to my magnificent estate."

Stasz writes that London "had taken fully to heart the vision, expressed in his agrarian fiction, of the land as the closest earthly version of Eden ... he educated himself through the study of agricultural manuals and scientific tomes. He conceived of a system of ranching that today would be praised for its ecological wisdom." He was proud to own the first concrete silo in California, a circular piggery that he designed. He hoped to adapt the wisdom of Asian sustainable agriculture to the United States. He hired both Italian and Chinese stonemasons, whose distinctly different styles are obvious.

The ranch was an economic failure. Sympathetic observers such as Stasz treat his projects as potentially feasible, and ascribe their failure to bad luck or to being ahead of their time. Unsympathetic historians such as Kevin Starr suggest that he was a bad manager, distracted by other concerns and impaired by his alcoholism. Starr notes that London was absent from his ranch about six months a year between 1910 and 1916 and says, "He liked the show of managerial power, but not grinding attention to detail .... London's workers laughed at his efforts to play big-time rancher the operation a rich man's hobby."

London spent $80,000 ($2,280,000 in current value) to build a 15,000-square-foot (1,400 m2) stone mansion called Wolf House on the property. Just as the mansion was nearing completion, two weeks before the Londons planned to move in, it was destroyed by fire.

London's last visit to Hawaii, beginning in December 1915, lasted eight months. He met with Duke Kahanamoku, Prince Jonah Kūhiō Kalaniana'ole, Queen Lili'uokalani and many others, before returning to his ranch in July 1916. He was suffering from kidney failure, but he continued to work.

The ranch (abutting stone remnants of Wolf House) is now a National Historic Landmark and is protected in Jack London State Historic Park.

Animal activism

London witnessed animal cruelty in the training of circus animals, and his subsequent novels Jerry of the Islands and Michael, Brother of Jerry included a foreword entreating the public to become more informed about this practice. In 1918, the Massachusetts Society for the Prevention of Cruelty to Animals and the American Humane Education Society teamed up to create the Jack London Club, which sought to inform the public about cruelty to circus animals and encourage them to protest this establishment. Support from Club members led to a temporary cessation of trained animal acts at Ringling-Barnum and Bailey in 1925.

222

Death

London died November 22, 1916, in a sleeping porch in a cottage on his ranch. London had been a robust man but had suffered several serious illnesses, including scurvy in the Klondike. Additionally, during travels on the Snark, he and Charmian picked up unspecified tropical infections, and diseases, including yaws. At the time of his death, he suffered from dysentery, late-stage alcoholism, and uremia; he was in extreme pain and taking morphine.

London's ashes were buried on his property not far from the Wolf House. London's funeral took place on November 26, 1916, attended only by close friends, relatives, and workers of the property. In accordance with his wishes, he was cremated and buried next to some pioneer children, under a rock that belonged to the Wolf House. After Charmian's death in 1955, she was also cremated and then buried with her husband in the same spot that her husband chose. The grave is marked by a mossy boulder. The buildings and property were later preserved as Jack London State Historic Park, in Glen Ellen, California.

Suicide debate

Because he was using morphine, many older sources describe London's death as a suicide, and some still do. This conjecture appears to be a rumor, or speculation based on incidents in his fiction writings. His death certificate gives the cause as uremia, following acute renal colic.

The biographer Stasz writes, "Following London's death, for a number of reasons, a biographical myth developed in which he has been portrayed as an alcoholic womanizer who committed suicide. Recent scholarship based upon firsthand documents challenges this caricature." Most biographers, including Russ Kingman, now agree he died of uremia aggravated by an accidental morphine overdose.

London's fiction featured several suicides. In his autobiographical memoir John Barleycorn, he claims, as a youth, to have drunkenly stumbled overboard into the San Francisco Bay, "some maundering fancy of going out with the tide suddenly obsessed me". He said he drifted and nearly succeeded in drowning before sobering up and being rescued by fishermen. In the dénouement of The Little Lady of the Big House, the heroine, confronted by the pain of a mortal gunshot wound, undergoes a physician-assisted suicide by morphine. Also, in Martin Eden, the principal protagonist, who shares certain characteristics with London, drowns himself.

Plagiarism accusations

London was vulnerable to accusations of plagiarism, both because he was such a conspicuous, prolific, and successful writer and because of his methods of working. He wrote in a letter to Elwyn Hoffman, "expression, you see—with me—is far easier than invention." He purchased plots and novels from the young Sinclair Lewis and used incidents from newspaper clippings as writing material.

In July 1901, two pieces of fiction appeared within the same month: London's "Moon-Face", in the San Francisco Argonaut, and Frank Norris' "The Passing of Cock-eye Blacklock", in Century Magazine. Newspapers showed the similarities between the stories, which London said were "quite different in manner of treatment, patently the same in foundation and motive." London explained both writers based their stories on the same newspaper account. A year later, it was discovered that Charles Forrest McLean had published a fictional story also based on the same incident.

Egerton Ryerson Young claimed The Call of the Wild (1903) was taken from Young's book My Dogs in the Northland (1902). London acknowledged using it as a source and claimed to have written a letter to Young thanking him.

In 1906, the New York World published "deadly parallel" columns showing eighteen passages from London's short story "Love of Life" side by side with similar passages from a nonfiction article by Augustus Biddle and J. K. Macdonald, titled "Lost in the Land of the Midnight Sun". London noted the World did not accuse him of "plagiarism", but only of "identity of time and situation", to which he defiantly "pled guilty".

The most serious charge of plagiarism was based on London's "The Bishop's Vision", Chapter 7 of his novel The Iron Heel (1908). The chapter is nearly identical to an ironic essay that Frank Harris published in 1901, titled "The Bishop of London and Public Morality". Harris was incensed and suggested he should receive 1/60th of the royalties from The Iron Heel, the disputed material constituting about that fraction of the whole novel. London insisted he had clipped a reprint of the article, which had appeared in an American newspaper, and believed it to be a genuine speech delivered by the Bishop of London.

Views

Atheism

London was an atheist. He is quoted as saying, "I believe that when I am dead, I am dead. I believe that with my death I am just as much obliterated as the last mosquito you and I squashed."

Socialism

London wrote from a socialist viewpoint, which is evident in his novel The Iron Heel. Neither a theorist nor an intellectual socialist, London's socialism grew out of his life experience. As London explained in his essay, "How I Became a Socialist", his views were influenced by his experience with people at the bottom of the social pit. His optimism and individualism faded, and he vowed never to do more hard physical work than necessary. He wrote that his individualism was hammered out of him, and he was politically reborn. He often closed his letters "Yours for the Revolution."

London joined the Socialist Labor Party in April 1896. In the same year, the San Francisco Chronicle published a story about the twenty-year-old London's giving nightly speeches in Oakland's City Hall Park, an activity he was arrested for a year later. In 1901, he left the Socialist Labor Party and joined the new Socialist Party of America. He ran unsuccessfully as the high-profile Socialist candidate for mayor of Oakland in 1901 (receiving 245 votes) and 1905 (improving to 981 votes), toured the country lecturing on socialism in 1906, and published two collections of essays about socialism: The War of the Classes (1905) and Revolution, and other Essays (1906).

Stasz notes that "London regarded the Wobblies as a welcome addition to the Socialist cause, although he never joined them in going so far as to recommend sabotage." Stasz mentions a personal meeting between London and Big Bill Haywood in 1912.

In his late (1913) book The Cruise of the Snark, London writes about appeals to him for membership of the Snark's crew from office workers and other "toilers" who longed for escape from the cities, and of being cheated by workmen.

In his Glen Ellen ranch years, London felt some ambivalence toward socialism and complained about the "inefficient Italian labourers" in his employ. In 1916, he resigned from the Glen Ellen chapter of the Socialist Party, but stated emphatically he did so "because of its lack of fire and fight, and its loss of emphasis on the class struggle." In an unflattering portrait of London's ranch days, California cultural historian Kevin Starr refers to this period as "post-socialist" and says "... by 1911 ... London was more bored by the class struggle than he cared to admit."

Race

London shared common concerns among many European Americans in California about Asian immigration, described as "the yellow peril"; he used the latter term as the title of a 1904 essay. This theme was also the subject of a story he wrote in 1910 called "The Unparalleled Invasion". Presented as an historical essay set in the future, the story narrates events between 1976 and 1987, in which China, with an ever-increasing population, is taking over and colonizing its neighbors with the intention of taking over the entire Earth. The western nations respond with biological warfare and bombard China with dozens of the most infectious diseases. On his fears about China, he admits, "it must be taken into consideration that the above postulate is itself a product of Western race-egotism, urged by our belief in our own righteousness and fostered by a faith in ourselves which may be as erroneous as are most fond race fancies."

By contrast, many of London's short stories are notable for their empathetic portrayal of Mexican ("The Mexican"), Asian ("The Chinago"), and Hawaiian ("Koolau the Leper") characters. London's war correspondence from the Russo-Japanese War, as well as his unfinished novel Cherry, show he admired much about Japanese customs and capabilities. London's writings have been popular among the Japanese, who believe he portrayed them positively.

In "Koolau the Leper", London describes Koolau, who is a Hawaiian leper—and thus a very different sort of "superman" than Martin Eden—and who fights off an entire cavalry troop to elude capture, as "indomitable spiritually—a ... magnificent rebel". This character is based on Hawaiian leper Kaluaikoolau, who in 1893 revolted and resisted capture from forces of the Provisional Government of Hawaii in the Kalalau Valley.

An amateur boxer and avid boxing fan, London reported on the 1910 Johnson–Jeffries fight, in which the black boxer Jack Johnson vanquished Jim Jeffries, known as the "Great White Hope". In 1908, London had reported on an earlier fight of Johnson's, contrasting the black boxer's coolness and intellectual style, with the apelike appearance and fighting style of his Canadian opponent, Tommy Burns:

> [What won] on Saturday was bigness, coolness, quickness, cleverness, and vast physical superiority ... Because a white man wishes a white man to win, this should not prevent him from giving absolute credit to the best man, even when that best man was black. All hail to Johnson. ... superb. He was impregnable ... as inaccessible as Mont Blanc.

Those who defend London against charges of racism cite the letter he wrote to the Japanese-American Commercial Weekly in 1913:

> In reply to yours of August 16, 1913. First of all, I should say by stopping the stupid newspaper from always fomenting race prejudice. This of course, being impossible, I would say, next, by educating the people of Japan so that they will be too intelligently tolerant to respond to any call to race prejudice. And, finally, by realizing, in industry and

government, of socialism—which last word is merely a word that stands for the actual application of in the affairs of men of the theory of the Brotherhood of Man.

In the meantime the nations and races are only unruly boys who have not yet grown to the stature of men. So we must expect them to do unruly and boisterous things at times. And, just as boys grow up, so the races of mankind will grow up and laugh when they look back upon their childish quarrels.

In 1996, after the City of Whitehorse, Yukon, renamed a street in honor of London, protests over London's alleged racism forced the city to change the name of "Jack London Boulevard"[failed verification] back to "Two-mile Hill".

Eugenics

London supported eugenics, including forced sterilization of criminals or those deemed feeble minded. His novel Before Adam(1906–07) has been described as having pro-eugenic themes.

London wrote to Frederick H. Robinson of the periodical Medical Review of Reviews, stating, "I believe the future belongs to eugenics, and will be determined by the practice of eugenics."

Works

Short stories

Western writer and historian Dale L. Walker writes:

> London's true métier was the short story ... London's true genius lay in the short form, 7,500 words and under, where the flood of images in his teeming brain and the innate power of his narrative gift were at once constrained and freed. His stories that run longer than the magic 7,500 generally—but certainly not always—could have benefited from self-editing.

228

London's "strength of utterance" is at its height in his stories, and they are painstakingly well-constructed. "To Build a Fire" is the best known of all his stories. Set in the harsh Klondike, it recounts the haphazard trek of a new arrival who has ignored an old-timer's warning about the risks of traveling alone. Falling through the ice into a creek in seventy-five-below weather, the unnamed man is keenly aware that survival depends on his untested skills at quickly building a fire to dry his clothes and warm his extremities. After publishing a tame version of this story—with a sunny outcome—in The Youth's Companion in 1902, London offered a second, more severe take on the man's predicament in The Century Magazine in 1908. Reading both provides an illustration of London's growth and maturation as a writer. As Labor (1994) observes: "To compare the two versions is itself an instructive lesson in what distinguished a great work of literary art from a good children's story."

Other stories from the Klondike period include: "All Gold Canyon", about a battle between a gold prospector and a claim jumper; "The Law of Life", about an aging American Indian man abandoned by his tribe and left to die; "Love of Life", about a trek by a prospector across the Canadian tundra; "To the Man on Trail," which tells the story of a prospector fleeing the Mounted Police in a sled race, and raises the question of the contrast between written law and morality; and "An Odyssey of the North," which raises questions of conditional morality, and paints a sympathetic portrait of a man of mixed White and Aleut ancestry.

London was a boxing fan and an avid amateur boxer. "A Piece of Steak" is a tale about a match between older and younger boxers. It contrasts the differing experiences of youth and age but also raises the social question of the treatment of aging workers. "The Mexican" combines boxing with a social theme, as a young Mexican endures an unfair fight and ethnic prejudice to earn money with which to aid the revolution.

Several of London's stories would today be classified as science fiction. "The Unparalleled Invasion" describes germ warfare against China; "Goliath" is about an irresistible energy weapon; "The Shadow and the Flash" is a tale about two brothers who take different routes to achieving invisibility; "A

Relic of the Pliocene" is a tall tale about an encounter of a modern-day man with a mammoth. "The Red One" is a late story from a period when London was intrigued by the theories of the psychiatrist and writer Jung. It tells of an island tribe held in thrall by an extraterrestrial object.

Some nineteen original collections of short stories were published during London's brief life or shortly after his death. There have been several posthumous anthologies drawn from this pool of stories. Many of these stories were located in the Klondike and the Pacific. A collection of Jack London's San Francisco Stories was published in October 2010 by Sydney Samizdat Press.

Novels

London's most famous novels are The Call of the Wild, White Fang, The Sea-Wolf, The Iron Heel, and Martin Eden.

In a letter dated December 27, 1901, London's Macmillan publisher George Platt Brett, Sr., said "he believed Jack's fiction represented 'the very best kind of work' done in America."

Critic Maxwell Geismar called The Call of the Wild "a beautiful prose poem"; editor Franklin Walker said that it "belongs on a shelf with Walden and Huckleberry Finn"; and novelist E.L. Doctorow called it "a mordant parable ... his masterpiece."

The historian Dale L. Walker commented:

Jack London was an uncomfortable novelist, that form too long for his natural impatience and the quickness of his mind. His novels, even the best of them, are hugely flawed.

Some critics have said that his novels are episodic and resemble linked short stories. Dale L. Walker writes:

The Star Rover, that magnificent experiment, is actually a series of short stories connected by a unifying device ... Smoke Bellew is a series of stories bound together in a novel-like form by their reappearing protagonist, Kit Bellew; and John Barleycorn ... is a synoptic series of short episodes.

Ambrose Bierce said of The Sea-Wolf that "the great thing—and it is among the greatest of things—is that tremendous creation, Wolf Larsen ... the hewing out and setting up of such a figure is enough for a man to do in one lifetime. "However, he noted, "The love element, with its absurd suppressions, and impossible proprieties, is awful."

The Iron Heel is an example of a dystopian novel that anticipates and influenced George Orwell's Nineteen Eighty-Four. London's socialist politics are explicitly on display here. The Iron Heel meets the contemporary definition of soft science fiction. The Star Rover (1915) is also science fiction.

Apocrypha

Jack London Credo

London's literary executor, Irving Shepard, quoted a Jack London Credo in an introduction to a 1956 collection of London stories:

> I would rather be ashes than dust!

> I would rather that my spark should burn out in a brilliant blaze than it should be stifled by dry-rot.

> I would rather be a superb meteor, every atom of me in magnificent glow, than a sleepy and permanent planet.

> The function of man is to live, not to exist.

> I shall not waste my days in trying to prolong them.

> I shall use my time.

The biographer Stasz notes that the passage "has many marks of London's style" but the only line that could be safely attributed to London was the first. The words Shepard quoted were from a story in the San Francisco Bulletin, December 2, 1916, by journalist Ernest J. Hopkins, who visited the ranch just weeks before London's death. Stasz notes, "Even more so than today journalists' quotes were unreliable or even sheer inventions," and says no direct source in London's writings has been found. However, at least one line, according to Stasz, is authentic, being referenced by London and written in his own hand in the autograph book of Australian suffragette Vida Goldstein:

Dear Miss Goldstein:–

Seven years ago I wrote you that I'd rather be ashes than dust. I still subscribe to that sentiment.

Sincerely yours,

Jack London

Jan. 13, 1909

In his short story "By The Turtles of Tasman", a character, defending her "ne'er-do-well grasshopperish father" to her "antlike uncle", says: "... my father has been a king. He has lived .... Have you lived merely to live? Are you afraid to die? I'd rather sing one wild song and burst my heart with it, than live a thousand years watching my digestion and being afraid of the wet. When you are dust, my father will be ashes."

"The Scab"

A short diatribe on "The Scab" is often quoted within the U.S. labor movement and frequently attributed to London. It opens:

After God had finished the rattlesnake, the toad, and the vampire, he had some awful substance left with which he made a scab. A scab is a two-legged animal with a corkscrew soul, a water brain, a combination backbone of jelly and glue. Where others have hearts, he carries a tumor of rotten principles. When a scab comes down the street, men turn their backs and Angels weep in Heaven, and the Devil shuts the gates of hell to keep him out....

In 1913 and 1914, a number of newspapers printed the first three sentences with varying terms used instead of "scab", such as "knocker","stool pigeon"or "scandal monger"

232

This passage as given above was the subject of a 1974 Supreme Court case, Letter Carriers v. Austin, in which Justice Thurgood Marshall referred to it as "a well-known piece of trade union literature, generally attributed to author Jack London". A union newsletter had published a "list of scabs," which was granted to be factual and therefore not libelous, but then went on to quote the passage as the "definition of a scab". The case turned on the question of whether the "definition" was defamatory. The court ruled that "Jack London's... 'definition of a scab' is merely rhetorical hyperbole, a lusty and imaginative expression of the contempt felt by union members towards those who refuse to join", and as such was not libelous and was protected under the First Amendment.

Despite being frequently attributed to London, the passage does not appear at all in the extensive collection of his writings at Sonoma State University's website. However, in his book The War of the Classes he published a 1903 speech entitled "The Scab", which gave a much more balanced view of the topic:

> The laborer who gives more time or strength or skill for the same wage than another, or equal time or strength or skill for a less wage, is a scab. The generousness on his part is hurtful to his fellow-laborers, for it compels them to an equal generousness which is not to their liking, and which gives them less of food and shelter. But a word may be said for the scab. Just as his act makes his rivals compulsorily generous, so do they, by fortune of birth and training, make compulsory his act of generousness.

> [...]

> Nobody desires to scab, to give most for least. The ambition of every individual is quite the opposite, to give least for most; and, as a result, living in a tooth-and-nail society, battle royal is waged by the ambitious individuals. But in its most salient aspect, that of the struggle over the division of the joint product, it is no longer a battle between individuals, but between groups of individuals. Capital and labor apply

themselves to raw material, make something useful out of it, add to its value, and then proceed to quarrel over the division of the added value. Neither cares to give most for least. Each is intent on giving less than the other and on receiving more.

Legacy and honors

Mount London, also known as Boundary Peak 100, on the Alaska-British Columbia boundary, in the Boundary Ranges of the Coast Mountains of British Columbia, is named for him.

Jack London Square on the waterfront of Oakland, California was named for him.

He was honored by the United States Postal Service with a 25¢ Great Americans series postage stamp released on January 11, 1986.

Jack London Lake (Russian), a mountain lake located in the upper reaches of the Kolyma River in Yagodninsky district of Magadan Oblast.

Fictional portrayals of London include Michael O'Shea in the 1943 film Jack London, Jeff East in the 1980 film Klondike Fever, Aaron Ashmore in the Murdoch Mysteries episode "Murdoch of the Klondike" from 2012, and Johnny Simmons in the 2014 miniseries Klondike. (Source: Wikipedia)

NOTABLE WORKS

NOVELS

The Cruise of the Dazzler (1902)

A Daughter of the Snows (1902)

The Call of the Wild (1903)

The Kempton-Wace Letters (1903) (published anonymously, co-authored with Anna Strunsky)

The Sea-Wolf (1904)

The Game (1905)

White Fang (1906)

Before Adam (1907)

The Iron Heel (1908)

Martin Eden (1909)

Burning Daylight (1910)

Adventure (1911)

The Scarlet Plague (1912)

A Son of the Sun (1912)

The Abysmal Brute (1913)

The Valley of the Moon (1913)

The Mutiny of the Elsinore (1914)

The Star Rover (1915) (published in England as The Jacket)

The Little Lady of the Big House (1916)

Jerry of the Islands (1917)

Michael, Brother of Jerry (1917)

Hearts of Three (1920) (novelization of a script by Charles Goddard)

The Assassination Bureau, Ltd (1963) (left half-finished, completed by Robert L. Fish)

SHORT STORIES

"An Old Soldier's Story" (1894)

"Who Believes in Ghosts!" (1895)

"And 'FRISCO Kid Came Back" (1895)

"Night's Swim In Yeddo Bay" (1895)

"One More Unfortunate" (1895)

"Sakaicho, Hona Asi And Hakadaki" (1895)

"A Klondike Christmas" (1897)

"Mahatma's Little Joke" (1897)

"O Haru" (1897)

"Plague Ship" (1897)

"The Strange Experience Of A Misogynist" (1897)

"Two Gold Bricks" (1897)

"The Devil's Dice Box" (1898)

"A Dream Image" (1898)

"The Test: A Clondyke Wooing" (1898)

"To the Man on Trail" (1898)

"In a Far Country" (1899)

"The King of Mazy May" (1899)

"The End Of The Chapter" (1899)

"The Grilling Of Loren Ellery" (1899)

"The Handsome Cabin Boy" (1899)

"In The Time Of Prince Charley" (1899)

"Old Baldy" (1899)

"The Men of Forty Mile" (1899)

"Pluck and Pertinacity" (1899)

"The Rejuvenation of Major Rathbone" (1899)

"The White Silence" (1899)

"A Thousand Deaths" (1899)

"Wisdom of the Trail" (1899)

"An Odyssey of the North" (1900)

"The Son of the Wolf" (1900)

"Even unto Death" (1900)

"The Man with the Gash" (1900)

"A Lesson in Heraldry" (1900)

"A Northland Miracle" (1900)

"Proper "GIRLIE"" (1900)

"Thanksgiving on Slav Creek" (1900)

"Their Alcove" (1900)

"Housekeeping in the Klondike" (1900)

"Dutch Courage" (1900)

"Where the Trail Forks" (1900)

"Hyperborean Brew" (1901)

"A Relic of the Pliocene" (1901)

"The Lost Poacher" (1901)

"The God of His Fathers" (1901)

""FRISCO Kid's" Story" (1901)

"The Law of Life" (1901)

"The Minions of Midas" (1901)

"In the Forests of the North" (1902)

"The "Fuzziness" of Hoockla-Heen" (1902)

"The Story of Keesh" (1902)

"Keesh, Son of Keesh" (1902)

"Nam-Bok, the Unveracious" (1902)

"Li Wan the Fair" (1902)

"Lost Face"

"Master of Mystery" (1902)

"The Sunlanders" (1902)

"The Death of Ligoun" (1902)

"Moon-Face" (1902)

"Diable—A Dog" (1902), renamed Bâtard in 1904

"To Build a Fire" (1902, revised 1908)

"The League of the Old Men" (1902)

"The Dominant Primordial Beast" (1903)

"The One Thousand Dozen" (1903)

"The Marriage of Lit-lit" (1903)

"The Shadow and the Flash" (1903)

"The Leopard Man's Story" (1903)

"Negore the Coward" (1904)

"All Gold Cañon" (1905)

"Love of Life" (1905)

"The Sun-Dog Trail" (1905)

"The Apostate" (1906)

"Up the Slide" (1906)

"Planchette" (1906)

"Brown Wolf" (1906)

"Make Westing" (1907)

"Chased by the Trail" (1907)

"Trust" (1908)

"A Curious Fragment" (1908)

"Aloha Oe" (1908)

"That Spot" (1908)

"The Enemy of All the World" (1908)

"The House of Mapuhi" (1909)

"Good-by, Jack" (1909)

"Samuel" (1909)

"South of the Slot" (1909)

"The Chinago" (1909)

"The Dream of Debs" (1909)

"The Madness of John Harned" (1909)

"The Seed of McCoy" (1909)

"A Piece of Steak" (1909)

"Mauki" (1909)

"The Whale Tooth" (1909)

"Goliath" (1910)

"The Unparalleled Invasion" (1910)

"Told in the Drooling Ward" (1910)

"When the World was Young" (1910)

"The Terrible Solomons" (1910)

"The Inevitable White Man" (1910)

"The Heathen" (1910)

"Yah! Yah! Yah!" (1910)

"By the Turtles of Tasman" (1911)

"The Mexican" (1911)

"War" (1911)

"The Unmasking of the Cad" (1911)

"The Scarlet Plague" (1912)

"The Captain of the Susan Drew" (1912)

"The Sea-Farmer" (1912)

"The Feathers of the Sun" (1912)

"The Prodigal Father" (1912)

"Samuel" (1913)

"The Sea-Gangsters" (1913)

"The Strength of the Strong" (1914)

"Told in the Drooling Ward" (1914)

"The Hussy" (1916)

"Like Argus of the Ancient Times" (1917)

"Jerry of the Islands" (1917)

"The Red One" (1918)

"Shin-Bones" (1918)

"The Bones of Kahekili" (1919)

SHORT STORY COLLECTIONS

Son of the Wolf (1900)

Chris Farrington, Able Seaman (1901)

The God of His Fathers & Other Stories (1901)

Children of the Frost (1902)

The Faith of Men and Other Stories (1904)

Tales of the Fish Patrol (1906)

Moon-Face and Other Stories (1906)

Love of Life and Other Stories (1907)

Lost Face (1910)

South Sea Tales (1911)

When God Laughs and Other Stories (1911)

The House of Pride & Other Tales of Hawaii (1912)

Smoke Bellew (1912)

A Son of the Sun (1912)

The Night Born (1913)

The Strength of the Strong (1914)

The Turtles of Tasman (1916)

The Human Drift (1917)

The Red One (1918)

On the Makaloa Mat (1919)

Dutch Courage and Other Stories (1922)

AUTOBIOGRAPHICAL MEMOIRS

The Road (1907)

The Cruise of the Snark (1911)

John Barleycorn (1913)

NON-FICTION AND ESSAYS

Through the Rapids on the Way to the Klondike (1899)

From Dawson to the Sea (1899)

What Communities Lose by the Competitive System (1900)

The Impossibility of War (1900)

Phenomena of Literary Evolution (1900)

A Letter to Houghton Mifflin Co. (1900)

Husky, Wolf Dog of the North (1900)

Editorial Crimes — A Protest (1901)

Again the Literary Aspirant (1902)

The People of the Abyss (1903)

How I Became a Socialist (1903)

The War of the Classes (1905)

The Story of an Eyewitness (1906)

A Letter to Woman's Home Companion (1906)

Revolution, and other Essays (1910)

Mexico's Army and Ours (1914)

Lawgivers (1914)

Our Adventures in Tampico (1914)

Stalking the Pestilence (1914)

The Red Game of War (1914)

The Trouble Makers of Mexico (1914)

With Funston's Men (1914)

POETRY

A Heart (1899)

Abalone Song (1913)

And Some Night (1914)

Ballade of the False Lover (1914)

Cupid's Deal (1913)

Daybreak (1901)

Effusion (1901)

George Sterling (1913)

Gold (1915)

He Chortled with Glee (1899)

He Never Tried Again (1912)

His Trip to Hades (1913)

Homeland (1914)

Hors de Saison (1913)

If I Were God (1899)

In a Year (1901)

In and Out (1911)

Je Vis en Espoir (1897)

Memory (1913)

Moods (1913)

My Confession (1912)

My Little Palmist (1914)

Of Man of the Future (1915)

Oh You Everybody's Girl (19)

On the Face of the Earth You are the One (1915)

Rainbows End (1914)

Republican Rallying Song (1916)

Sonnet (1901)

The Gift of God (1905)

The Klondyker's Dream (1914)

The Lover's Liturgy (1913)

The Mammon Worshippers (1911)

The Republican Battle-Hymn (1905)

The Return of Ulysses (1915)

The Sea Sprite and the Shooting Star (1916)

The Socialist's Dream (1912)

The Song of the Flames (1903)

The Way of War (1906)

The Worker and the Tramp (1911)

Tick! Tick! Tick! (1915)

Too Late (1912)

Weasel Thieves (1913)

When All the World Shouted my Name (1905)

Where the Rainbow Fell (1902)

Your Kiss (1914)

PLAYS

Theft (1910)

Daughters of the Rich: A One Act Play (1915)

The Acorn Planter: A California Forest Play (1916)

CPSIA information can be obtained
at www.ICGtesting.com
Printed in the USA
LVHW020236150920
665985LV00001B/105